3/15

Books should be returned or renewed by the last date
above. Renew by phone **08458 247 200** or online
www.kent.gov.uk/libs

Libraries & Archives

SOULPRINT

MEGAN MIRANDA

BLOOMSBURY

LONDON NEW DELHI NEW YORK SYDNEY

Bloomsbury Publishing, London, New Delhi, New York and Sydney

First published in Great Britain in February 2015 by Bloomsbury Publishing Plc
50 Bedford Square, London WC1B 3DP

First published in the USA in February 2015 by
Bloomsbury Children's Books
1385 Broadway, New York, New York 10018

www.bloomsbury.com

Bloomsbury is a registered trademark of Bloomsbury Publishing Plc

A CIP catalogue record for this book is available from the British Library

ISBN 978 1 4088 5540 9

Printed and bound in Great Britain by CPI Group (UK) Ltd, Croydon CR0 4YY

1 3 5 7 9 10 8 6 4 2

For Alexa and Jake

prologue

THERE IS A SAYING, an old one, from before me—before June even: *To know your soul is to become it.*

True or not, it's the main reason most people don't check who they were in the past life, when given the choice. Such a luxury, that choice—I hope they appreciate it.

I would give anything not to know.

I'd trade everything I have, every drop of information I surround myself with, down to the hope I hold tight like a blanket.

I'd trade it all for my parents sleeping in the next room and an alarm clock waking me before dawn to catch the bus for school. For a heavy backpack and a forgotten umbrella as I walk through the rain up the front steps on the first day of class. For bumping into strangers in the doorway who mumble half apologies, for running straight down the hallway as the bell rings. For a girl catching my eye when I walk in late and grinning in a secret understanding. For the empty seat that she has saved beside her. For the teacher looking at the class roster and then back at me, and asking *Alina?* because he doesn't know.

Because nobody knows.

What I'd give for that.

I'd trade you my next life, and the one after that. I'd trade you every one of them—for however long my soul should last—for this life.

Just this one.

chapter 1

THERE HAS REALLY BEEN only one official attempt on my life—two, if you count the time when I was ten, but that one was eventually ruled an accident and lost its official status. Really, if I had any say, they wouldn't count that first one from my father, either. I guess it doesn't matter. It's the perceived threats—not the official attempts—that got me stuck in this prison.

That's not a metaphor.

Prison, noun: a place or condition of confinement. This counts.

The threats are a nice excuse, I suppose. Something to make themselves feel better, to appease their collective conscience, to garner public support. But I am not here for my safety. Not really.

I am the perceived threat.

I was not born on this island, but I can't remember anything before this. Not the foster family that took me in for a while when nobody else would—they must've been saints in a past life, honestly—and definitely not any time before that.

My mother spent more than half my childhood in jail—because she dug the tracker out from beneath a layer of skin and fat under my third rib when I was a baby, in a reckless attempt to free me from my past. My father was also sent to jail a few months later, after he tried to end my life—to *save* me—so that I might start fresh. So that I might be a person with no history.

I wish I could meet them, these people who loved me so fiercely. Who believed my soul was my own.

They are the only ones.

I wish I could remember a time before this, a place before this, other than in my imagination, because that's not the same as a memory. I'm imagining my mother's face right now, with my eyes closed, as I listen to the footsteps move across the room. It could be anyone. For the moment, it could even be her. But then someone speaks and the moment is gone and ruined.

I open my eyes, and I am still here.

Three women stand strategically throughout my kitchen—trying to pretend, for the moment, that they are family, or friends maybe, and not guards. One of them smiles in my general direction, her eyes skimming over my own so quickly I might've imagined that, too. "Wait until you see the cake," she says. Another nods in agreement.

A cake. My life for a cake. I make myself uncurl my fingers from the corner of the table. "Can't wait," I say.

I don't know her real name, or any of their names. They call each other Jen or Kate or something equally common and fake. It's pointless anyway. They've been here thirteen—no, fourteen—days. They'll be gone in fourteen more. Some will rotate back in, a few months or a few years from now, in a pattern I cannot decipher no matter how many ways I approach it. Some I will never see again.

Sometimes I think I'm onto it, the pattern, if there is one—the new rotation will be starting that morning and I'll think, *the green-eyed one, the one who jumps every time I speak, the one who goes by Mary*—and then I'll see her as part of the group stepping off the bridge after screening. But maybe that's just coincidence—my mind trying to find meaning where there is none.

A girl with shoulder-length dark hair enters the room, averting her eyes from me as she carries the cake to the counter. She tucks her hair behind her ear and wipes her hands against the sides of her pants. The bottom of her pants are frayed on one side, near her heel, and I feel my heartbeat pounding against my ribs. *Her*. It has to be her. I remind myself to look away. To look anywhere else—*at* anything else. The ceramic floor. The dark stone counters. The older woman inspecting that white cake.

They are right about the cake, though. It's iced to perfection, and *Alina* is written in sprawling, loopy cursive. I imagine a mother preparing this, licking the icing from her knuckle, cupping her hand over a match as she holds it to the candlewick, but I know this cake was made in a bakery by a stranger, and the woman lighting my candles now has never made eye contact with me.

There are seventeen candles, and they flicker, they burn. The smell of smoke carries through the otherwise pristine room. It's a smell that always surprises me. Like something changing, something happening. Maybe because it's so rare, and burning candles always means my birthday, and a measure of time, and one year closer to getting out.

I used to think that, anyway. But I'm not a child anymore. I understand the truth—that even though for now I am here and "cared for" because my own parents were deemed unfit and for now this legally falls under the guise of child welfare and protection—there's no way they will ever let me out. It will be for another reason next year. A loophole: words that have been twisted to alter meaning, a law that has been bent to contain me.

I wonder, for a brief second, what I could do with seventeen burning candles. I wonder how much of this house—this island—is flammable.

Not nearly enough.

One of the women places a glass of water in front of me. Then she holds a walkie-talkie to her mouth and says, "Please proceed to the house."

Everyone here calls this place a house, and I guess that's not exactly a lie. It has a kitchen and a bedroom, a game room and a television room, all of which I'm allowed to roam through freely. And a basement, which I am not. There's a yard—a big one—stretching from rocky cliff to rocky cliff.

Nobody ever calls it a jail, even though I'm not allowed to

leave. Nobody calls it a punishment, either, even though that's exactly what this is. The worst term anyone here ever uses is "containment."

Like I need an island and thirty-two guards to contain my soul.

I hear the television turn on in the next room as we wait for everyone to come inside, and I assume it's one of the guards from the basement—someone who doesn't typically have access to one, someone who treats today like a holiday. He's almost right. It's a memorial, and we are the topic.

I hear June's name on the television, like music, like nails on a chalkboard, humming through my blood, scratching at my nerves. They haven't gotten to me yet. But it's coming. Today is the seventeenth anniversary of the day that June Calahan died. And the day her soul was reborn, twelve hours later, six miles away, in me.

Most souls are free of their pasts. Of their crimes and transgressions, their love and hate. Because a soul has no memory, and that's a scientific fact.

Still, most people agree it's better not to find out who you once were. And if you do find out, it's best to keep that knowledge to yourself. Because while the soul has no memory, the world does, and that is usually enough.

I didn't have a choice. I'm being contained because it's too dangerous for my soul to be free. That's what they say every year on my birthday, on every news station and half of the non-news stations, too. And this year will be no different. Whether my freedom is too dangerous for *me* or for *them*, I guess it depends on the filter you're looking through.

I've been avoiding the television all day. The endless debating—every year the same words, the same sides—and nothing ever changes. Someone says, *Alina Chase is being held because she's dangerous.* Something about June leaving me with information to continue her crimes, which is ridiculous, because June is dead and I am here, and I have nothing. But then someone else says, *Alina Chase is being protected, because who would care for the soul of June Calahan?* And for some reason, that one feels worse. Whichever way the news spins, it all comes back to June—the girl with the blond curls, the bright eyes, too young and too beautiful to look guilty. *Her* crimes. *Her* life.

When June died, they tested all the newly born with a lumbar puncture—the fingerprint of your soul in the sample of spinal fluid they draw out in the enormous needle. There was no option, no choice to opt out of the database like usual, though most everyone chooses to leave a record anyway. They sedated the babies, and they tested them all, any born within a hundred-mile radius, though souls rarely ever travel that far. Not unless they have to. Not unless there's no one around. They tested everyone, checking the results *right then*—instead of waiting until the children turned eighteen and made that choice for themselves. They screened them all and ran the results, against the parents' wishes, to find June.

There are laws against this now, privacy laws meant to protect, but they're a little too late for me.

And now all this talk is a waste of air, of thought, of time. All the talk in the world, and nothing ever changes.

The only thing that ever changes here is me. My anger. My hate.

It's perhaps the biggest irony of all that the main reason why soul fingerprinting still belongs primarily to science and not yet to the public is because of this very fear: that revenge, hate, guilt, *punishment*, could be carried over into the next life, because a soul never dies, it just takes a new form. And if I pay too much attention to the words on the television, if I listen too closely, if I feel the words as some people argue that I am not June Calahan but Alina Chase, I won't be able to hide the anger. I won't be able to hide the hate.

And I have to hide it.

Today, most of all, I have to hide it.

The kitchen fills with more people—people who work here in the house and on the grounds. People who are never allowed in here on most days. People who are no longer at their posts. I have been counting on this.

They sing "Happy birthday, happy birthday, dear Alina," and I breathe in the smoke and relax my clenched fists, and I smile.

That's one of the skills I taught myself with the hours and days and years of time. I can understand Spanish. I can run the perimeter of the island in just under eighteen minutes. And I can bury my anger beneath sedate indifference.

"Make a wish," someone says. I smile. I choose not to make a wish—words, whether spoken or thought, never change a thing.

They applaud as I blow out the candles, the smoke rising and blurring their faces. They are all the same anyway. They are everyone and no one. The people who work here rotate out every month, lest they get too attached, like when I was ten. Lest they grow soft. Lest I manipulate them into letting me out. June Calahan would've been able to. She would've talked and talked until her words felt like theirs, her ideas their own. *She* would've been able to see the pattern of guards, if one exists.

I may have her soul, but I am not her.

I am *not*.

As the applause winds down and the noise drifts away with the smoke, the only sound left besides the plastic dishes and cups and utensils being spread across the counter is the ridiculous television news program from the next room. They are still discussing June, but they're really discussing me. My God, it's the same thing every year. The discovery of soul fingerprinting, the scientific studies that followed, the development of the Soul Database, the privatization of the information, and the construction of the presumed unhackable Alonzo-Carter Cybersecurity Data Center to house it. And the study of violence—the one that showed a high statistical correlation in criminal history from one generation to the next. The study June used to ruin lives. Ruining her own, and mine, in the process.

Every year, they show our pictures side by side on the news, and I look nothing like her. My picture changes every year, but hers remains the same—stuck at the age of nineteen, as old as she will ever be. Alongside her, our faces splitting the screen, I always look like her shadow. My hair is nearly black, and my skin is darker than hers—my mother was, *is,* Hispanic. But I think my eyes are a problem. They confuse people. Make me unplaceable. Dangerous.

Year after year, they show my eyes as they zoom in on my picture, and it makes people see her. They are so light they are almost clear. Like you could look through them to see my soul.

Straight to June.

The girl with the short dark hair serves me a piece of cake. Her hand shakes as she places it on the table—the plate wobbles on the surface before settling. Someone else looks at her. At me and her. I pick up my spoon and force a bite into my mouth, and I change my mind about that wish. I look at the girl, who is now serving someone else, and I think: *Please don't screw up.*

I swallow the cake and watch as others do the same. Last year I assumed it was something in the cake they give me every year that made me pleasant and malleable when the press showed up—permitted to visit on this one day a year. That I was drugged by something other than sugar and iced perfection. Something that kept me from crying out about the injustice of it all. Something that kept me from screaming that speech I practiced last year—that my name was Alina Chase, and that my incarceration (*not* containment) was unconstitutional, unjustified, and inhumane.

So I didn't eat the cake last year, but it didn't matter. The press showed up just before sunset, and I just grinned and waved from the front entrance. No speech. I felt content and slow and indifferent. The articles the next day said my soul was gloating.

So this time I'd eat the cake. I just wouldn't drink. I could not afford to be content or slow or indifferent today. I'd been drinking from the tap in my sink, but that was it.

I hold the cup to my mouth, feel the water touch my lips, and bring it back down to the table.

The cake is delicious. I'm not going to lie.

In the lull of inactivity, as people scoop cake into their mouths and remark on the taste or the texture or something else completely safe and meaningless, someone in the next room switches from the news station to that movie, the only thing I'd want to hear less.

Of course it's on today. *June of Summerton*. Like Joan of Arc or Helen of Troy. But it's barely even about the crimes, or the fact that she was once considered a hero before she was the villain. It's a love story, which is apparently more interesting.

Liam White is beautiful in the movie version, but in pictures, he is not. It's this fact that people always came back to: that she was so beautiful, beautiful and charismatic, and he was so not—and because of that, she could convince him to do any-thing. She could convince him to hack one of the most secure systems in the country, to commit the most notorious crimes of her generation with her. To keep her secrets. Help her escape. Sacrifice himself, even.

The movie ends with Liam begging June to run as the police surround their building. Whispering that her soul was not meant to be in a cage, that he'll be okay, that they'll be together again someday.

She clutches at his shirt as she wavers. But June is strong. She is strong enough to run. To let him go. She promises him that her soul will find him again. That she'd know him anywhere.

And then he does it. It's Christmas Day, and it's starting to snow, and there are lights strung up in the windows behind him. He runs for the barricade lined with police cars as she sneaks onto the roof and down the fire ladder, and he pulls a weapon at the last minute, and the sound of gunfire accompanies June as she races frantically through the woods, as tears run down her cheeks.

The credits roll as his blood seeps into the thin blanket of snow surrounding him, beside the weapon that turned out not to be a weapon at all but a metal recorder. Liam White, the goddamn martyr. The snow will continue to fall until the screen goes white.

I know the movie by heart.

The movie doesn't show June in hiding for the next year and a half. It doesn't show her dying a very unbeautiful hit-and-run death when she suddenly reappeared. Not the baby being born twelve hours later, or the tracker implanted on its third rib, or the parents begging no. It does not show the house where I am kept.

Anyway, the whole thing has to be a lie. Liam White must've orchestrated everything. I feel it in my soul, like something whispering to me. I am not capable of such darkness, despite what science says. I'm sure of it. And now his soul is free and I am stuck here, even though I have done nothing. *Nothing.*

"Can someone *please* turn that off?" I ask. And then I realize my mistake. I should be content and slow and indifferent by now. "Because my head feels funny," I add. And then I make myself smile. "More cake?"

Someone places another slice onto my plate.

"If there are leftovers," I mumble, digging my spoon into the *A* of my name, "I'm having this again for breakfast."

Someone forces a laugh, and I force another piece of sickeningly sweet birthday cake into my lying mouth.

Because today is my seventeenth birthday.

Today is the day we agreed on.

The girl with the short dark hair watches the clock over the table.

One hour and twelve minutes to go.

And then I will escape.

chapter 2

THERE ARE THINGS THAT must happen first. I know this. I look at the clock and imagine the spot on the underside of my third rib, under the scar where my mother dug out the tracker the first time, under the scar where they replaced it and stitched me back up. It must come out. I wonder, not for the first time, if I'm supposed to do this myself.

I've been waiting seven months for today. I've been waiting seven *years* for today, if I'm being honest. Since I first understood that escape was a thing that was possible. I was ten when it happened, when Genevieve, my longtime guard, tried to sneak me out in the back of a supply van, crammed in a compartment underneath the trash. The entire memory reeks of decay. We didn't even make it over the bridge, and all that attempt got me was a change in protocol—a steady stream of changing faces, so no one would see me as anything other than their one-month assignment.

Well, it got me that, a gash in my forehead, and a fire

continually burning in the pit of my stomach: the possibility of escape, filling my head and my heart and my bones for the last seven years. *Escape.* The word taking meaning, gathering context, becoming more than letters on a page but a promise, whispering in my ear.

Sometimes I imagine it's June speaking to me. *Go*, she says in the voice I have heard in five different documentaries and countless news programs. *Go.* I hear it at night, when I wake up and the island is still. I feel it stirring under my ribs, restless and wanting.

And now, it's really happening. This time, I'm ready. It's been seven months since I deciphered the first message—hidden inside a strand of DNA code in my schoolwork. A simple and boring assignment: to decode the nucleotides of a DNA strand into the corresponding chain of proteins. The C-A-T was a histidine, designated by an *H*. Next: A-T-C, coding for isoleucine, written as *I*. On and on, until I stared at the protein strand on my page: H-I-A-C-I-S-E-E

Hi, A.C., I see.

Hi, Alina Chase. I see.

I must've stared at it for an hour, doing nothing but hoping, which is a very dangerous thing. It could've been a message or maybe just a random combination of letters that I was stringing my hope on.

But I don't get a lot of chances here.

So at the next problem, when I was supposed to do the entire procedure in reverse, translating a random string of letters back into its original DNA strand, I ignored the letters assigned to me and substituted them with: HELP. And I sent back the corresponding DNA strand.

Someone responded in my assignment the next week. READY, it said, when I decoded it. Like a statement, or a question. *For what?* I wanted to respond, but there's no codon designation for the letter *O*, and while I was thinking of how to rephrase that, I changed my mind. YES, I sent back.

But that was seven months ago, and there was only so much information we could exchange during the few weeks when I studied DNA. This is the grand summation of what I know of the plan:

DEATH DAY

GIRL IN FRAYED PANTS

DETACH TRACKER

DISTRACT

ESCAPE

Seven months of waiting. Seven months of anticipation.

And now I'm faced with the reality of the tracker lodged under my skin, under my muscle, and what exactly DETACH TRACKER will entail. There are no sharp objects in the house. It's a subtle thing, though. Something I didn't realize for a long time. Not until I went looking for something I could use.

It's for my own protection, I've been told.

No knives. No pieces of furniture that can be unscrewed and fashioned into anything. Food is cooked and brought in on supply vehicles that get screened on the other side of the bridge. We use battery-powered razors. The guards don't even carry weapons. The only sharp item that I'm aware of is the point of the needle they use to administer drugs on the rare occasion when I become unmanageable.

I turn the spoon over now, feeling along the dull end. I'm wondering if I'll have to use a fork, if the ends will bend before they pierce my skin—and I don't think it's the cake that's making me suddenly nauseated—when the girl with the shoulder-length hair hands me a napkin.

"To wash the cake off," she whispers.

I push back from the table and announce to no one, to everyone, "I'm going to get ready."

The older woman who inspected the cake looks at the clock, ticking closer to sunset. "One hour," she says.

"I know," I say. Oh, I know.

I wonder if the girl managed to sneak something inside. Something she has whittled into a point and left in my bathroom. It's the only place, in addition to my room, with no surveillance. The cameras, too, are for my own protection, I am assured.

There are no locks, so I slide my dresser in front of the door when I shut it behind me. Then I step into my bathroom. There's a man. No, a boy. No, a man. Whatever he is, he's standing beside the sink. He must be stationed on the grounds or in the basement or in security, because men or boys or this in-between variety are no longer allowed in my house. Definitely not in my room. Not since the fiasco with Ellis. At least, I think that's his name. The other guards called him Mark, but he said his real name was Ellis. I'm still embarrassed by the whole thing, that I trusted him so quickly, so readily.

But he was looking for someone else, someone other than me. He was looking for June—for her information, like everyone else. I'm not sure why I was surprised. I'm not sure why I was upset. I blame it on hope.

I don't know what happened to him afterward, exactly. After they dragged him out of my room, shaken and only partially conscious. I assume he got in a lot of trouble. I didn't. I am already in trouble.

Women only from then on. A core group of guards. Precise and watchful. I was hoping my birthday would be an exception.

It is.

I shut the door to the bathroom behind me now and waste no time. I know what he's here for. I pull my shirt over my head. His gaze doesn't linger too long. He doesn't look surprised. He opens his mouth and looks away as his fingers unscrew his eyetooth, pulling out a small metallic blade where the root should be. I wonder absently whether it hurt.

It occurs to me in that moment that this is about to hurt me.

He flips the blade, and it is now twice the length. He turns on the shower, but I'm not sure why. Then he takes a washcloth and balls it up, and I'm not sure why. He grips my chin and holds it to my mouth. I understand, biting down on the towel. But I still don't understand the shower. If he needs water, the sink is right beside him.

He lowers me onto the cold tile, and I lie back. My head is on the hard floor. He's leaning over me, his breath on my chest. Dangerously close. I feel his fingers trace the ribs as he counts them, then he takes a breath and the metal slides into my flesh. It stings in a shocking, sudden way, and I have this moment where I realize that, though this place has kept everything from me, it has also kept pain from me.

The blade slides under the bone and I feel it scraping at something, at the inside of me, and then I understand the need for the shower. For the sound of it.

I'm crying.

I grit my teeth into the towel, trying, trying, trying not to make this sobbing sound that seems to come from the deepest place inside me. Trying not to make any noise at all. But the pain builds, and it will smother me if I don't let it out. If I don't scream it out. "It will be worse if I take a break," he says, I guess as an apology.

But he doesn't stop. And I feel the pain, and I bite back the scream until it tastes like vomit, and it chokes me from the inside until everything turns gray.

I wake up under the lukewarm water on the floor of the shower. "No time for stitches," he says from the other side of the glass. He turns away as I examine the damage to my rib.

"I'm still bleeding," I say, almost in surprise. And it still hurts. Burns. Throbs. I hold my fingers to the skin around it.

"You'll keep bleeding until it's stitched."

I start to panic. The blood keeps coming. It's not a big cut, but any cut here is quickly tended to and treated. I needed stitches across my forehead when I was ten, after the failed escape. But someone gave me a shot and I slept through the stitches and my forehead was kept numb for days. I also sprained my ankle once when I fell from the tree outside my bedroom window, but the leg was braced and I was medicated before I could even explain what happened.

"Are you going to pass out again?" he whispers as he glances at the black watch on his wrist.

"No," I say, pushing myself to standing. He goes to leave, and I notice he's not wearing the same uniform as the guards. He's got a media badge, but his clothes look close enough to blend in anywhere on the island. He puts a big wad of gauze on the sink counter, and a roll of tape. The tracker sits beside them both. I'm not sure how he plans on sneaking out, but he can't. Not yet. "I don't know what to do next," I say.

"Just press down on the wound. And get ready," he says, and his fingers grip the side of the doorway on his way out. *READY*, someone wrote.

YES, I responded.

"Wait," I say, before I can stop myself from sounding desperate. "I . . ." He doesn't turn around at first. A boy. He's still a boy. And the girl out there, she's still a girl. And they are terrified.

"What's your name?" I ask. I'm not good at putting people at ease. It takes practice. It takes me doing the opposite of everything instinct tells me to do. Right now, I want to beg him to stay with me. Right now, I want to cry that this is not a prank, or a dare, or an assignment. That this is my goddamn life. I want to tell him that I'm terrified, too.

"Cameron," he says. He's still standing in the doorway, and

I notice that one of the muscles in his upper arm is twitching. I notice that his dark hair is starting to curl at the nape of his neck from the moisture in the room. I notice that he's gripping the wall so hard that his knuckles blanch white.

"Cameron." People always respond better when you use their name. Which is probably why nobody here uses their real names. I take another breath, to steady my words. "Cameron," I repeat, "I need you to help me." I look back down again, at the watery blood running down my stomach. At my shaking hand covering the wound. I grab a towel and swallow my panic and relax my face into calm and brave before he turns back around.

He keeps checking his watch, and he keeps moving, moving me, as fast as he can.

"What's the girl's name?" I ask as Cameron tears the tape with his teeth. He's not much taller than I am, and I notice the eyetooth is back in place. I wonder what it feels like inside his mouth. If he screamed when they dug into his flesh, like I did. Or whether he was already unconscious.

He pauses, the tape an inch from my stomach, before he says, "Casey." She means something to him. I can tell by the way he looks down and mumbles her name, like he doesn't want me to know. Like her name belongs to him alone.

"Which one of you have I been communicating with?" I hold a dress out to him, asking him to help me with it. In truth, this is not what I need help with. I need help with finding out what the hell is going on, but I'd rather have him think it's the dress.

He tugs it over my head, helps me snake my arms through without loosening the bandage. "Neither," he says. He clears his throat, whispers even lower than he has been. "You've been in touch with Dom. He's the one who will pull you from the water."

I suck in a breath, and Cameron apologizes, trying a different angle of my arm. I don't tell him that I have no idea what happens under the broad heading of *escape*. I don't tell him I have no idea what to do when he leaves this room, only that there will be a girl with frayed pants, that there will be a distraction and we will escape. I've only received words, or short phrases, in the code. I don't tell him that I don't really know the plan at all. That I've only been guessing. That I lie on my bed and stare out the window, with the perfect angle—past the tree—to the sky, imagining racing across the bridge or being snuck out in the back of one of the media vans. But the bridge is a mile long, and the media vans are left on the other side of the bridge before each person is screened for potential weapons. Once, I imagined a helicopter, but I knew it would be nearly impossible to sneak one through restricted airspace.

"I have to go," he says, as he zips up the back of my dress.

"Thanks," I whisper. My heart races as I imagine the ocean—the calm blue that stretches straight to freedom. It races no matter how I picture being pulled from its depths: an arm reaching under the surface to grab me; a man throwing a rope as I strain to keep my head above water. *You can do it*, I tell myself as Cameron walks away.

I don't tell him I'll see him later, because I'm not sure if I will. I don't tell him good luck, because luck has never been on my side.

And I sure as hell don't tell him that I don't know how to swim.

chapter 3

CAMERON LEAVES THROUGH MY window. I shouldn't be surprised. It's not difficult, once you get the hang of the tree. I've done it myself before. But I am surprised that there's nobody there to see him do it. The guards stationed outside always make sure that I know they see me, and I pretend not to notice. Not that there's anywhere for me to go, but I like to see how far I can push them. What I can get away with, what they report back on later, and what they approach me about right then.

So I expect them to be there watching, but they're not. The press must be waiting out front already. The guards must be restationed. It must be almost time.

The press come every year, because the public likes to see that I'm treated well. Kept safe. Proof that this is not a punishment but a humanitarian effort. My parents cannot care for me, so the state must watch over me. This is their mistake, after all—that everyone knows who I am—and now they are responsible. The pictures from when I was younger, eating my cake and laughing, hugging a stranger, kept the public content. Except now that I'm older, I no longer smile and laugh and hug strangers. I have seen the headlines. Now I make them nervous.

It's not my fault that I am what I am, and so, like the mentally ill, they like to see that I am both contained and cared for. Like if you cross your eyes and look through the blurry filter, maybe I am even free. And so the guards will look like people who keep me company today. They will watch the press very closely. They will watch *me*, probably following my blip on the computer screen from somewhere in the basement. They will not watch my window, or see the guy jumping from it, or the trees he disappears into.

I consider doing it myself. I can see straight to the section of woods. I could hide there for a bit, now that the tracker is out. Create some chaos as the media sets up their cameras. Make a scene. Make that speech I've been saving since last year. Wait for people to rise up in support, to lobby for my cause, to fight for me. But I'm not June. I'm not good at the same things that she was, despite what science claims about the elements fully bound to a soul: left- or right-handedness; the results of standardized personality tests; areas of extreme giftedness.

Whatever. All the charisma in the world couldn't save her. She couldn't persuade her way out of death. There was no equation to be solved that would extend her life, no pattern she could find that would keep everyone from turning on her.

And my father has tried. He had appealed to the masses from behind the bars of his cell. And when he was released five years ago, he came a step too close to me—a violation of his parole—and ended up back in jail.

There's a plan. There's a plan, there's a plan, and I'll stick to it. *READY. YES.*

There's a knock on the door just as Cameron disappears into the distance. He runs like he's been training for it, like someone taught him how to move his arms and the perfect length of a stride. He doesn't look back.

I've been training, too. But nobody teaches me how to run faster. All I can do is imagine someone after me, someone who trains every moment I'm thinking of taking a rest. I always outrun them. My muscles twitch with adrenaline just thinking of it.

"Just a sec," I say as I move the dresser away from the door.

The girl—Casey—is there. She looks at my dress, at the spot where my third rib sits underneath, and she says, "All set?"

"Yes," I say, even though it's an effort not to hunch over, to hold my hand against my rib cage.

She touches my hand, and I flinch. Then I feel her fingers spreading, and something cold and hard that she presses into my palm. "Under your desk," she whispers. "And I need the tracker."

She shifts her weight from foot to foot and casts a quick glance over her shoulder. I want to tell her to calm down, to not draw attention to herself, but I realize I'm doing the same thing. My fingers tremble as I place the small cylinder under my desk. I wonder how she got this inside. It looks like a candle, all waxy on the outside, but without the top. And then I real-ize: the cake. No wonder she was nervous when she brought it in.

I guess this is what they meant by DISTRACT.

I told them no casualties, and at this point I have to trust that this is just that—a distraction. That it won't destroy every-thing. Just this. My computer. My journal. My life.

Everything I've been for seventeen years will be gone. Everything I've known for seventeen years . . .

I open the bottom drawer and grab the picture buried near the bottom. The newspaper clipping with my mother's photo that I printed off years ago, and I fold it up and shove it into the sleeve of my dress.

I grab my journal from the desk.

Casey watches me from the doorway. She frowns and says, "You can't take that with you."

I nod. Of course I understand. It's too bulky, too noticeable, and I'll be in the water at some point anyway. But my nails dig into the softened spine. I know it's just words, but they are my words. I know the people here can and probably do read it, but I don't even care. It's the words of Alina Chase, not June Cala-han, and in a way, it's the only tangible evidence of my exis-tence. It's proof that I am something other than the soul of June Calahan. Her soul may be mine, but my mind is my own.

I clear my throat and dart to the bathroom, tossing the journal behind the toilet, hoping it survives. I want it to exist. Even if I never see it again, whether it's peeled back and exposed for everyone to see, or whether it's kept locked up in some closet of evidence, I want to know it's *somewhere*.

I retrieve the tracker from the bathroom, balling it up in my fist, preparing to hand it to her the same way she passed me the candle.

Casey frowns as our hands connect. "Your hair is wet," she says.

"I took a shower." Not a lie.

"Turn around," she says. She pulls an elastic band from her wrist and holds it in her teeth. I do as I'm told. I feel her hands in my hair, dividing it up, weaving it together. She spins me around and smooths back the sides of my hair. I catch a glimpse of myself in the mirror as I leave my room for presumably the very last time.

A braid runs down my back, and my dark hair looks just that—dark. Slick, like it was styled that way. And with the dress, I look like I cared that there were cameras coming. That my face would be splashed on every network today. And in the coming days.

Jen or Kate or whoever stands at the end of the hall. "You look lovely, Alina," she says, eyes flat and full of dispassion. "Leigh will take you out to see them now."

I look in the hall, wondering who this Leigh is, and then I realize: she meant Casey. Cameron gave me her real name, and I'm wearing her elastic, and she did my hair. I hear both of us breathing over my pounding heartbeat. I try to slow it, to be calm, act normal, but nothing is working.

I feel my mother's picture crumpled against my shoulder, and I concentrate on that. Not on the fact that I am following her, the girl in the frayed pants—a person with a real name—and I am walking away from my room for the very last time, down the hall for the very last time, out the door for the very last time.

I hear the shutter of camera lenses as I step outside. I shield my eyes for a moment—from the sun on the horizon in the distance, from the flashes at the edge of the path. Casey walks down the steps, and I follow.

"Alina," a reporter shouts. "Do you have anything to say?"

I picture June and that speech she made when she was barely older than I am now, appealing to the people. *I am not the danger. I am not the threat. I am the bell, tolling out its warning. I am delivering a message.*

She had such poise, such grace. She made people believe in her. She made them believe that a criminal past life should be public information. That the warning she delivered justified the crime she committed to provide it.

Casey guides me down a step. Last year I made it only to the first step. Nobody led me anywhere. But Casey keeps moving. We walk down the rest of the steps, down the brick path, much closer to the press than I've ever been before. It's not that we want to be close to them, it's that we want to be away from the house. They smile widely, holding microphones out to me.

I see a few guards look at each other—questioning glances that I haven't seen since they found that guard Ellis in my room.

This is not part of Casey's instructions, I am sure. And I'm supposed to be slow and malleable and content. I am not. I can see it in their eyes—they can see *I am not*.

They start to move closer. "One," Casey whispers.

They won't get here in time.

"Alina," someone shouts again. "What did you get for your birthday?"

"Two." I see her hand reach into her pocket.

I glance at Casey. Her face is bare. The cameras see her as much as they see me. This is the last moment I will be complicit in my own imprisonment. This is the last moment she will be anonymous.

What I'm about to gain, she is about to lose. "You're about to see," I say.

"Three."

The explosion is more than just noise—it's a rush of air and a flash of light and, yes, noise. Everyone drops to the ground instinctively.

Except Casey, who has a grip on my arm, pulling me against instinct, dragging me away.

ESCAPE.

I leave my shoes behind, my feet calloused from months of training, and I run. I can't breathe. The air is full of dust and dirt, and then suddenly it's worse—smoke. I glance behind me quickly, but the house is fine. Still standing. The window from my room is missing and there's a gaping hole in the bricks surrounding it.

People are moving toward us.

And then I can't see anymore because smoke settles down from above. From the trees. I can't see at all, but that must be the point. I wonder if Cameron is up in the trees somewhere. Or if he's running with us right now.

I hear shouting, hear footsteps, feel the ground vibrating beneath my feet.

"Close your eyes," she says, her hand still on my arm. I don't know how she can tell where she's going with her eyes closed, but she does. She counts as she runs. Stopping. Turning. Counting again.

I run with my eyes closed. I didn't train for this. If they had told me to memorize this island blind, I would have. I would've been ready, and not just someone who had to be dragged. I know this island. I know it better than anyone.

Casey slows, and I open my eyes. We've broken through the smoke and are deep in the trees—almost to the cliffs. She stops abruptly and rips her shirt over her head. "Switch!" she yells at me. "Hurry!" A wig comes off with her shirt, and a long dark braid weaves down her back. Her body is lean and muscular under her clothes as she tosses them my way. If I catch a glimpse of her from just the corner of my eye, she looks like me.

"Now!"

I tear off my dress, and the picture of my mother drifts away, and with a single gust, it flips over the edge of the cliffs and it's gone. I pull on her pants. Her shirt. She tugs at my hair, yanking the elastic out, and I understand, shaking out the braid.

She looks out over the edge. "This is where you jump," she

says. I look down, but I shouldn't have. The waves crash against the rock, and the sea swirls and foams.

This is the edge of my world, and it looks exactly like an edge of the world should look.

I imagine my eyes are huge when I look back at her. "No. Over here." She points behind her, and I lean over the edge. There's a small cove. It looks still, as far as oceans go. "Swim to the entrance." She must be talking about the mouth between the rocks.

I thought I could do it, but there's no way. It's suicide. If I jump I'll be too deep, and how do you swim for the surface? Is it instinct? People drown every day, even people who know how to swim. I can't do it.

"There's netting, and—" And I can't swim. But they have made a mistake beyond that. There's no way out. It looks just like an island, and the guards look just like people, and the mile-long bridge doesn't need guns or barricades, because it lifts—it ceases to be a bridge unless a bridge is needed. This is a prison, and I am its captive. The air above is restricted airspace. And below the water, there's a cage. Steel netting, hooked into the floor, and it rises up out of the water, attached to steel posts. Everyone knows this. Algae and seaweed make it look natural. Beautiful, even. But this is a prison. There's no way through it. I'd have to climb up over the top, and everyone would see. Then again, I'd have to be able to swim there in the first place.

"Trust me," she says as she zips up the dress and backs away.

"You're not coming with me?" I ask.

I cover my face as another round of smoke drops over us. Over the whole island. Cameron darts out of the clearing. "Let's go," he says to her, not even looking at me.

"We jump somewhere else," she says. "With your tracker."

And then I understand. She will be running through the smoke with another person, dressed like me, carrying my tracker. She is the diversion.

"I can't," I say. I grip on to her, like she'd been doing to me.

"You have to," Cameron says. "You can't see him, but Dom's there. He's outside the cove. Under the surface. He's waiting for you."

"Okay?" Casey says, but I shake my head. Not okay. There must be another way. I've been training. I am strong, but I'm seized with the fear of water in my lungs. With the fear of never resurfacing, of drowning, of dying, of becoming nothing. I can't will myself to jump—to trust that I can reach the surface, to trust that someone is waiting for me.

"We're behind schedule," Cameron mumbles. He turns me around, facing the water, and I realize what he's about to do the second before he does it.

"I can't swim!" I scream, but it's too late. His hands are already on my back, and his weight is already behind it, and I'm leaning over the edge—my feet kick up dirt, and I feel Cameron's fingers grasping at my shirt. He's too late. I'm too far. I feel air, and my feet clamber for nothing. My hands, for nothing.

But then I feel him still, his fingers tightening on the

fabric, and then his arm around my waist, but I'm still falling. No. *We* are falling.

We hit the water, and it's colder than I imagined it would be. And it slams into my side—or my side slams into it—at the same moment my head collides with Cameron's. Either way, it feels nothing like freedom.

chapter 4

THE SHOCK OF COLD wears off, and my head throbs, and my eyes burn, but the cut on my rib burns far more. I feel Cameron pulling me by the waist, his legs moving below, and I keep mine still, against instinct, so I don't make things worse. We break through the surface, and I suck in air. Except the water crests up at the same moment, and I take in salty water, burning a path to my lungs.

Cameron lets go of me as he turns his face to the top of the cliff, and I start to slip under. I reach up and throw my arms over his shoulders in a panic, taking him down with me.

He pushes me off under the water, then comes up coughing, holding me by my arm. I follow his gaze to the top of the cliff and see Casey leaning over the edge. He waves vigorously for her to go, and she disappears.

"*Shit*," he says. "Shit, shit, shit." Then to me: "Float. Can't you even do that?"

My face burns. My stomach burns. I didn't expect

everything about the ocean to burn. It seems like it should do the opposite.

I try to do as Cameron says. I lie back, but my hips dip first, and then the rest of me, like my body mass is off. Over the last year, I've traded in most of my curves for muscle, most of the give of my body for a tense resistance, but people don't notice under the nondescript clothes. The doctor comes every year after my birthday. She has not seen what I have become yet.

Everyone has seen me run—my soul is understandably restless—but I've hidden the fact that I do nothing but push-ups and sit-ups and lunges in my room, deep into the night, and I hide the results even more. I thought it would help me escape, but it's weighing me down. I haven't done a thing on my own.

His arm is around my chest again, and I'm on my back, and he's swimming on his front, cursing repeatedly under his breath. He pauses and pushes me against the rocks. I reach around and dig my fingers into the crevices, supporting myself for once.

A person's head, covered in black material, rises up beside us. I assume this must be Dom. His hand rests on my shoulder. His lips smile around the breathing apparatus in his mouth. But he stops abruptly when he sees Cameron beside me.

"She can't swim," Cameron says through clenched teeth.

Dom has a face mask over his eyes and, with that thing inside his mouth, I can't tell the level of his annoyance or disappointment—not like I can see on Cameron.

Like it's my fault.

"Excuse me for not spending the last seventeen years

anywhere near a goddamn swimming pool!" I slap at the water with one hand, the words pouring out before I have a chance to weigh them, like I usually would, and I momentarily lose my grip on the side. I dig my hand back into the slick rock. "I don't even have a bathtub."

"I have to go back for Casey," Cameron says, but looking at the slick rock, at the concave cliffs, I know it's impossible. He knows it, too. I think he just needs someone else to tell him he can't.

So I do. "You can't," I say, as my fingers tremble to keep me above water. No one can. It's a *prison*, which nobody seems to understand but me. He knows it's true, but he focuses all his anger at me.

Dom looks at the sky, points to his watch. I hear his breath, slow and loud, through the device. He hands Cameron a face mask, a set of flippers, and an air tank with a hose attached. "She'll be fine," Cameron says, but he's saying it to himself, I'm sure.

Dom disappears under the surface, but not before holding out a long piece of rope. I feel him under the water, like a shark brushing against my skin. His hand grips on to my bare ankle. And then the rope tightens, which is more than anyone here has ever done to me. They don't need to. When I used to act up, to fight, to push back, all it would take was a sedative shot. And when I trained myself to bury it—to hide it—instead, they mostly stopped needing the shots as well.

In the water, where I can't swim, with a rope held by a stranger, I fear what I have traded everything for.

Dom gives a thumbs-up, and Cameron comes very close.

He shows me the breathing device, and he straps the tank onto my back. "Five breaths. Slow and steady. Then pass it back." He hands it to me, and I place it between my lips, nodding at him.

"And whatever you do, don't let go."

I remove the mouthpiece for a second and say, "There's always the rope." It may be to hold me, but it will also keep us from getting lost, being left behind.

But he turns away and whispers, "For you." And I realize the power I have, as I wrap my arms around his neck, and my legs around his waist, preparing to dip under the water. If I let go of him, he could be stranded in the middle of the ocean with nothing.

"Do not let go," he says again, trying to be stern. But he is asking. As he lowers the mask around his face, I see it in his eyes. He is pleading.

"I won't," I say. I have never held on to something so tightly in my entire life.

The muffled sound of blades cuts through the wind. I know that noise. They came for me once before, when we were in the path of a hurricane. They didn't even need a rope then—just a shot beforehand. But it didn't help with the motion. I threw up in the back of the helicopter. I feel Cameron's pulse pick up through my palms that are pressed so tightly to his chest. I feel like throwing up again, because this time they are not coming to save me.

He drops us both under the surface, into the dark.

From the cliffs, from my home, the water looks clear. A blue calm stretching into the distance. But Cameron has the face mask, and my eyes burn and see nothing when I open them. There's nothing to guide us, nothing to direct us, but the rope stretching before us. Cameron breathes slowly, calmly, and my lungs start to ache long before he hands the device back. And then I take breaths too quickly, too desperately, and have to give it back too soon.

I keep my eyes squeezed shut, trying not to hear the blades over the surface or the sound of the air I'm draining from the tank. I try to picture my mother, like she looked in the newspaper clipping. Not the photo from after she was arrested.

I did not print that one out.

I imagine her humming a song, as she shushes me with a lullaby, as she cuts into my skin. In my head, I do not scream, even though I'm sure I did. I was just a baby. In my head she takes out the tracker and holds me to her, wrapping a blanket around my body. In my head she tries to run.

In my version they do not arrest her at home, like the article claims.

In the article, they say she put the tracker in the garbage disposal. That she knew they would come for her. That she must've been *hoping* they'd come for her. That she didn't want to be responsible for the soul of June Calahan.

Like June's family did for their own safety, severing ties, taking new identities, leaving the country, so they would never be associated with her name again.

I wonder if they would've let me grow up there, with my

mother, with my father. If she hadn't been so blatantly defiant.
If he hadn't held a pillow to a baby's face and then changed his
mind, unable to go through with it in the end. He brought me
to the hospital. They never returned me.

I hold my breath and press my head into Cameron's back,
imagining a time before all of this, before I was June—that
first day, when I could've been anyone—before the needle in
my back. I can hear my mother, and only her, as if my ear is
pressed to her chest, as she sings me to sleep.

Duérmete, mi niña . . . and the pain, the cold, the entire
world falls away.

Something is wrong.

We've stopped moving. Cameron's body shifts to vertical,
and he pulls me toward him, and then past him, until I feel my
forearms scrape against cold metal—we've reached the steel net.

My fingers tangle with the metal wires, and I press my face
against them as my lungs beg for air. Cameron moves the mouthpiece to me, and I breathe too much. Too fast. We're trapped.

I feel the tank being pulled away from me, off my back, and
I start to panic. I claw my way up the netting toward the surface. I need air. I need out. But someone grabs my leg, trap-
ping me between his body and the netting. He puts a mask
over my face. A new breathing device in my mouth, and turns
me around to strap it on my back.

But I still can't see. The mask is full of water. He's trying to
tell me something, tapping at my mouth, tapping at my mask.
I think he means to use the air to push the water away, but

when I remove the device, he puts it back in my mouth. Then he taps my mouth once more, traces his finger up along my cheek, to my forehead, down my nose—tracing the path the air might take. He presses against the top of my mask, and I understand. I take a breath through my mouth and let it out through my nose, and the water pushes out the bottom, and I see Cameron in front of me, nodding.

I see.

I see the netting behind me, covered in algae, but I can't see much farther because it's nearly dark. I see Dom in the wetsuit rising up from the bottom with another tank, and I watch as Cameron switches it out. Cameron illuminates his watch and presses himself against the netting as beams of light pass across the surface of the water.

We wait.

Dom has another set of equipment in his hands that must be for Casey. Beside me, Cameron leans forward, as if he's waiting to see her swim out of the darkness. I understand. Cameron and Casey were supposed to meet up with us here, but I have screwed that up.

We breathe underwater for a long time. Long enough for us to hear the motor of a boat ripping overhead. Long enough for me to stop worrying about Casey and instead worry about running out of air.

Dom disappears into the darkness below us again, comes back with another set of tanks, and my fingers grasp ineffectively at the straps. I am a prune. I am a bleeding, blind prune, and I start breathing too fast, unable to control the panic. Because I am sure I will either become prey to something that has caught the scent of my blood, or else I will surely suffocate under here, in the darkness—and they will pull up my body a few days from now, and they'll test all the newly born, and they'll put my soul in a cage again.

And then just like that, Cameron touches my shoulder and points up. Dom is near the surface, waving at us. I claw at the steel, pulling myself up out of the water. It's as dark on the surface as it was underneath. This must be what we were waiting for.

Darkness.

I burst through the surface and spit out the mouthpiece, sucking in real, salty air. Waves, water, move around me, and I feel exposed, despite the darkness. My fingers tighten around the steel, digging through the algae. Cameron is still close, but he has his own equipment now. I wonder if he forgot that he doesn't need to rely on me anymore.

There are lights in the distance, from the island. And there are lights through the steel netting, from boats on the other side. And in the distance, far away, I see land. There is no way we will make it with this canister. I realize that, having gone through two already. There is no way we will make it without being seen.

I wonder if this is a suicide mission.

I wonder what will happen to my soul.

The others have removed their mouthpieces as well, speaking in quick, low voices to each other.

"What's the plan?" I ask, as the current pushes my body into the steel.

"We climb. And then we swim," Cameron says.

I look, wide-eyed, at Cameron.

"There was a robotic sub," he whispers quickly, "that we left just outside the cage, on the other side. Casey put your tracker on it." He nods, as if he's convincing himself she made it. "They're not looking over here."

I want to believe him, but the beam from a boat cuts across the surface, and we all dive underneath for a moment. When I resurface, I expect them to make a new plan.

"Climb," Dom says.

I have come this far. They have come this far with me. My muscles twitch in anticipation, because this is something I can do. And so I climb.

This I do faster than either of them. I make it to the top and hook my legs over the other side, flattening myself against the netting, and see nothing but dark water, waiting to swallow me up.

The boats cast their beams of light across the surface in a steady pattern. If light hits us, we are found. We need to get back into the water. Back *under* the water. I count the seconds in my head. The light moves in a steady, obvious pattern. Automated and predictable, but still, they need to move faster.

The rope on my ankle tugs as I slip down the other side. The ocean is dark, except for the beams of light cutting across in the distance, heading this way. I wait for Dom and Cameron to come over, but they're arguing as they climb.

"I need to wait," Cameron says, watching the water.

"There's not enough air," Dom says. His voice cuts down to my stomach, or maybe that's just the seawater. He's holding something that looks like a walkie-talkie with a screen in one hand and his breathing device in the other. "Not for you to wait without being seen." He points to the beams of light, stretching across the surface of the water periodically. "Not enough for both of you." Cameron nods, like of course he knew that. Of course he does.

He slips down the rest of the steel, not worried about drowning when he hits the water again. He comes back up beside me.

He looks like he's about to throw up.

He looks like he's about to break down.

"She'll make it," I say. He didn't see the way she grabbed my arm and ran with single-minded focus. Or the way she did my hair, or switched our clothes. She's going to make it.

"Of course she'll make it," he says. And then he readjusts his mask, grabs on to a slack of the rope, and disappears under the surface again.

For a second I wonder whether I'm expected to know how to swim now. Or whether I'll be dragged by the rope. I see a beam of light coming, and I dip under the surface.

Swimming feels like it should be easy. I push off from the cage, and I move my arms like I felt Cameron doing, and I kick my legs like he did, but mostly I'm just moving water around. And sinking.

Then I feel his hand on my arm as he pulls me toward him, as he hooks my arm around his shoulder, and we start moving.

We keep a slow pace—I don't know how we know where we're going, or how we're going to get there with the air we have, but I don't have any more options. Eventually Cameron stops, grasping a rope that's tethered to a buoy, still under the water. I grip on to the rope as both of them follow it down, disappearing from my vision. I close my eyes. I am alone in the ocean, underwater. I count to ten, and I imagine shadows, shapes, circling me. Thirty seconds, and the water grows colder. *Forty-nine* . . . I jump when someone grabs my hand, pushing fresh equipment toward me. I open my eyes and the shadows disappear. Cameron holds his thumb up and keeps it that way, like he's asking me. I do the same, mirroring his movement, and he nods.

READY? YES.

We switch out our tanks, leaving one behind for Casey, and we start moving again.

I realize that's what Dom has in his hand. A GPS, leading us on a marked trail that they had set up previously. Like a path with lights along the way. We stop at two more points, swim some more, but by this point I am numb past the point of shaking. I no long worry about being found. Being captured. I no longer worry about if we will . . . *if we will* . . . I breathe through the mouthpiece, and the endless ocean falls away.

Duérmete, mi niña, duérmete, mi amor . . .

The water shifts. It *moves* us. It pushes at us more and then pulls, in a rhythm. I open my eyes to darkness just as we are thrust against it. A darkness that is real and solid.

A wall.

I push off Cameron's back. I am at the end of something. Or the start of something. An edge. I start clawing my nails at it, and one breaks off on the brick as I slide farther down. My eyes burn, even through the mask, as if I'm staring at the sun and trying not to blink.

Someone pulls at my arm—I can't feel it, only the pressure—and leads me toward a metal pipe. He pushes me inside first. It's still full of water, and it's pitch black, but it doesn't matter that I can't swim now—there's barely enough room for me. My hands and feet push at the narrow, curved sides, propelling me along the steady incline.

I start to breathe too fast, and I imagine the air running lower, running out, and I understand in a way I can feel that this is it: this is the last air, and this is the last step, and this pipe leads to something I want desperately.

I feel something other than water—the absence of water— on my back, and I clamber onto my knees. I pull the mask from my face and shake the tank off my back and suck in air. Humid, dank air, but air. Dom says, "Don't leave this behind," so I pick it back up and crawl onward. "You, too, Cameron."

"Why not? They know who I am," Cameron says.

"They know who *she* is," he corrects, his voice deliberately quiet, but it still echoes through the tunnel. "They don't know where we've been. They don't know anything but your face so far, if that. Don't give them anything more. They don't know who you are."

Cameron laughs. "What I *am* is a dead man walking."

But he's wrong. In fact, what we are right now, crawling through a pipe under the earth somewhere, is the exact opposite of dead.

The pipe ends, and the room opens up. I see light filtering from somewhere beyond. And I hear water dripping, echoing, along with our movements. There's stagnant water in a pool in the middle of the room, and we stand, silent, on the concrete ridge over top. There are clothes, in piles, shoved against the walls, curving upward. Clean, dry clothes. Cameron doesn't speak as he pushes one pile my way with his foot. I'm wobbly on my legs, and my entire body is shaking, so I press my hand against the wall to steady myself as I undress.

When I pull the wet shirt over my head, the bandage comes with it, and I let out a sound. The wound starts bleeding again, dripping down my stomach, and I wipe it away quickly, hoping nobody else notices.

I look over my shoulder. Dom, in the wet suit, is facing the pipe we came through, pulling the black material down his chest. Cameron stands halfway between us, and he's watching me. He walks closer, half-changed, and whispers, "Casey will take care of it. Soon as she's back."

I nod and instinctively look at the untouched pile of clothes against the wall. Cameron finishes changing with his back to me. It's funny, I think, the things people are supposed to keep hidden about themselves.

My entire life has been on display since forever.

"I'll wait here for Casey," Cameron says, speaking across the room. Dom turns around, his mask gone, and steps out of the shadow. He shakes out his hair, and I freeze. His mouth twitches when he sees that I see.

I try to grasp my bearings. To grasp the upper hand. But I feel instead as if I'm falling over the edge of the cliff again. I try to mimic his condescending gaze. I weigh the words before I speak them, so that I am sure of them. "Hello, *Ellis*," I say. Emphasis on the lie he fed me to hide my shock.

"Always the skeptic," he says, with a sad smile. He sticks his hand out, as if I would consider taking it. "Dominic Ellis," he says. "Did you miss me?"

I sense, but do not see, that Cameron is stepping closer. I wonder if he's as confused as I am. If he knows that I know this man. *Knew* this man. That he was a guard and I liked him. That he snuck into my room and we talked. And then, when I realized he wasn't there for *me,* I did something more, something worse.

Dominic Ellis's crooked grin turns into a full-on smile, and my heart plummets into my stomach, ruining that fleeting feeling of freedom. And I realize that I have made a terrible mistake.

chapter 5

THE SADDEST THING ABOUT this moment, as I finish dressing myself, as Cameron watches Dominic Ellis watching me, is that when he says those words, I realize I do, in a way. I did miss him. I missed the very idea of him—that there could be an ally in a prison, that he could see through the *thing* that I am portrayed to be to the person I am instead. When he showed up last year, he seemed closest to me in age, though I know he must've been at least eighteen. Maybe it was the way he didn't distance himself, lacking the formality, or the way he smiled when he thought no one was looking—but it's true, I missed him.

I miss the person I thought he was for the first three weeks of his assignment. I miss the guard I thought I knew, even though it was all a lie.

But he was not there to help me then, and he is not here to help me now. I am sure of it.

I need to get out of this sewer. *Now*.

"Dominic," I say, leaving off the Ellis, the part that makes it seem as if he didn't lie, not entirely. "Nice to meet you," I say, and I grit my teeth together and force my lips to smile.

He laughs, which sounds strange in this place full of stale, standing water. "Sweetheart, I'm pretty sure we met good and official in your room last year."

Cameron looks at me, and heat rises to my cheeks, even though there should be no reason for that to happen. I want to defend myself. To tell the truth. But I don't yet know this person, and I have to remind myself of that. Because there's something odd about clinging to someone's back for several hours while you escape from the only place you've ever known—it tricks my mind into thinking that I *do* know him, or that he knows me, but that is not the case.

Dominic Ellis wanted something from me, and now he has me. Facts are weapons. So is silence. Right now, the silence lingers dangerously throughout the room, but I can't grasp onto its source. Whether it's Dominic. Whether it's Cameron. Whether it's me.

"I'm ready," I say when the tension starts to feel dangerous. If Dominic expected something more from me, some apology, some begging, then *he* has made a mistake. "Where to?"

"What?" he asks. "No *thank you*?"

My gaze slides away from his, because I'm remembering the Ellis I knew before. He comes closer, reaches out like he's about to touch me. I try to keep the discomfort off my face, but he must notice because he grimaces, his hand hovering beside my arm. "You're welcome, Alina."

"You're wasting time," Cameron says, and Dominic gives

him this look that makes me truly understand the dynamics of this group. "I mean," he starts again, "she needs to move. And I need to wait for Casey."

Dominic tilts his head to the side. "You're not waiting for Casey."

"I'm not doing *anything* until—"

"I am fully aware of what you will and will not do for her. Which is exactly why *I* will wait for her. And why *you* will escort the lovely Ms. Chase to Point B. You will go straight there. You will get her there, and you will keep her there, until I arrive—as a function of this contract. Do you understand?"

Cameron doesn't look much younger than Dominic. But he nods before looking away.

"And," Dominic adds, "you will not listen to a word she speaks. Are we clear?"

I slide my feet into the sneakers that they have left for me, but there's a gap between my heel and the back of the shoe. "Sorry," Dominic says, like he didn't just talk about me to Cameron as if I were a thing instead of a person. "We didn't know your size."

I misjudged him. I hate that I misjudged him.

I hate most of all that he's the one who freed me.

Cameron and I stuff our wet clothes into a plastic bag, which he then places inside a canvas bag that he slings over his shoulder and across his chest. He looks instantaneously carefree, like the kids on TV shows who talk effortlessly, who smile effortlessly, who laugh effortlessly.

He gestures toward a metal ladder, and I step onto the first rung. "It's an alley," he says. "And the street connected to it will be very busy this time of night. We're going to walk in plain sight. We're going to blend in, in plain sight. Got it?"

"Got it," I say, and I pull myself up the rungs of the ladder. It sounds like a horrible plan. I try to imagine eyes skimming over me, but I can't picture it. I see the press, eyes fixed. I see the guards, who watch me without making eye contact. If they look away, it's for a reason.

And I feel Dominic Ellis's eyes following me, rung by rung, as I climb.

The walls around us narrow until I can't see Dominic and he can't see me, and our breathing and our steps echo off the brick walls. There's a metal circle above me, and I hear the sound of muffled screaming—or maybe laughter—carrying through.

Cameron touches my calf briefly before speaking. "They won't know you," he whispers. "They're done with work or school, and they're out—they aren't watching the news."

The idea seems so foreign, that there's this world that exists without me, and yet even as I think it, I know that it's entirely egotistical and selfish of me. But in my world, on my island, there does not exist a time when I am not at the center, when I am not the axis.

Cameron climbs up the other side of the ladder, his feet carefully avoiding my feet. His hands avoiding my hands. I have my elbows hooked over the final rung, but I'm frozen. "But look at us," I say. Meaning our wet hair, our wrinkled fingers, our chattering teeth.

"People only look," he says, his hands flat against the metal circle, twisting it gently, "if you give them a reason to." He tests the lid, which gives easily, and a rush of fresh air flows in before he sets it back down again. "We're going to be together. Just two people walking home." Then he nods at me, gives my elbow a squeeze, and I flinch. "Ready?"

But he doesn't wait for me to answer, probably because he knows that I am not. Probably because he remembers how he had to push me over the edge of the cliff. Possibly, but I'm not sure how, he understands how overwhelming and terrifying that big expanse of freedom actually is when you get there.

Cameron pushes the lid and lifts himself effortlessly out. He reaches his hand down for me—just one hand, one person, one step—and I take it. *YES.*

And then, before I can process the magnitude of this moment, I am out. We're in a narrow street and there are people walking, lots of people walking, by the entrance to this alley. Cameron kicks the lid back in place, and the sound of metal on metal makes someone pause. Makes someone look.

His hands are on my waist, and every muscle in my body freezes. Then they twitch with adrenaline again, waiting for the signal to run, but instead he comes closer, and I feel the brick wall against my back, and his body pressed close to mine, and I'm trying to move because there's too much all at once, but there's nothing but an unforgiving wall. I feel his breath in my ear as he says, "It would help if you pretended to like this."

So I move my hands to his back, and I hear a giggle from the mouth of the alley, but the muscles in his back do not relax.

"You're nervous," I whisper back. He's not supposed to be nervous. He made it seem like this was the easy part.

"Not about this," he says.

I know he's thinking of Casey, even as he runs his fingers down my arm and takes my hand as he backs away.

"You don't like Dom," I say, not as a question.

He pauses. "I don't trust him." Neither do I.

"Then let's go back. I can help."

He looks at me quickly and then away again as he snakes an arm around my waist and pulls me even closer as we exit the alley. "I don't trust you either."

It should hurt when he says it, but it doesn't. I understand. The feeling is mutual. And somehow, his harsh honesty makes me trust him just a little, just enough to keep going.

We step onto the street, and there are tons of people— laughing, yelling, weaving in and around us. We blend in, and my heart races. We walk, and nobody sees me. Just a girl who maybe drank too much and can't walk straight, like I've seen in movies. Just a boy taking a girl home after a night out. I lean into him. We reek like the stagnant water from the sewer, and our hair is still wet, and our fingers are wrinkled, and I still can't shake the chill. But I look up at him, and this sound escapes my throat—I think it's laughter.

He smiles.

I smile.

I am not even faking it.

This street goes on forever in a straight line, like that mile-long bridge connecting my island to the rest of the world. *The rest of the world.* I'm finally here. Walking through it. Watching things *change* just by walking. Where there had been restaurants and bars, now there are houses and convenience stores. The crowd has thinned out, but a few people walk this way still, following signs for a bus stop. I can finally hear the thoughts swirling through my head. *We are through it. We are through it all.*

Moss hangs from the trees along the sides of the roads, looking black now that the lights have faded. Even the houses are dark here. Children tucked into bed by someone who cares for them. Not lights that have been automated, like on my island, after they realized I was flashing my lamp in Morse code like a beacon.

I see the shadow of a child in an upstairs window, and I lower my head, as if she might recognize me. But she seems to find the moon more interesting than me. For a moment, I picture the window I will never look through again, with the perfect angle past the tree to the sky. I spent hours last night watching the moon, unable to sleep. Just imagining . . . and now I'm here. The adrenaline has worn off, and though I tell myself we have made it through the danger—*I have survived*—I can't shake the lingering fear lodged in the center of my chest.

I am thinking of the fact that, even though it took a long time, law enforcement still eventually found June and Liam. I realize, then, how traceable I am. Cameras in the streetlights to catch traffic violators, catching the angles of my face, like a fingerprint. My prints on the ladder rungs in the sewer. My DNA in the blood I've been leaving in my wake.

My soul that can be screened from the base of my spine.

I wonder how soon they will find me.

I wonder if I will be safer on my own. Without Casey's face, and Cameron's face—without a group of people hiding, but one person moving.

But most of all, I wonder why Dominic has come back for me. If this is the most dangerous element of all.

"He's going to leave her," I tell Cameron.

His body tenses, but he keeps walking. There's another alley up ahead, past a sign and between two dark and silent houses. I bet it cuts into more alleys, more homes. I can see them, stacked up behind one another. I could lose him right here. I could make it. But instead my words make his arm tighten around me, his steps speed up.

"No," he whispers, and then his fingers dig into my hip. "You're trying to distract me, and then you're going to run. I know because it's exactly what I would do. Right up there." He jerks his head toward the alley I had spotted.

"Maybe," I say, because I want him to believe me. "But it's true. I know you're not supposed to listen to me, but I know him. He's going to leave her. I swear it." I know I sound convincing, because I mean it. He would. I understand him now. Not like I thought when he was the guard with the crooked smile and the secret notes. He is selfish, and he was using me then, and so he must be using them now. If, as science claims, the nature of a person doesn't change from life to life, then it definitely doesn't change within the *same* one.

"No," he says, never once faltering. "You don't understand. If I don't bring you directly there, then she's screwed. We're both screwed."

"She's screwed anyway," I say. I'm not trying to win anymore, just trying on the truth. Her face will be plastered on every news station by tomorrow morning. "Why are you doing this for him, then? If you don't trust him?"

"I'm not doing it for *him.* I'm doing it for *her.*" Of course. Love. People always do stupid things for love.

My parents were sent to jail.

Liam White is dead.

June Calahan is dead.

"Well if you *love* her—" I start.

"Stop talking now. Dom told us how you work. You take information, and then you use it."

It's such an absurd statement, I have no idea how on earth to respond. Isn't that exactly what you're supposed to do with information? Do people just collect it and store it, spouting out facts when prompted like a computer?

I can't argue the point, so I don't.

Instead I stop walking. Someone bumps into my back, mutters an apology, and continues past. He looks behind him as he walks past, as if I'm a memory he can't quite grasp.

"What are you doing?" Cameron asks through his teeth, but it doesn't look like he expects me to answer. In fact, it looks like he knows exactly what I'm doing. He grabs my arm and tilts his head back toward the sky, like he's aggravated at the big expanse of blackness instead of me. "Listen, he's not going to leave her. It would not go well for him if he did."

"You're sure?" I ask. But I look at him instead of the sky. I want to see his reaction. I want to know what he's thinking, even if he's not saying it.

He's not sure. Not even close. "She's going to make it," he says. "Please don't screw this up for her," he adds. The same way he asked as we were dipping under the water. *Don't let go,* he pleaded.

He frowns at his hand, which is wrapped around my arm and pressed against my side. He holds me with his other arm, brings his fingers to his face, and rubs them together. "You need stitches," he mumbles.

My blood has seeped through this shirt to his fingers. "We can't just stand here," he says. As if the world is conspiring to prove him right, we hear the sound of a helicopter, the blades cutting through the air a few streets away. His eyes go wide, and then he tries to hide it. I start to run, but he tightens his grip again. "If you run, they'll know. Get on my back," he says.

"What?"

"Trust me," he says, even though we've already established that neither of us trusts the other.

I hop onto his back, and his hands hook under my legs, and he weaves across the street as if he's drunk. As if he's a carefree kid. As if we're not afraid of making a scene, of looking like fools.

I laugh into his ear, because I understand him, even if I am terribly afraid in that moment. I laugh because I know he's afraid as well—I can feel it in the way he's holding on to me, and the way his heart is pounding through his back. And now I know he's smart. He's not so different from me, actually.

I've spent the last seven months acting like a mindless fool so nobody would notice, too.

chapter 6

CAMERON DROPS ME UNCEREMONIOUSLY after he veers off the street at the next block. I hear the helicopter circling back around. I risk a quick glance behind us and notice them everywhere. Far away, near the island. Over the water. Over land. They're searching, but they're moving without purpose. Without tracking us.

I press a hand to my rib and imagine the tracker under the water somewhere. Everyone following a piece that they've cut out of me instead. I put pressure on the wound, but it feels dull and far away—something that has happened in another lifetime.

I follow Cameron as he cuts through a patch of trees without looking back, and it seems as though we're in a real neighborhood now. The homes are large, with high, metal gates, complete with decorative spikes on the tops. Like people trying to carve a section of the world out for themselves, and only them.

Cameron punches a set of numbers into a keypad beside a high metal gate covered with ivy, and the sound of a lock catching breaks the silence. My island is made like this. A code, an emergency switch, and everything within the house latches. My window. The locks. Nothing gets in, nothing gets out.

They had to use it only once. After the incident with Dominic Ellis—

"Come on," Cameron says, pulling me through the sliver of an opening. He closes the gate behind him, and it locks automatically.

"Where are we?" I ask.

"Home, for now," he says.

I don't ask whose home, and I don't ask for how long. "Shouldn't we go farther away?"

Cameron looks over his shoulder at me, as if he knows something I don't. He knows a lot of things I don't. I hate the feeling.

He thinks that I don't realize that I'm still in a prison. The things used to keep people out can turn in an instant to keep people in instead. The island, my island, had once been a fort. A layer of protection, a first line of defense against the outside, many years ago. Then it was supposed to be a safe haven. A safe place *for me*—somewhere nobody could reach me. Where revenge and anger and hate must stay on the other side of the steel netting. But it has become my prison.

The gates on the outside can keep people out, but they can also keep me in.

The inside of the house is dark, and he doesn't turn a light on. The house is colder than it was outside, as if it's been closed up tight with no heat for ages. "Watch the couch," he whispers as he weaves in front of me. "The table," he says next. My hand brushes fabric, not wood, and even in the dark, I can see the outline of sheets hanging over all the furniture, softening the edges of their shadows. It's a ghost of a house, and I can tell from just this room that there's no other life inside.

When we're deep in the center of the house, he pulls me into a room and shuts the door. Only then does he flip a light switch. My eyes shut instinctively, and when I reopen them, I see that we're in a bathroom. As far as bathrooms in abandoned houses go, it's pretty fancy. All tile and curved metal and fancy towels. Cameron looks at my shirt, and I follow his gaze. There's a dark stain through the black material, and it's not from the water.

"It doesn't even hurt anymore," I say, as he pulls the fabric away from my skin. I hear it pull—like something detaching—and feel a delayed sting.

"That's really not a good sign," he says. He sighs to himself. "Casey is better, but I can do it."

My fingers are numb and trembling as I reach for the hem of my shirt, and underneath, my entire body is shivering, covered in a uniform layer of goose bumps. Cameron opens the cabinet under the counter—designed to look like shutters—and grabs all the contents. There's a white box with a red symbol on the lid—a first-aid kit—much like the one we have on the island. He tears open a packet of pills and holds one out to me, but I shake my head. "No," I say. No way. I will not let anyone drug me. Not again.

"It's for the pain," he says.

"It doesn't hurt," I say.

He tilts his head, holds it out to me again. "*This* will."

Oh. Still. "No," I say, maybe a little too forcefully, leaving no room for discussion. I will not be calm and malleable and content. Not again.

He wrinkles his nose, and it makes him seem years younger. Now that he's not in mission mode, with his perfect stride and his single-minded focus, he looks like a different version of himself. His brown eyes roam, and he looks a little lost. His dark hair falls across his forehead as he leans over to rifle through the white box, and his entire face takes on a look of uncertainty, despite his words. His teeth catch his lower lip as he tears open a disinfectant wipe, and he becomes someone else.

I imagine him in the kitchen of a house, grabbing half a bagel from the toaster, holding it between his teeth as he searches for his books, tossing them into his bag, like a familiar scene I have watched on the television. I imagine him running out the front door, shouting a good-bye to his parents over his shoulder, and Casey waiting for him on the porch.

I imagine too much, I know this.

"Uh," Cameron says, looking behind me at the glass shower, not unlike the one in my room. The glass here is clear but distorted, as if there's a film obscuring it. "Hot shower. Take one. You can't get the stitches wet after, and I want to try to prevent infection as much as possible . . . and, no offense, but you reek." He wrinkles his nose again. "Also, you don't look so good."

He turns on the water for me, and the pipes groan. Cameron shifts nervously on his feet as I attempt to peel the shirt over my head. "I'm sorry," he says, turning around. "I'm not allowed to leave you alone."

But I don't care at all. I want in the hot shower, and I'm already mostly undressed. "I'm used to it," I say. He acts as if I'm not used to people watching me all the time. I barely even notice him as I step under the hot stream of water, his outline hazy on the other side of the glass.

There's a bar of soap, and I use it on my knotted hair, on my grimy skin, under my brittle nails. I clean around the wound as best I can, though it makes me wince. The hot water stings my scalp, and nothing has ever felt so good. I brace myself against the walls of the shower and let my entire body relax. I let myself breathe. I am out. *I am out.*

I can see Cameron, blurry through the glass, still facing away. "You okay?" he asks.

"Yes."

I see his leg bouncing, but I don't want to leave the water yet. "So . . . ," he says, "how do you know Dom?"

I wait a moment before I speak. "How do *you* know Dom?" I respond.

And I'm surprised when he answers. "I don't. I didn't. Casey did. I'm here to help Casey." It's like he needs to tell me that he is not my ally here. I appreciate the honesty, but I already understood that.

"He was a guard," I say, giving him a piece of information for the piece he has given me.

"Yeah, I know. But it seems like you know him better than that," he says, like he's accusing me, though I can't be sure why he is or why I care.

It's embarrassing, is what it is. It's embarrassing to admit how I know him. That I was naive. That I wasn't thinking. That I trusted so easily. "I don't know why he'd want to rescue me," is all I say, because it's true.

"Guess you made an impression," he says, and I turn off the water.

I laugh, and it sounds fake, like how I'd laugh back on the island. For a purpose. For a reaction. I grab a towel off the rack, wrap it around myself, and stand in front of Cameron. His head is tilted to the side, and his brown eyes are looking into mine, as if he can see through them. I close my eyes and look away.

"He pretended to be my friend," I say. And I decide to tell him. I'll tell him so he knows that I will not fall for it again.

"He used to leave me secret messages," I say. I had my head in a book when he passed me a note on the first day, a slip of paper taped to the inside of my cup when he set it before me, so only I could see. I saw the paper before I saw him, and so I liked him even before I set eyes upon him. The paper said: *I'm Ellis.* I looked up at him then, and he was looking right at me, right into me, with half a smile—so unlike anyone who had ever worked there before. When everything is the same, the different can blindside you. And then another guard said to him, "Mark, take out the trash." And it felt like a secret, a code, that he was giving just to me.

"And?" Cameron says. He looks away again, I guess because

I'm standing in nothing but a towel. "You had a fight because you found out he was pretending?"

A fight? Oh, if only. When I don't respond, he looks at me again. I smile at him the same way he looked at me over his shoulder when we walked into this place—like I know something more than he does.

He notices. "How did you find out?" he asks, trying a different approach.

"He gave himself away," I say. The notes had continued, every day, same as his smile. They'd say things like, *Where's the junk food?* And I knew he could've just asked anyone, but it was like a game, or a test, maybe. So I'd go to the cabinet and grab the chips, eat half the bag, and then leave them out in the middle of the table when I left the room. We were communicating in code. Establishing trust.

I'd hide the notes in my pockets, flush them when I was back in the privacy of my bathroom, something wild and hopeful running through my veins.

"I found out," I say, "when I caught him in my room a few days before the end of his assignment."

"Aren't there cameras?" Cameron asks.

"How did *you* get in?" I ask. "Same way, I assume."

Ellis—no, *Dominic*—acted surprised when I opened the door, with his hands still hovering over the keyboard of my computer. He froze. Then he hit a few buttons, turning the monitor to black. He put his hands in his pockets, and he smiled.

It was the same way he smiled at me the first day—crooked and personal, as if he were talking to me without making a sound. It was the way he looked at me, like I was a girl he saw walking by, not an assignment. But that was the moment I knew that he was pretending—that he had always been pretending. I guess maybe I had been pretending, too.

"Do you ever think of getting out of here?" Dominic had asked, looking anywhere but at my computer. It's not like the guards never go through my things. They do, all the time, but they don't hide it. This was the first time I realized that maybe computer searches weren't private. And I was thinking about the things I'd been researching.

"No point," I'd said. I thought about it every second of every day. I thought about it as I looked at the sky, at the sea, at the blackness behind my eyelids, but I made a point never to say the things that were merely hope, things that might burst if I gave voice to them, stranded out in the air by themselves.

"You don't want to?"

I didn't understand at first. I thought I did, I thought he was going to help. And then his eyes shifted from one electronic device to the next: the computer, the printer, the light fixture, the clock.

I felt the truth seep into my bones, like acid.

"Are there cameras in here?" I asked, turning away so I could mask my expression. Turn it to calm. How else would he know?

"No," he said, "and you know that." It's true. The humanitarian groups are allowed to screen this island twice a year, to make sure I am treated humanely. Like an animal. *You can keep her forever, just give her the decency of some privacy*. What a joke.

I had been researching what I could make with batteries, with the pieces of the electronics I'd taken apart and put back together. If I could make a radio. A phone. Or a bomb.

How to start a fire.

And he knew.

How did it not occur to me that computers were monitored? That just because it was in my room didn't make it mine? Of course later I found out about search histories and remote access, but I didn't know as much about computers when he was a guard eight months ago. Just that I had one and it was *full of information*. Lots of information. Information is free to me, I just can't send it out. Just like in a prison.

I felt my anger grow, and I buried it under my indifferent expression.

At first.

"Do you ever get messages from the outside?" he asked.

June. Like everyone else, he was looking for June.

I set my jaw, set my resolve. "Yes," I'd told him, "but you can't tell." I gave him a small smile. "And not through the computer."

If he was playing me, I was going to play him right back. "How, then?" he'd asked, leaning toward me, the light from the window catching off the blue of his irises. His whole face seemed to glow.

"I don't know how exactly, but sometimes at night, there are words shining directly onto my wall." I pointed to the wall opposite the window for emphasis. "It says, 'In the ocean is the key.' What do you suppose that means?" The lie slipped out as

effortlessly as it manifested in my head. I walked closer, studying his reaction.

Dom was mumbling to himself. "I don't know." Then he
refocused on me, searching my face. "I can help you," he said,
"but I need something from you. Just one thing." He pulled
the needle out of his pocket—the one they use to administer
shots—but it had been refashioned in some way, so the syringe
was instead a glass tube. "I need a sample."

And then the rage clawed its way up from the depths. He
knew I was June. They *all* knew I was June. Who the hell did
he think he was, coming in here, thinking he could mess with
me, thinking he could *use* me? Who the hell did he think *I*
was? Some easily manipulated kid who'd let him take everything and leave me here to rot? I walked closer to where he
stood leaning against my desk, but he must've been confused,
because when I got within reach, he put an arm around my
waist. He leaned down, and he paused—just for a second—and
then he kissed me. And I let him. I kissed him back, as I
reached behind his back to my desk, to my clock . . .

When I glance back at Cameron, his eyes are on my
knuckles, which are turning white from gripping my towel,
and the steam filling the room makes him feel closer. Makes *us*
feel closer.

I wonder now if Cameron is pretending. If Casey is pretending.

Cameron gestures to my clothes on the floor and looks
away. After I dress, I tell him, like a warning, "The last time I
saw him, he was being dragged from my room, unconscious."

It's not a lie, but it's not all of the truth, either. I leave out the kiss, and the fact that I was screaming at him, full of rage and nonsense, as his body shook on the floor. I leave out the lies I told and the part where the entire island went on lockdown. My words, unchecked. My actions, unchecked. They were so careful about blades and points and weapons on the island, but when you need something to use, none of that matters. Everything could be a weapon.

And I *had* been able to make something from the batteries and simple circuits I found in the room, from the careful wiring.

I can still feel it, the power of it, in my hand. I can still see the surprise on his face, the way everything about him changed as I held the base of the clock to his back and the current ran through him.

"I had turned my clock into a stun gun," I say.

Cameron starts laughing, and instantly it is my new favorite sound. It's surprisingly fast, and real, and his eyes narrow like he can't control the rest of his face. I smile back at him without even thinking. "You have no idea how much I would've loved to see that," he says. Then he holds up the needle he must've just threaded. "Ready?"

"Yes," I say. This time, at least, I don't have to lie on the floor. He sits me on the counter, and I lean back against the mirror to give him more access. I hold up my shirt, and his hand shakes as he nears my skin.

"Sorry," he says. "I'm cold."

But he doesn't try to warm them up. He takes a deep breath to steady himself, and then he pushes the needle through my skin, over and over, as if I were a piece of fabric. I should've taken the pill. I know it. He knows it. But he doesn't say anything as I choke on my cries, or as I tense with each new stitch, and he doesn't mention the fact that there are tears rolling down my cheeks. He pretends not to notice that I'm gripping on to his shoulders in a way that must hurt, but he doesn't flinch.

When he finishes, before he looks up at my face, he moves the side of his hand across my cheeks in a quick motion, and he smiles to himself. "Not too bad," he says, "for my first time."

"You were practicing on my rib cage?" I ask, feeling a pull each time I breathe in.

"I was," he says, trying not to smile. He dabs some sort of ointment over the top. "There. Done."

And then we're stuck there, with nothing more to do. It's just him and me, inches apart, my bare skin on display in front of him. He must notice at the same time, because his hand reaches for the bottom of my shirt, still held over my ribs, and he pulls it down and backs away.

I make him nervous.

I'm not entirely sure why.

He's still watching me, but I guess that's his job. "Look—" But Cameron's gaze quickly shifts to the wall—to somewhere beyond the wall—where I hear a faint beep. He opens the bathroom door and holds his breath. I hear Dominic whispering in the house. I hear Dominic whispering *to someone* in the house, and so does Cameron, who runs out of the bathroom into the dark.

I hop off the counter and stand in the doorway. Cameron already has Casey in his arms, and his shoulders are shaking as if he's laughing, and Casey is pushing him away saying, "Yeah, yeah, oh ye of little faith." Then he picks her up and spins her once, and I want to run to her, too. I'm overwhelmed with that same feeling. Of relief. Of happiness. Of wanting to go to her.

But I stay in the doorway to the bathroom, watching them instead.

Then Casey starts laughing, and even Dominic Ellis is smiling. Casey spots me over Cameron's shoulder, her eyes twinkling, her face smiling as her chin rests on Cameron's shoulder. She is contagious. I am laughing with her. With them. "We made it," Casey says.

"Of course we made it," Cameron says.

"Shh," Dominic says, but he is smiling, too. And his steps are the loudest of us all. His gaze shifts to me, but his smile never falters—crooked and personal. In the dark, with only the light from the bathroom, he nods at me once, coming closer. I force my spine straighter, taller. I force my smile to remain, to reach my eyes.

I force myself to act as if I don't understand that he is smiling at me like a man who has already won.

chapter 7

AFTER THE REST OF them take turns in the shower, we shut off all the lights again and head down to the basement. There's only a single lightbulb hanging from the ceiling, and there's a small television in the corner, which Dominic turns on but keeps the volume so low he has to lean forward to hear it. There are mattresses along the floor and a stash of food, and I don't wait for anyone to offer it to me. I rip open a granola bar and devour it in two bites, downing an entire bottle of water afterward. I focus on the door at the top of the stairs. It's closed, but I didn't notice anyone lock it. Still, I don't know where to go. What to do. I can't think of a single person who would take me in. Who would keep me hidden.

"Let me see your rib," Casey says. "We need to disinfect and stitch it up."

I shake my head, swallowing the last of the water. "Cameron did it."

She raises her eyebrows, and one side of her mouth lifts along with it. "Did he now?"

"I have many talents," he says from across the room.

She puts one hand on her hip and says, "I bet outrunning three guards and outswimming a motorized boat aren't on *your* list of talents."

Cameron is enraptured as she tells us the story of how she raced across the island, through the smoke, and dove off the cliff. She says her hands brushed the air tank on her way down. "It was just . . . perfect," she says, as if the whole world was conspiring to enable her escape. She must've looked like a girl who died under the surface, never coming back up. By the time they realized the tracker was still moving, she was probably already halfway to the cage.

There were too many boats, she says, after she put the tracker on the sub, and she couldn't get to the next tank in time. She ran out of air. And so she stayed near the surface, with her nose peeking above the water with every dip of the wave— breathing, when she could, right in front of everyone. "I was *right there*," she says, wide-eyed. She laughs, almost out of breath, as if she can't believe her own luck. She says she didn't dare move until dark. She hit the rendezvous point at the steel netting after we'd already left. She had her own GPS. And she swam through that dark ocean by herself, crawled through the pipe by herself, found her way to freedom by herself.

Seeing her now, standing before me, the others watching

her with awe, I wish I was more like her. More competent, more capable.

"So," she says. "I'm beat." And she flops back against a mattress, smiling at the ceiling.

"Wait," Dominic says, turning up the television a notch. We're on the screen. Casey and I. I look wild, feral, as my eyes smile before the explosion. They zoom in on Casey's face after, because everyone already knows me. "According to her file, Elizabeth Lorenzo, age nineteen, joined the guard unit about six months ago," the woman's voice says, but the picture stays zoomed in on Casey's face.

She pushes herself up on her elbows. *Elizabeth,* she mouths to Cameron, like it's funny.

"But we have reason to believe that this information is false."

Her mouth twitches as a number appears at the bottom of the screen.

"If you have any information about the identity of this woman, please call the number below."

"Well," Cameron says, arms crossed over his chest. "There goes your identity."

Casey turns to Cameron and says, "I'm Nobody, who are you? Are you Nobody, too?" She laughs at her own joke, but he looks away.

She laughs louder, and pushes him in the shoulder, but he still doesn't say anything.

"Then there's a pair of us, don't tell," I say, completing the poem by memory. Casey turns to me and looks surprised, as if maybe she thought I had something better to do over the last seventeen years rather than to read and read and read some more.

Casey tilts her head to the side and smiles at Dominic Ellis. "I like this Alina Chase girl, Dom. Can I keep her?"

Dom turns the television off, turns the light off. He locks the door at the top of the stairs and pockets the key. "Sleep," he says. "We leave early."

I lie on the mattress, but I cannot sleep. I eventually hear Dom's breath go slow and steady, and then I see Casey stand up and tiptoe over to Cameron's mattress. I see them lying side by side, and I hear faint whispering, and I want to shut them out. In this basement, with three other people, freer than I've ever been, I have never felt so alone. I put the pillow over my head, and I hear nothing but my own breathing.

And then I listen for my mother, who I believe is alive somewhere out there. I wonder if she's seen the news. If she's somewhere nearby. If she's in the country still, if she knows that I am out. *I am out.*

Duérmete, mi niña, duérmete, mi amor, duérmete, y nos vemos en la tierra de sueños . . .

There's light from across the room. I wake up completely disoriented. Where are the walls, keeping me in, keeping me safe? Where is the window, with the perfect angle past the tree to the sky? My bed with a space carved out for me, my mother's picture seven paces away, the world with me at its axis?

I feel the hard ground as I shift on the thin mattress, and the walls are gray and cold. There is no window. I feel as if I do not exist.

I see Casey, hunched in a ball in front of the silent television. Her face is on the screen. They show it from every angle. They show the explosion, the smoke, people scrambling to their feet, running at an angle across the screen—the camera on the ground somewhere.

Casey is rocking slowly, back and forth in front of the television. I walk silently across the floor—I am good at moving silently—and I see a tear track down the side of her face. I don't know whether to say something or pretend I don't notice, but before I can decide, she seems to catch sight of my reflection on the screen.

She jumps to standing, then puts a hand on her heart before wiping away the tears with the back of her hand. "You scared me to death," she whispers, then shakes her head to herself and shrugs at me with one shoulder. "Long day, you know?" she says as explanation.

I point to the television. "Do they know anything? Did they follow us?" I whisper.

She puts her finger to her lips. Comes closer. Her fingers brush my arm as she goes to hold my shoulder, and I jump. She narrows her eyes and leans closer, as I lean back. "What have they done to you, Alina Chase?"

But I don't understand what she means.

She steps back, moves her hand away from me, and whispers, "They found the tracker, but that's it. Haven't mentioned a thing about Cameron." I catch a faint smile, and then it's gone. "He came in with the media. His name—well, the name he was going by—was on the list, and he joined them on the other side of the bridge. But he doesn't belong to any of them. The guards probably think he's media, and the media think he's a guard. Nobody misses him yet. They're backtracking now. Looking for what really happened. But it's still dark. In the daylight, they'll probably find the discarded air tanks." She looks at her watch, the same one that Dominic and Cameron have. "We'll be gone by then."

As if on cue, there's some sort of vibration coming from Dominic's mattress. He jerks up, presses his finger to his watch, and quickly scans the room. Casey's body goes rigid beside me, and I feel mine do the same in response. He's on his feet as soon as he sees us. "What are you doing?" he asks, but he's looking at Casey, not me.

She feigns indifference. Slouches. Puts a hand on her hip. "She has to go to the bathroom," she says, like it's obvious.

"And you were going to *take her*?" he asks incredulously. Dominic looms over us both—I have to tilt my head up just to watch his face. By now, Cameron is awake as well, and also on his feet.

"Does it look like I'm taking her?" Casey says. "I told her we needed to wait, especially since you have *the key*, so I put the television on, and here we are. Waiting. With the television on. God, paranoid much?" she asks, and then she turns around, and I turn around with her, and I see she's trying to compose herself. I see that she's terrified.

"All right, Ms. Chase," Dominic says, and I feel him coming closer. My body tenses like Casey's did before. "Let's go."

Casey narrows her eyes at him and follows us both.

"Can I help you?" he asks Casey over his shoulder.

"I thought we weren't supposed to leave her alone," she says.

"I don't intend to," he says. I want to tell her that I don't care, that if he's trying to intimidate me by following me into the bathroom, it won't work. But I *do* care. I care because it's him. Lack of privacy is fine when it's impersonal and meaningless. But I cannot stand the thought of him watching me now. My stomach twists at the thought.

"I have to go anyway," she says, brushing by him, not giving him a chance to argue.

I see why Cameron loves her, I do.

We're all packed up before sunrise. The mattresses are stacked in a corner, the food is in a bag, and there's nothing to show that we've been here. Of course, that's not true. I picture stray hairs with my DNA, and my fingerprints on the sink faucet. If someone knows where to look, they will see my path. They will find me.

"What is this place?" I ask, as we pass by the furniture with the white sheets spread atop, the layer of dust across the mantel.

"A friend's house," Dom says. "They're gone, though."

There are no pictures and no books. Nothing on the walls, nothing on display. "Second home," he explains, as he sees me taking it all in. I can't imagine why one wouldn't be enough.

We exit through the back door into a yard overgrown with weeds, and moss hanging from trees, clinging to the fences.

Dom leads us to a garage, where there's a red car with no top. He manually lifts the garage door, wincing at the noise it makes. The sun is just starting to color the sky a dark pink. And there's a chill in the air, even though it's summer. I feel goose bumps form across my arms. Dom puts the car in neutral, and he and Cameron push it out of the garage, out the gate, to the long driveway still shielded by hanging moss and tall shrubs. He locks the garage back up and opens the trunk.

My eyes go wide, and my stomach flips at the thought. "No. I can't."

Casey jumps in. Apparently we're both supposed to. Except then Cameron slides in beside her, and I realize that his face might be known, too, caught on someone's camera during the escape. He has disappeared with us as well, and someone must know he was there and then not. That he is now tied to us, and we to him. Even if he's not on the news yet, eventually he'll be discovered, and then he can be traced back to us. I imagine the facial recognition software, the streetlights we must ride through, and storefronts we must pass.

"I'm going to be sick," I say, not as an excuse but as a warning. "I get motion sickness."

"We crawled through a storm sewer. I think we can handle you getting sick," Cameron says.

I almost smile. I climb in beside him. There's barely any room, and when Dominic closes the trunk, I have a moment of complete and total fear. I suck in a breath, and someone brushes the hair back from my face.

I don't know who, and I don't even care. But I imagine, in

the dark, that it's my mother, soothing me. I try to will myself to sleep, but I cannot.

The engine comes to life, the material at the base of the trunk feeling rougher as it starts to vibrate against my bare face. I strain to focus on the voice in my head instead. Truthfully, I've heard it only once, and not even in the song I imagine her singing. I know my mother's voice not from my memory of her but from the memory of an interview when she was first released from prison. She ignored all the reporters' questions, their microphones held out to her as she walked straight for a waiting taxi after seven years in prison. Until she got to the door, and someone said, "Do you have anything to say to your daughter?"

And her eyes, just like mine, stared right into the camera, piercing right into me, as she said, "I used to sing her a lullaby. Same as my mother used to sing to me. She can find me there, in her dreams."

It was Genevieve who sang me the song after that. I never heard from my mother again.

Just a few words, that's all I've ever heard her say. The rest I must be imagining.

The car begins to move, slowly at first, but I can no longer conjure the sound of her voice.

"How long?" I whisper, but nobody answers.

I realize why later. Much later. Because it's been hours and we're still moving. True to my word, I've been hovering on the edge of sick the entire time, but nobody has said anything about the noises that escape my throat, or the fact that I keep shifting, trying to find relief, leaving them with even less space. I moan again, and I feel an arm on my arm, holding me. I flinch for a moment, and then relax. The car lurches back and forth, as if we're going around curves—I'm going to lose everything in my stomach, and this time I won't be able to stop it.

Someone rubs my upper back, and the feeling passes. I take a deep breath through my mouth. I wonder, for a moment, if we knew each other in a past life. Everything feels so effortless with them. They know what to do without asking.

But I know that's impossible. Souls have no memory. But I wonder, for the first time, if they can still be drawn to each other. If we wander restlessly until we find one another again. If some of us are full of a yearning, driving us to keep moving, searching for something we can't quite name. I understand completely, in that moment, why the Soul Database was formed in the first place. Why people wanted it, wanted a record of themselves—a permanent, eternal history. So the people you've made a connection with can find you again, just in case. Because I suddenly don't want to leave this trunk—let alone this life— even though another wave of nausea is beginning.

I wonder if the soul of Liam White would want to see me again, in this body. If he could look through my eyes straight to June. He wouldn't want to, not at all, if he knew why I wanted to see him.

The car slams to a stop, and we become a pile of bodies. Of arms and legs, twisted and crushed.

And then the trunk pops open, and I squint against the

glare of the sun. Dom doesn't spare more than a glance before he says, "Out."

I climb out first, since I'm closest to the edge. But the stillness and the solid ground don't help. The ground spins, the horizon tilts, the axis shifts. I fall to my knees in the dirt and lose everything in my stomach.

Then I put my hands on the earth and look around. We're in the mountains somewhere. I see them, stretching peak after peak, past a still body of water in front of us. There's another car, dark colored and partially rusted, parked in the trees off the side of the road. I hear crickets in the grass and in the trees. These are not the trees I'm used to seeing. They are tall and thick and the leaves rustle in the gusts of wind.

I have no idea what lurks behind the first layer of trees. Whether there are animals or people or nothing at all.

I can hear the wind stirring up everything in its path, seconds before it reaches us, like a warning. Cameron and Casey stretch beside me, shielding their eyes from the bright light. But nobody else seems to notice the mountains that go on forever, or the wind that comes from deep in the woods, the way the sky seems to move if you stare at it too long—

"I think she needs some food," Casey says as I stumble, bracing myself on the hood of the car.

I keep waiting for freedom to feel like something else. Something not so disorienting. Something not so terrifying.

Something *more.*

chapter 8

DOMINIC PLACES A HAND on my elbow and squats to my level. He hands me a bottle of water, which I take, even though I hate to take anything from him. I rinse my mouth and spit in the dirt in front of me. "Where are we?" I ask as I pull myself to standing.

Casey pulls her shirt away from her skin, obviously as overheated as I am. "In the middle of—"

"Nowhere," Dominic cuts in. "We're nowhere." But he's holding a GPS, and I see the latitude and longitude numbers across the top, marking our location. Unfortunately, they mean absolutely nothing to me. I want to go back and tell myself how to prepare. *Learn how to swim. Run blind. Study the latitude and longitude coordinates of the world.* Seven months of preparation and I am helpless and lost. Seven months of preparation and I have traded everything I've ever known, tossed it in the air like a coin, and shrugged as it came back to the earth. Seven months of preparation and I am left at the whim of another, yet again.

Cameron throws our bags out of the backseat, and Dominic says, "Ditch the car."

Cameron stares at him, as if he cannot believe the request. I can't either. The car must be worth a lot of money, and it belongs to someone else. But after a prolonged look, Cameron disappears into the woods. He comes back out with a thick branch, which he wedges inside the driver's side, against the gas pedal. He releases the parking brake as he jumps away from the car.

The red car drives straight into the lake, churning and angry, and the water bubbles as it goes deeper. It sinks slowly, sputtering, and we all watch it go. We watch from the dirt road until the surface of the lake is still again. And then Dominic swings a bag onto his shoulder and starts walking. "Let's move," he says. I don't ask. I am so far beyond asking.

I just move.

These shoes they've given me are slowing me down because they don't fit, blisters already forming against my ankle, so I stop to take them off even though the path is rocky. The callouses should help.

Cameron is behind me, and he looks at my feet as I step out of my shoes and bend to pick them up, and for a second I think he's going to say something. To offer something. "Bad idea," he says, but I ignore him. He waits for me to move again, and I hear his steps behind me.

Ten more minutes of walking and I'm beyond irritated because Cameron was right and I'm trying not to show it. Walking in socks through the woods where there's no path was a really bad idea. *Obviously.* I try to distract myself by watching my surroundings, and I try not to let him see me wince when I misstep.

I attempt to memorize our route, looking for markers along the way. A tree with a knot that overtook its trunk. A rock extending over our path, like a cliff. But this place is enormous, and most everything looks the same. Stumbling upon this mangled trunk or that sharpened rock again would be a miracle in and of itself. The world has never seemed so vast. I'm not sure I can find my way back out.

I *need* to find my way back out.

I sit on a rock when Dominic and Casey stop for a rest, and I use the opportunity to put the shoes on again. I don't look at Cameron, but I'm sure he sees. They're all watching me.

We keep moving. I wonder what will happen if I just . . . stop. If someone will throw me over a shoulder and bring me anyway. I wonder what will happen if I run. If I could survive out here, at latitude 34.88 and longitude –83.17. If maybe I could find a way out, find a friendly face, a safe place. I think of my mother, who is the only person I can imagine helping me, even though she has all but disappeared—at least, from the news, from the Internet, from the world I have access to. There's a small article about her violating parole, but I don't know if anything ever came of it. But she's not in jail, and her death was never reported, so I believe she's out there. Alive.

I don't suppose I have anyone else. June didn't have any allies left, at the end. Maybe from before she got tangled up with Liam White, but not any longer. Like her family, I'm sure they don't want to be associated with her any longer.

She and Liam were famous once. They were the kids who broke into the unbreakable system—a challenge originally set up to test the security of the Alonzo-Carter Cybersecurity Data Center. I've seen the original report, watched the interview with the creators. Two men, Mason Alonzo and Paul Carter, arrogantly declaring it unhackable and issuing the challenge as the final test. I mean, come on. That's just asking for it.

Nobody knows how they did it exactly. But June and Liam got in. They released a screenshot as proof. That should've been the end of it.

But they didn't stop once they were in. All that knowledge, just there waiting for them. I want to believe it was just curiosity at first that made them look. But then it turned into something they couldn't unsee.

All that information.

All that truth.

She had to warn people. It was the right thing to do.

They searched out the names of dead criminals from the generation before, and they found the record of their current lives. It was a public service, they claimed, much like warning residents of a local ex-con, but there were reasons the privacy laws were in place. Scientists had studied the correlation between generations, and they did find a high linkage of violent crimes committed by past criminals in their next life when all other factors were stripped out. Not 100 percent. But a correlation. The famous study, the one that started all the debates, showed a violent crime correlation of 0.8, with 1.0 being complete.

Part of the debate over using this information is that the studies were flawed by the very nature of the data used—criminal records. It didn't take into account anything else. And the law says you can't punish someone for something he or she might do. The very idea of it threatened the foundation of justice. Thinking bad things does not equate guilt. Words mean nothing. Action, everything.

Still, 0.8 is high. Higher than the genetics of IQ and the heredity of height.

A dangerous soul is dangerous.

It wasn't a conviction, June claimed. It was a warning. We had a right to know who we lived with, who our neighbors were, who our *leaders* were. It was for our own safety. We had a right to the information.

And at first, the world loved them for it. For allowing them to be on guard. For putting the information into their hands.

I've watched that speech that June delivered over the airwaves from an undisclosed location more times than I can count. *I am the bell, tolling out its warning.* She was very convincing.

People supported them. People hid them, sheltered them, provided them with money. Meanwhile, the people whose names they released became unemployable, the targets of numerous threats. And still the public supported June and Liam. Until they released names of children, of *people's* children. When slowly the vigilante groups began to form against the names on her list.

When people stopped just listening to the warning and started acting on the information instead, hurting people who had done no wrong in this life, seeking revenge from the crimes of the past, the tide began to shift in public opinion, turning on Liam and June.

That part, that's her own fault. June was too impulsive. Too proud. Too self-righteous. Too selfish. Watch one of the many documentaries and take your pick of flaws.

She was an idealist, believing that information belonged to everyone. That people should be free to draw their own conclusions from it. That knowledge should never be hidden behind closed doors and firewalls and passwords. Personally, I think she just had too much faith in humanity, releasing that information to begin with.

As if knowledge would be used only for good.

And when that tide began to shift with public opinion, it shifted in them as well. People claimed that June and Liam started to use the information for blackmail instead. They stopped releasing the names at all, instead allegedly black-mailing the wealthy or powerful with that information and taking their money to disappear. June's name appeared on accounts the few times the crime was reported, the few times people tried to call their bluff. I have to believe that was Liam. I have to.

They didn't bluff. They released the names, like a hit list, to the vigilante groups.

And then how the people turned. Oh, how they turned.

No more protection. No more public support. No, it was a witch hunt. Liam was dead within two months, when they were caught on a security camera of a computer warehouse and surrounded on Christmas Day. June escaped but was killed when she resurfaced a year and a half later, run down in the street as she raced for the woods. A generation later, and countless threats to any foster parents who dared to care for me, and I am a prisoner on an island for my own safety.

This is what a belief can do to you. It can drive you, without reason, without cause. It drives you more than law, more than love. It drives you until you *are* the belief. Until your very soul becomes imprisoned by it.

"Not much farther," Dominic calls, and I'm relieved to hear that this walk has taken something out of him. My limbs are shaking, but that could just be from the adrenaline of the last day.

We don't stop until we reach the cabin. I didn't even see it until I was on top of it. The logs are the same color as the trees, the windows dark and unassuming. We're all out of breath, even Cameron, who seems as if he's in the best shape of all of us. They drop their bags on the wooden porch, and Dominic does a quick loop around the house. I see windows, doors, woods that I can disappear into. No fence. No gate. No cliffs or steel cage or mile-long bridge.

I see chances, an opportunity for later. So when they sit down on the ledge of the wooden porch with smiles of relief, I do the same.

"We made it," Casey says, that same expression of pure joy across her face.

Cameron smirks at her. "Of course we made it," he replies.

I tilt my head back, with my eyes closed, and pretend not

to notice Dominic's shadow cross my face, or his steps as he settles in beside me.

"Did you know, Alina," Dominic begins, "that people have stayed hidden in these woods for years?"

I stop smiling. My stomach clenches at the word "years." I have already been waiting years. I cannot stand to wait another hour. But I'm also seized with the realization that I have nowhere to go. And the things I want—no, the *thing* I want—isn't a location at all. June is still a chain around my ankle, shackling me to dark rooms and car trunks and hidden cabins.

"June disappeared in them. For over a year. Nobody found her," I say.

Nobody found her until she made a mistake. Until she chose to come out of the woods. A huge, epic mistake.

"Did you *also* know," he says, leaning back on his arms, "that you could wander the woods for weeks and never find your way out?" It's like he can read my mind, or my fears, and give voice to them. "I'm not the enemy," he says, but I'm not sure how he expects me to trust him yet again. "You'll be safe with us."

Every part of me wants to bite back with a sarcastic remark, something to wipe the smile off his face, to knock his ego or confidence, to gain a step forward, but instead I put the water bottle to my lips. Control my words, control the situation. I will speak only when the emotion has passed.

I swallow too much water, and it hurts going down, but it forces down the tension that has been clawing upward. "And if I ever do get lost," I say, keeping my eyes fixed on Dominic's mouth, "I'm grateful you shared the coordinates with me." I'm trying not to smile, but I'm losing. I see Cameron over his shoulder, the surprised grin on his face.

Dom's mouth tenses and he stands up, and for a second I wonder if he's going to lean over and shake me, but instead he begins to laugh. "I can tell why people listened to you," he says, like someone who has watched June's movie way too many times. "I really can." He stands and opens the front door, which apparently does not need a lock—my heart races to see—and he says, "Grab your stuff and come inside."

I stop smiling when I walk inside. The cabin is equipped with a stash of water bottles, a long wooden counter, a wood-burning stove, and stacked cans of food. There are also bags of clothes, all the color of the woods—like we're kids playing out some military mission. But then I remember that Dom and Casey *were* members of the National Guard, since that's where my guards are pulled from. That they *are* old enough, and that they're definitely trained.

I wonder how long we're supposed to stay here. It doesn't look like this place has electricity, but there must be, because there seems to be some sort of television screen.

I pretend not to notice the rope on the counter. But Casey finally sees it, and I sense her shoulders stiffen from across the room. I pretend not to hear the lock turn on the door—not to notice it's a key instead of a latch system. Or that the windows are covered in meshed wire, nailed into the wood.

I pretend not to notice that I am being held against my will, once again.

There's a brown sectional sofa, which looks as if it hasn't been cleaned in a decade or longer. Cameron sinks into it, a cloud of dust rising up around him, and he coughs into his closed fist. There are three doors beyond this main room, one of which has rolled-up sleeping bags leaning against it. I'm hoping one of the others is a bathroom.

Casey picks through a bag of clothes, pulling out a pair of camouflage pants, which she frowns at. "Oh, good, just my style," she says, tucking her hair behind her ear. Her hair has a wave to it, I'm noticing now, that makes it look lighter than mine. And it falls in wisps from behind her ear, softening the sharp angles of her face. She throws a pair of clothes at me, gesturing toward the blood on my shirt. She wrinkles her nose as she does, reminding me of the expression Cameron makes.

I turn around, facing the wall—like Cameron or Casey might do—as I change from the black, blood-stained shirt to the forest-green T-shirt she's thrown my way.

I don't understand what they intend to do with me, and I don't want to stick around to find out. I need to move. I need to get outside, and I need to disappear. These clothes—the way they're made to blend in with the surroundings—will probably help.

"Where is this place?" I ask, as I slide my legs into the new pants. I pull the drawstring tight around my waist, and when I turn around, Dominic is the only one looking at me. He's watching me as if he's confused by me. Like I'm a puzzle he's intent on solving.

"Nowhere," Dominic says for the second time. "It's nowhere, sweetheart."

The fact that he calls me sweetheart makes me nervous. The fact that I am essentially locked in a room with him makes me nervous.

The presence of the rope and the wire makes me nervous.

The fact that I cannot orient myself, that I am not at an axis, that the world is moving and existing and changing without me at the center makes me feel small and insignificant and lost, and I recite the facts in my head to keep calm: *There were thirty-two guards on the island, and I escaped.*

Here, there are only three. There are only three. There are only three . . .

"Can't say I'm a fan of this place," Casey says, tossing the bag of clothes on the couch beside Cameron.

"It's temporary," Dominic says. *Temporary.* That can mean nearly anything. Days, months, years. Now that we know that the soul doesn't die, it could also mean a lifetime.

June's hiding was "temporary," too. That's what they call it on that one documentary. A year and a half, and then she came out and was killed.

Even now, nobody knows how June and Liam got in the database. Rumor has it that after they got inside, they set up a secondary shadow-database, one that copies directly from the original source, so they could have unlimited access to it at all times. Somewhere only June and Liam knew. That's what people are worried about now. That I might somehow know how to find it again. That I might continue where June left off.

"Okay," Cameron says, "then let's get on with it."

Dominic holds his arm out, gesturing toward the back room.

Casey skips ahead into the back room and says, "Give me ten minutes."

Dominic nods and heads for the second closed door. He sends Cameron a look. "Watch her," he says.

I catch the tail end of Cameron's eye roll and find myself involuntarily smiling at him. He looks away first.

Well, I do have ten minutes. I open the kitchen drawers, one at a time, but they're empty. Though the drawers are old and removable, and I bet I could pry a nail or two loose if I had a few minutes to myself. I slam them closed and run my fingers along the mesh wiring, pulling at it to see if it gives.

"What the hell are you doing?" Cameron asks.

"Looking around," I say, not pausing.

I check under the brown couch, but the wooden legs seem to be firmly attached.

"Stop," Cameron says.

"Why?" I ask, but he doesn't answer. He of all people should understand after helping me escape. I will not be slow and malleable and content. I will not wait for someone to come. This time, I will be ready by myself. I'm used to people watching me. What's he going to say? *Alina was looking under the couch*? So what. It would be stupid if I didn't. It would be a waste of time for us to stand here staring at each other, pretending like I am not still being held against my will.

There are four lantern-shaped lamps that I'm assuming

are battery powered. Inside each is a tiny lightbulb. I wonder if they will break. When they're on, I wonder if they will burn. I try to pry the top off one, but it's glued on pretty tightly. I look for anything that will shatter into shards that I can store in the pockets of my pants until someone opens the front door.

They are not careful enough.

Everything is a weapon.

I will not stay here long.

"Stop," he says again, but lower. "Before he comes out."

My eyes lock with his, and I wonder, not for the first time, what he's doing here. I place the lantern back on the counter, wondering just how far I can push him, trust him. "Just . . . ," I say, "one more thing."

I take the rope off the counter, and Cameron comes closer, his hands held out like he must stop me from something, but he's not sure what. Like I might use it on him. I'm not stronger than he is, I know I'm not. But still, he comes closer as I walk toward the couch with it.

"Don't," he whispers, but I have no idea what he wants me to stop doing, or why. He has my elbow in a grip just as I'm lifting a couch cushion, and he looks completely confused but doesn't let go. I shove the rope under the cushion with my free hand and drop it back down just as Dominic enters the room again.

"Wow," he says, eyeing Cameron with his hand on me, standing perfectly still, so close I can feel his breath on the side of my face. "What the hell happened in that trunk? No, don't tell me, I bet I know."

My entire face is burning. I know what he's going to say from the way he's leering at me. I shouldn't be ashamed of kissing him. I did it to distract him, so I'd have a moment to think, to act.

I kissed him, and then I ruined him, and I cannot look him in the eye. I can't look at Cameron either.

"She got carsick," Cameron says, a second before Dominic speaks. "And then she hiked four miles across the state border." My pulse races, because he's giving me information. I know he knows it, too. And he hasn't said anything about the rope or my search of the room. "She needs something to eat."

I pull my arm away, let my eyes wander the room like I'm mindlessly assessing it. I know better than to hope blindly, but I relish the information.

I will use it.

Casey pokes her head out of the back room, swinging the door open. "All set," she says. But she doesn't smile, and so neither do I.

There's something humming in a back room. It sounds like ten refrigerators, and I really hope that's the case, because I really am starving. On the island, someone would've brought me food by now. Someone would've made sure I had enough.

My stomach growls and my legs are shaky from the hike, but all thought of food leaves my mind as I enter the room behind Cameron. There's a generator, I think. Something to power this place, so far off the grid. It's humming, and the computer it's hooked up to is humming, too. There's another machine with a computer screen attached, but it's long and

rectangular and has a pin dropping out of an alcove in the middle, currently resting in a beaker of something. Maybe water.
Maybe not. But the most uncomfortable part of this room is
not the things that are unfamiliar. It's the thing I know: a narrow cot, a metal tray covered in Saran Wrap, a box of gauze, a
bottle of disinfectant.

Dominic comes up behind me and places a hand on my
tense shoulder. "Relax, Alina, it won't hurt much."

But my shoulders go tense because I don't understand.
"What the hell is this?" I ask. Nobody looks me in the eye.
"Casey?" I say, but she keeps herself busy at the screen. Dominic wanted a sample from me in my room as well. He didn't
tell me why then either. "Cameron?" I say.

Cameron cuts his eyes to Dominic. "I thought you said she
wanted this," he says.

"Wanted what?" I ask, panic rising, rage rising. "Wanted
what? You think I'm not her?"

Dom looks at me with something close to compassion. "No,
I know you're her. Calm down, Alina," he says, but that only
succeeds in making me even less calm, because he's also blocking the door.

We all know June's soul is mine; what more do they intend
to see? There *is* nothing else to see. That's the problem with
soul fingerprinting. We still don't know what it can do, what it
can tell us. All we can do is find a match.

There have been several studies on the nature of the soul,
but it's not information that comes from the soul fingerprint
itself—there's no secret revealed in the readout; it's like seeing

a DNA strand but having no idea what it codes for. The only way science has learned anything so far is by linking the soul with a person, monitoring each generation, and seeing what traits correlate from life to life. Science explains the correlations the same way it explains DNA markers. In the same way that some sequences in a DNA chain indicate an increased likelihood of developing certain multifactor diseases like Alzheimer's, there's no certainty. And here, they're not even using hard facts—no markers in the soul fingerprint they extract in the spinal fluid itself. The "markers" they use as evidence are personality tests, self-surveys, or in the case of the famous study, specific types of criminal records tied to each soul. But there are only a few generations in the database, and it's no secret that even these so-called markers are flawed. People could be committing crimes and not getting caught. People could be caught and not convicted. People could be framed. But it's the best they can do. A human being isn't quantifiable. So they study those markers from generation to generation to assess the correlation. Seems a lot less like science to me. Most of the results were reported during June's lifetime.

They already know the nature of my soul.

The only thing they can get from that needle is knowledge they already have.

Dominic flips a switch on the side of the rectangular box, and the liquid in the beaker begins to disappear, sucked inside the machine as it stutters to life. "It's time to see exactly what you're worth, Alina Chase."

chapter 9

"NO." I BACK UP toward the door, but Dominic is blocking my way.

Cameron turns around but doesn't look at me. "She doesn't want this."

Dominic comes closer and says, "Of course she wants this. She's June. This isn't to hurt you, Alina. It's to access your money."

"What money?" I ask, even as the pieces are falling into place. I know what he's trying to do, to see if June has left herself an inheritance. But to check funds, to *transfer* funds, you need to have this procedure done at a bank to prevent fraud.

It's rare, truth be told. Most everyone leaves their assets to their children, their spouses, their loved ones. It's only the lonely people who do this. The people who have no one else. Something cold settles through my bones, and I hope that the account is empty.

"Won't it be frozen anyway?" I ask.

"That's the beauty of privacy," Dominic says. "It's not tied to any names. Your soul fingerprint is the username and password. The banking system merely searches for the match. The money is just sitting there, waiting to be retrieved." That way, either life can retrieve the cash. Nothing else may be passed along. No messages, no notes, no confessions or last words. Just a sum of cash. Nearly everyone checks it on their eighteenth birthday, because why not?

But I'm not eighteen and I'm not in a bank, and if I were, surely I would be arrested before I could get the money, regardless.

Surely June would've been arrested had she walked in to make a deposit.

"That's it?" I ask. "You just want the money?" It's a price to pay for my escape, I suppose. It's not really mine, anyway. Honestly, I could use it. But I'm not June, and I don't want her blood money.

"No," he says. "But we're going to *need* the money."

We're on the run, after all. Money is necessary for survival. I understand this on some academic level, but I've never had it, and I've never needed it. But it must have cost them a considerable amount of money to pull off that escape.

"I owe you money, though. Isn't that right? How much do I owe you?" I ask.

I want there to be a price—a price I can pay and be free. But nobody responds as I crawl onto the table and hike my shirt up to my ribs and pull my knees to my chest, like I've seen done on television a hundred times before. I've had this procedure done three times, but I don't remember any of them. The first, when they were searching for June. The second time, by request of my parents, to double-check. Dumb hope. The third, by request of the state when I was placed in their care.

June Calahan, every time.

When I was younger, I tried to prove I wasn't her in other ways: June was right-handed, so I sat on my right hand and wrote with my left, until it felt natural. Left- and right-handedness transferred at a correlation of .99, and so I fought it. I refused to study the things June was good at, skimming over math problems and pretending I didn't see the patterns in the IQ test. I was quiet when she was loud, and I stayed far away from anything she liked to do, according to all the documentaries.

Didn't matter.

Still June.

Even though I don't remember having this procedure done, I've seen it enough on TV.

Every year, there are at least three movies that deal with the "what ifs" of soul science. Like when DNA, and all its implications, was discovered, and there were movies on human cloning and scary government regulations and selecting for perfect traits and an end to life as we knew it. None of which happened. Life stayed pretty much the same, and science was pretty much used for the betterment of all: disease prevention, genetic screening, criminal evidence. Sometimes there'd be news of a couple who screened their embryos for a perfect match for their sick child, and there'd be some ethical debate about it, but mostly people did what they did for their loved ones. It was all still a matter of privacy. And sometimes there was more knowledge than we really wanted. Did we really want to know if we were going to die from a horrible disease? Did it change anything, other than provide a ticking clock? And that was something that privacy law protected as well. It's your decision to check such things. It's only your information to know.

And this is no different. It exists, and we know it, and there are movies about understanding the nature of the soul, of quantifying and labeling people, and there are movies about souls trying to reach some nirvana, and about illegal screening and revenge scenarios and government plots, none of which have happened. No, I am the only mistake.

So I know what to do, to pull my legs up so my spine sticks out, so they can ease the needle between my vertebrae and extract the clear liquid from the base of my spine, that they can run through the spectrometer and see the color spectrum the marker of the soul emits, in a pattern that is unique to itself. Like a fingerprint.

I wonder what mine looks like. If it's all blues and purples, which is how I feel inside. Whether the colors mean anything. Personality. Predisposition. Good. Evil.

DNA was just a combination and pattern of nucleotides before we knew what they stood for, too.

I expect it to be Dominic who sticks a needle in my back, but he goes to the computer and his fingers fly across the keyboard. "Casey already has us remotely on site." I'm surprised to hear this, that she's the one who hacked into the bank. I don't know why, but I didn't want it to be her. "All we need is your username and passcode."

I feel something cool against my lower spine. And then the sharp smell of alcohol. "Hold very, very still," she says, and even Dominic stops typing. I feel a sharp pinch, and then pressure, so unlike when Cameron extracted the tracker from my rib, but at least it was a hurt I could quantify. This becomes a pull, the feeling that my nerves are moving in a way they shouldn't. It feels so very, very wrong.

"There," she says, and I feel the needle slide out from between my vertebrae. She applies pressure and tapes something over the top. I push myself up, but she puts a hand on my shoulder. "No, you need to lie still for a bit."

Casey carries a small vial filled with a clear liquid over to the rectangular machine, removes the beaker, and slips the test tube over the pin.

"Were you left anything?" I ask, because every piece of information is useful. The type of people they were, the type of people they are. I can use it all.

"No," Dominic says, and he looks exceptionally angry by the fact that his soul must've had loved ones, must've had a family or friends or a cause to donate to.

"Not me," Casey says.

I stare at Cameron, but he doesn't answer. "He never checked," Casey says. "He doesn't want to know."

"You could be a millionaire," I say, just to bait him into speaking.

He turns to me, tilts his head to the side, and says, "But I'm not." He holds my gaze as I lie on the cot, and I let his words sink in. *But I'm not.*

"There," Dominic says. Casey and Cameron crowd around the computer screen, and I can't see anything from this cot. "What the hell?" Dominic says.

"What?" I ask, pushing myself onto my elbows.

Dominic spins in his chair, narrows his eyes at me as if I have somehow done something to him. "It's just change. God-damn pennies."

Which makes me even sadder. That June felt the need to leave something to me, first of all, and that this was all she had left.

"Where is the money?" Dominic yells, as if I might know. Sure, June and Liam allegedly took in a lot of cash through the blackmail, but who knows what she did with it for the year and a half she was in hiding? Maybe she needed it. Maybe she gave it away. I let the sliver of hope work its way in that maybe she gave it back.

"Maybe Liam had it," I say, but Dominic rolls his eyes. I know, June was said to take off with it after his death, because none was found with him, but who knows if that was true.

"What's the point?" he asks, pointing at the screen. "What's the goddamn point? She even went through the trouble to make two deposits. Two. Pointless. Deposits."

I stand then, even though I feel the pressure drop from my head. I feel dizzy, but the screen beyond Dominic's head sharpens into focus. "Thirty-five dollars and thirty-one cents," he says. "Oh, look, another eighty-three. Wow."

"83.65," I say, because I see something he does not. I see the screen of the GPS as we were hiking—the numbers and decimals—and I feel someone whispering to me, someone real. It's the closest to June that I've ever been, right here, staring at those numbers. She's telling me something. Something only I see in this moment.

No, I'm not the only one who sees. Cameron's eyes are soft and focused, and he slides them over to me for a second. He sees it too. I shake my head at him, just the barest shake. But Cameron leans forward and puts his finger on the screen. He seems to change his mind, because he pulls back and says, "Dinner on June tonight?"

But not even Casey laughs.

I don't know what I've done to earn his silence, and I'm not sure if I trust it either, but I'll take it.

Because those numbers on the screen, they're coordinates. Put a negative sign before the second number, and it looks a lot like the coordinates here. The money doesn't mean anything.

It's a location.

June is trying to show me something.

I close my eyes and commit them to memory, the only place that has ever been safe for me. I close my eyes and recite them in a song, in the way I imagine my mother's cadence, which is how I commit everything to memory. But this time, it doesn't work. This time, I see June's mouth, close to my ear, reciting the numbers. Her white teeth and full lips with the hint of a smile, enunciating them with perfection: *35.31 –83.65, 35.31 –83.65, 35.31 –83.65.*

It works out the same. I know I won't forget.

Dominic kicks the machine, and Casey jumps. And I remember this version of him on the island as well. How his confidence, his entire demeanor, became unhinged when things did not go his way. I heard him after he recovered, trying to explain it all away while I was locked in the next room. I heard him kicking the furniture, tossing things to the ground, throwing out accusations that couldn't hold water. I refused to give any sort of statement at all, which made him even angrier.

I didn't go his way.

I didn't then, and I won't now.

The guards who cycle through are in a division of the National Guard, and most of them are fairly young. It's not a desirable position—twenty-eight days in, twenty-four-hour responsibility, and they must hold me on a tightrope—I am a human being, not a prisoner, but one who must be balanced and assessed and held at bay but not restrained. I am a portion of their training. I am a goddamn test.

And Dominic Ellis flunked the test.

He was too cocky. Too sure of himself. Too sure of *me*.

I was those things, too. But I was not the one being tested.

.   .   .

Now, I'm being tested. Not by someone else, but this is it. This is the only test that matters. Fail, and my only chance is gone. Will it be another seventeen years before I have another?

Dominic kicks the machine once more, but the machine doesn't budge. The vials of test tubes on the table beside him rattle and clang against one another when he leans on it to regain his composure. Casey's eyes are wide, and so are Cameron's, and he looks at her and nods his head toward the door.

"Nothing changes," Dominic says as they walk away. He smiles at me. "She hid it," he says. "She hid the money, just like she hid the clues to the database. The answers are in you, Alina. You're going to tell me everything."

I pretend to be scared—only I find I don't have to pretend at all—and I back into the table with the test tubes as he kicks it once more. My hand moves across the table behind me, the lone beaker falling to the floor and shattering, but Dom doesn't notice over the sound of the test tubes rattling around.

"I don't know anything," I say.

"That's what you think," he says.

The last time we were in a room alone, I had the upper hand. There was a perceived safety, that nothing bad could truly happen to me. That island kept me safe, just like it promised to. There's no one to protect me here. Only myself, and I don't know if I am enough.

I slide to the floor, my back against the machine, like I'm terrified. His face twists and he steps back.

"Get up," he says, backing away toward the door. He holds his hands up, palm out, toward me. "I'm not someone to fear, Alina."

I grope around behind me until I find the shards of glass from the beaker. I keep my hands clenched into fists as I push myself to standing, and I stick them inside my pocket and try not to move more than necessary until I can store them some-place safer.

Until I need it.

Dominic waits in the entrance, and he puts his hand on my back as I pass. I hold my breath until I'm out of his reach. I feel a sharp point against my leg, and my heart beats wildly.

Now I have glass.

Casey is crouched in front of a television—or maybe it's a computer screen—that she's setting up in the main room. She powers it up and watches the black screen as Cameron sprawls on the brown couch that looks like it's coated in a layer of dust.

She bites her lip and feeds a cable from the monitor into the back room, and a woman's face fills the screen. She's talk-ing to us through the camera and there's a red bar at the bot-tom with a phone number. The screen flashes to a picture of me. *Pictures* of me. Then back to her.

"Whoa, whoa," Cameron says. "Sound!"

"Working on it!" Casey yells back.

Dominic sits beside Cameron and leans closer to the screen, as if he's trying to read her lips. And then sound comes blaring from the speakers, and all of us jump at once. It's too loud, but nobody seems to care, because the woman is talking about me. About us.

"—believed to be traveling with nineteen-year-old Casey London." The screen flashes to Casey's guard photo with her false identity, but then to another picture from another time and place. One that was obviously taken by her friends or her family. One handed over, along with her identity.

"Damn it," Cameron whispers, and Casey has frozen beside me, standing behind the couch. They're zooming in on her face now, but not before I see the person beside her. It's Cameron, off to the side, not even realizing he's been caught in the frame, and he's talking to someone who looks just like Casey, but with heavier makeup and longer hair. Cameron seems younger, a little thinner. The camera zooms further, and they disappear from the edges of the screen. Casey is holding a glass plaque of some sort, smiling wryly at the camera.

"It's not yet known," the woman on the screen continues, "what their connection is. Only that Casey London is a talented computer programmer who unexpectedly, according to her teachers, dropped out of school last year after the disappearance and presumed death of her twin sister, Ava London, despite having a full scholarship to nearly any college of her choosing." I cast a quick glance at Casey, but she's riveted to the screen, her fingers digging into the back of the couch.

"It's unclear how she assumed a new identity, but she joined the National Guard six months ago as Elizabeth Lorenzo. We haven't been able to contact family yet for comment."

The air in the room is heavy with silence. With Casey's secrets. She pushes off the back of the couch and forces a laugh. "Foiled by academic awards. The irony."

"I'm glad you think this is funny," Cameron says, and Dominic shushes them both with a wave of his hand.

The number flashes on the bottom of the screen again. "Once again, law enforcement is currently offering a one-million-dollar reward for any information that leads to the capture of Alina Chase. Consider her dangerous if seen, and call this number immediately."

"Whoa," Cameron says.

Casey walks over and fidgets with the controls, turning the volume back to normal levels.

"Well," Cameron says, "I guess we know exactly what she's worth now."

Dominic leans back against the couch. "They don't want you out here for a reason, Alina. If it's worth a lot to them, it's worth a lot to us. Tell us everything." He looks at the number on the screen, narrows his eyes back at me, and says, "Don't tempt me, Alina."

chapter 10

I DON'T KNOW WHAT Dominic expects me to say—what they all expect me to say. *Oh, hey, I know where the shadow-database is hidden.* Or *I know how June and Liam hacked inside, no problem.* I was convinced the rumors were bullshit, but now I'm not entirely sure. I think of the coordinates. Even if it were possible, that information is poison. It destroyed my last life. I'm not going to let it destroy this one.

"I've been contained my entire life, how could I possibly know anything?" And I'm also growing painfully irritated. Even though I realize they haven't freed me for some altruistic reason, I still wanted it to be about *me*. Me, and not June.

"Has anyone tried to contact you?" he asks.

"Other than you, no," I say immediately.

"Think," he says, but I roll my eyes at him and catch Cameron grinning. Dominic thinks I haven't been looking for the last seven years? That I haven't looked for patterns in the guards' speech, in news programs, in the way my chicken was cut and positioned on the plate? That I haven't counted the time between the lights turning on and off in my own room, that I haven't spent nights awake watching the lights I could see in the distance? How else does he think I caught his codes? I was looking for them. I was *always* looking.

"June must've left pieces of information with different people. They must've been instructed to pass it along to you somehow," Dom says.

"How were they supposed to know who June became?" Casey asks. "I'm sure June didn't think she'd be sought out and contained for her entire life. Her identity wouldn't be public information."

Dominic doesn't want to hear it. He flicks his hand through the air, as if he can push the question aside. "It was her bargaining chip," he says. "June set it up, and she let them know. Kind of like blackmail. *If you kill me, I'll come back and haunt you.*"

Cameron says, "Looks like she was bluffing."

Dominic's face pulls into a scowl. "June didn't bluff."

Maybe not, but the only one she's haunting is me.

All these people believe they know June—what she would do, what she wouldn't do. I know her better than anyone. Better than *everyone*. I've spent my life learning about her, hearing about her, trying to crack through to the truth.

"That guard who tried to kidnap you when you were a kid. Did she tell you anything?" Dominic asks.

"She wasn't trying to *kidnap* me, she was trying to *free* me,"

I yell, and Cameron looks surprised by my outburst. "Unlike you," I add.

Dominic comes closer. "Sometimes you act older than your age, and sometimes you act like a child still. This? This is how you *get* freedom. What do you think happens the second you show your face out there?" He gestures into the wilderness, or maybe somewhere beyond. "You're Alina Chase, and I'm sorry to say that you cannot actually be anything you want. We all have to play the hand we're dealt. You've got a good hand. Use it."

He reminds me of someone, the way he speaks, so sure of his words and the meaning behind them. And then I realize: June. He reminds me of June. How she spoke those words with such conviction because she believed them. Right or wrong, she believed.

He should really already know this story, anyway. I'm sure this information is part of their training. The second attempt on my life, before it was ruled an accident. Casey must have heard it as well when she joined the guard. I have nothing to lose by telling him again.

"Genevieve. Just a guard," I say, in case Cameron doesn't know. "She didn't tell me anything."

"Are you sure?" Cameron asks. I'm surprised he's the one who asks. And for a moment, I am not anymore. He does that to me, makes me question what I know of myself. Makes me not trust my instincts. He makes me nervous, more than Dom does, and Dom has the power to hold me and keep me.

"I was ten. How should I remember?" But while that may be true, it's also true that I do remember all of it. When day after day is so much the same, the different takes on life, a string of individual moments burned permanently into my memory, all on its own.

Genevieve was probably my mother's age, and for the two years she was stationed there, she was the closest thing I had to one. On four days, off three. I had another guard for the three days Genevieve was gone, but she was older and her hands were dry, and she always smelled like licorice. They had been screened rigorously—no connections to June or Liam, their families or mine—and their identities were kept private for their own safety and their families' safety.

Liam's family blames June for his death. They are not on my side. June's family has fled, disappeared, and wants nothing to do with me. Not that I blame them—it's the safest option. I had two caretakers, but Genevieve was the only one who *cared* for me.

I trusted her—and I gave her a letter when she was leaving for her days off, a letter to my mother. I asked her to get it to her, but she squeezed her eyes shut, crumpled it in her fist, and put it back in my own. "Tell her yourself," she said, "when you're dreaming." Then she held me while I cried, and she sang me that lullaby, the one I like to imagine my mother singing to me instead.

Three weeks later, she smuggled me out. I had no warning, but I trusted her. She wrapped something stiff and cold around my arms and across my ribs as I was getting dressed. At the time, I thought it was some sort of bulletproof vest, like I'd seen in the movies. But now I know it was probably to block the signal of the tracker. I remember it was dark, and her fingers were tight on my arm as she led me into the back of the delivery van, the engine already running. I remember she was dressed differently, and that her nervous energy transferred to me. She lifted a lid on a container, helped me inside, and before closing me in, she touched her finger to her forehead, her heart, and both shoulders, in a gesture I didn't fully understand.

"Where are we going?" I asked.

She shook her head. "*Duérmete, niña,*" she said—*sleep, girl*—and the lid enclosed me in complete darkness.

But we never made it past the bridge. The wheels started spinning harder as I heard the gears of the bridge being raised up ahead. I couldn't see anything, couldn't orient what was happening, whether the van was hurtling through empty space or losing control on solid ground, and I'm not sure whether it was the motion, the disorientation, or the uncertainty of it all that made me so violently ill, but I now cannot sit in a moving vehicle without that same feeling every time.

The crunch of metal was loud and fast, and I felt the world becoming smaller, so it was just me with bags of trash and caved-in walls. I suppose I'm lucky, because the garbage cushioned me in, softened the blows as the container was tossed about in the back of the van.

They pried me out, and they did it quickly, hands grabbing and assessing, sharp whispers that settle like fog in my memory.

I wish I remembered some resistance from Genevieve or some bravery on my part, but I was sobbing, and Genevieve didn't fight. I remember only the blurry vision of faceless people and the smell of gas and dirt as they ran me back inside.

They were all gone the next day.

I knew enough not to ask for Genevieve, but even when I looked up the incident years later, I was unable to find any reference to her—just an attempt on my life, a plot from the inside, leading to a change of protocol, and the threat neutralized. No follow-up.

I looked up "*duérmete*" later, too, with the stinging hope that maybe it was a location and not just an order to sleep, but it turned out not to be a real place after all.

Like my mother, Genevieve only exists in my imagination now.

I feel a quick wave of anger, but then I push it away. My mother never speaks out. Never makes statements. I can find no trace of her on any Internet search, other than from our very notorious past. She has all but disappeared.

I'm glad for her. I am.

So I tell Dominic the story. I tell him all of it, about the letter I tried to send and her order to *duérmete* and the accident. And at the end I shrug and say, "Did they tell you about Genevieve? Is she in jail? Why don't you ask her?"

Casey and Cameron share a quick look, and Dom's head tilts just the slightest bit to the side, and he examines me as if he's trying to understand something. "I would, Alina. I would. But that woman is dead. They told us this story during our training. She died in the van, crushed from the impact. Don't you remember?"

But no.

That's not what happened.

That's not how I remember it.

The threat neutralized. No.

Genevieve is dead. I try the phrase on, watch my memory shift as it does. The van rolls and I am screaming, but I'm the only one screaming. They use a crowbar to pry me out with an urgency I don't understand, because I'm fine. Genevieve doesn't try to stop them, she doesn't resist, she doesn't run. The threat has been neutralized.

She is dead.

She's in the front seat, crushed, and she is dead.

I feel the nausea roll through me, like I'm trapped in the container again. Like I'm being tossed about, and when the motion stops I'm completely disoriented.

There was never any further story about this. It was dealt with by security on the island. I never knew her last name, so I couldn't find her even if I wanted to. There was never anything about her punishment, or a trial, because she was dead. Neutralized.

I don't like the fact that they lied in their omission, in their word choice.

I don't like the fact that my mind created a story that was wrong, that missed something, that was a single camera angle.

I feel even smaller. I didn't even understand everything about my island.

"I was ten," I say as an excuse once again. And I shrug like it's not a huge deal. Like my universe isn't shifting as we speak. Like I don't feel myself losing a grip on something, on myself.

"I bet her name wasn't even Genevieve," Casey says, which makes me feel even worse. I am responsible for another person's death, and I don't even know who she truly is.

"*Duérmete*," Dom mumbles. "Go to sleep? Seriously? Are you sure she wasn't trying to kill you both?"

That's what people thought at first, I think. Because they raised the bridge to stop her, and she didn't stop. What did she really believe was going to happen?

"You're contained because you can find the shadow-database, or you can figure out how to hack the original again," Dominic says. I kind of like that he believes the status quo statement is crap, but I don't like this alternative. "June left you clues," he says. "There *are* clues, Alina. There have to be."

"Why?" I ask. "Because otherwise I've been contained for some other reason, right? Because this is all some huge mistake, and I'm the only one who has to pay for it!"

"There are clues. There is money. I've staked my life on it, that's how much I believe."

I can't imagine believing something so strongly that I would stake my life upon it. I can't imagine trusting in an idea that much. I think of what June believed and where it got her. Where it got *me*.

"It's an urban legend," I say. "There are no clues."

I don't *want* there to be clues. I don't want to think of June

using me. I don't want to think of me and June in the same
sentence ever again.

But I see her mouth, and it's pressing closer to my ear.

35.31 –83.65, she says. And I wonder if this is the start.

They question me for hours. Mostly it's Dominic. But every once
in a while, Casey will pick up on something I say and dig and
dig at the sentence until it's completely dissected and we're all
sure it's useless.

They want to know about maintenance workers, but if
they came, I never saw them. They ask what happened in the
hurricane. Where did I go? *An underground bunker.* Who talked
to me? *Nobody.*

They ask about my tutors, but that conversation quickly
goes nowhere when I explain that I take distance-education
courses that have been taped years in advance. They know how
the homework thing works, since they were able to hack it.

They want to know if the doctor is the same every year—
she is—and what she says. Exactly. She's someone who's allowed
to be alone with me, who has the opportunity. But I can't take
their concern seriously. This is how my doctor visits go: *Any
complaints?* Let me list them. *Any questions?* Many.

It had become a game for me, to try to make the doctor
uncomfortable. And I do. I make things up, and she knows I
do it, but she has to take them seriously, just in case. *I see only
the color red. My left arm acts on its own accord. I think there's
something living inside my right lung. I can feel my heart throwing off extra beats. I can't feel my toes.* I say ridiculous things in

the hope she will have to take me to a medical facility, but she never does. They bring it to me instead, in a medical transport vehicle. So I gave up on that and started asking her ridiculous questions instead, which she insists on answering, just in case. But I make her uncomfortable, I can tell. It is not the doctor.

Dom asks about the humanitarian group—but I'm never present for their assessments—and about the media in years past. Do they shout things? Pass on information? Anything they say could mean something.

They exhaust every facet of my life, any contact I might have with the outside. They have run through the list, when Casey says, "What about your parents?"

"What about them?" I snap. She jerks back, and I try to play it off that I snapped because they've been questioning me for hours.

"Your mom was released ten years ago, and your dad was released five years ago, before being recommitted for breaking parole. Have they ever tried to make contact?"

"Never."

"Are you sure—"

"Don't you think I would know if the only people I want in the world had come back into my life? There's nothing. There's nobody else."

And then, at least, the questions stop.

Casey paces back and forth across the room, and Dominic follows with his eyes. "Hey," he says, but she's still pacing. "There's always the money. And that price? I guarantee it'll go up. I'll give you your share, enough to get out of here, go anywhere you want."

Casey stops and spins to face him. "I don't want the freaking money. You *promised* me."

"What do you want me to do? Shake it out of her?"

They're talking about me, right in front of me, as if I were a thing to extract information from. I think of Casey doing my hair, running with me, holding my hand. Casey protecting me and sticking up for me, and then all those moments are replaced with a bitter swipe. Her, using me. Of course she was using me. What did I expect?

Cameron clears his throat, and Casey looks over at him. He makes some slight expression, something so slight only someone who knew him intimately would be able to decipher it. I have no idea what it means, but Casey seems to relax, or at least she pretends to relax.

Dominic faces me again. "Don't you want the money?"

"No, I don't want June's money."

"*Your* money," he corrects.

"June's money."

"She said she doesn't," Cameron says. "So she doesn't. Why is that so hard to believe?"

Dom shakes his head, leans closer. "Want to know why people believe you're still the same person? Why they think you're June?" he says. "This is why. I see what you're doing. It's been two days, and already they listen to you." He gestures at Cameron and Casey. "They wait to hear what you're going to say, and they believe you. They don't see what you're doing."

"I'm not doing anything," I say, but Dominic keeps going like I haven't spoken at all.

"But they don't know you like I do. They don't know what you'll do next. Do you want to tell them about the night in your room, or should I?"

My jaw drops, and I shove a finger in his chest. "You betrayed me," I say. "That's what happened. You were *spying* on me, trying to find out about June. You were trying to extract information from me. You wanted June's money. You were *using* me."

"Really?" he says, but he's leering. "Then how come I'm the one without a job now? How come you're the one who had to be physically restrained? How come everyone is scared of you there?" Cameron is watching, and I want him to stop. But he keeps going. "The kiss of death, that's what you are."

I flinch.

I was screaming and the stun gun was still in my hand and the entire island went on lockdown . . .

Because he couldn't balance me. Couldn't hold me on the tightrope. Because he failed the test. It wasn't my fault.

"It's your first instinct, Alina. It's who you are. *You* come first. *Your* ideals, at the expense of everyone else. That's the soul, right? It's who you are. Who you'll always be."

I'm shaking my head. I've been shaking my head, and I'm still shaking it. But I have no words, only rage, fighting its way to the surface, inch by inch, and I can't shake it off.

"Yes, I wanted out," I say, my voice firm and practiced. "I always wanted out. Because I was being held, inhumanely and unconstitutionally." The speech I'd come up with last year pours out of me. "Because my soul is my own, and the world is punishing me for something that no longer exists. The world is the only one with a memory. Not my soul. June is dead. *I* am the only one here. *My* name is Alina Chase."

He starts to smile then, as I catch my breath. He looks back at Cameron and Casey with his eyebrows raised. "Well," he says. "If this isn't proof that the girl before us is June Calahan, I don't know what is. You sound *just* like her."

And then I have no more words. Only anger. I throw the closest thing I can find. It's that battery-powered lantern, and I hurl it at his head. He ducks just in time, and it hits the wall behind him. He rushes toward me, and I throw the second lantern, nailing him in the side of the skull. "A little help?" he yells, as he sinks to the floor clutching the side of his face.

Cameron rushes me from the side. He doesn't knock me over like I think he will. But he does restrain me. He wraps his arms around me, and I can't move. But his hand is rubbing my upper back, like I'm an animal he's trying to calm. It feels like it did back in the trunk . . .

On the island, this would be the point where someone would give me a shot and my emotions would fall to nothing. When I'd become complacent and malleable. I wait, with his arms wrapped around me. I wait for the emotion to fade, but it doesn't. Instead, it shifts.

Against all reason, I don't fight back. Against all reason, I begin to cry instead.

And this makes me even angrier. With my hands at my side, I reach one to the outside of my pocket, and I find the sharp edges of the broken glass. I reach inside and a shard scrapes against my knuckle, drawing blood. I feel for it between my fingers and position it in my fist. I give Cameron a warning, "Get your hands off me," as I prepare to slice at his arm. And surprisingly, he does. He listens. And I'm left there holding a handful of glass and nobody to use it on.

Dominic rises from the ground, still holding the side of his head. "There you are," he says, and he smiles. He turns to Cameron with the same expression. "See? There she is."

And then I realize they're talking about June Calahan, like a ghost, rising from the ashes.

I fall onto the couch, tears gone, something much worse in their place.

And just like I understood in the trunk of the car why everyone leaves a piece of themselves behind, I also understand completely why people rarely go check for results. It's not just the past-life message boards full of con artists, pretending to be long-lost loves. It's not just the people who seek you out with questionable motivations. It's because as I lie on the couch with Casey watching me with wide eyes, with Cameron looking anywhere but at me, and with Dominic holding a shirt to the side of his head, I lose the one thing I've always held on to.

I believe him. I believe that maybe the person I was is the person I am.

Because I feel it in me, that thing he's talking about. I used to believe this impulsiveness, this rage, was a product of my incarceration. Justifiable. Expected, even.

It's inside me, this instinct, and I'm constantly pushing it down. I'm constantly trying to hide it, along with my emotions, my intentions. But it's there, and he knows it.

But what if it runs deeper than the circumstances of my life?

If I believe that maybe I *am* nothing more than the soul of June Calahan, and if I believe that maybe she *was* capable of betrayal and selfishness and ruining lives . . .

Then I must believe that maybe I am capable of these things, too.

I don't want to be her. I don't want to be anything like her.

Dominic keeps talking, with the shirt still pressed to the cut on his head. "I get that, right now, you're holding on to information until you can use it for something. And you're not thinking of me, or Cameron, or Casey, who have risked our lives and given up our identities to free you. I get that your soul is unbearably selfish. I get that you'll trade it only for something worthwhile. So tell me what you want, and I'll trade you for it."

Isn't it obvious?

"I want to get away from you. I want to be free," I say, and even to myself, I sound like a child, throwing pennies into a fountain and wishing for fairies and ponies and magic. I guess while I'm feeling particularly tragic, I'll be completely honest with myself: I want my mother to come for me, and I want to wipe June Calahan from existence, and then I want to undo the last seventeen years and start again. But getting away from here with a fresh start is coming in a very close second.

Dom nods. We all want something; why should I be any different? Why should I not trade part of my soul for what I want? They're all doing it. Dominic wants my money. Casey wants *something*. Something she was willing to trade her identity for. I have no idea why Cameron is here still, but I'm sure it's not for me.

"Okay," he says. "Okay. Do this with us, help us, and you'll get a share of the money one way or the other, and Casey can work you up a new identity."

Cameron scoffs, and we all turn to look at him. "Everyone knows her face. She'll never be free." It's like he doesn't want me to agree. Doesn't want me to tell them what the numbers of my inheritance mean.

Dominic shakes his head. "The world is big, Alina."

It's just me. I am alone, like always. They want something from me, and now I want something from them.

Like the terrifying ocean, the only way to get past it is to go through it.

"The deposits," I say. "They're coordinates."

And just like that, I trade everything I have to bargain with for the tiniest sliver of hope.

chapter 11

DOMINIC TEARS THROUGH HIS things like a kid on Christmas, desperately searching for his GPS. I recite the coordinates for him from memory, and he plugs them in. "This is nearby," he says. Of course it is. This is where June disappeared for so long. "A day's hike. We go tomorrow. Bring food and a tent, we may need to stay the night."

I'm still clutching the glass, but only Cameron seems to notice. He waits for Dominic and Casey to disappear into the computer room, on some mission to look into different variations of a place that may be called Duérmete, or something similar. They won't find anything. It doesn't exist. I've looked.

I stand, spinning away from his gaze, from what I might see in it.

"What were you planning to do?" he asks.

I take a deep breath and turn to face him, but he's staring at my clenched fists, at the shard of glass sticking out.

"I don't know," I say. It's the truth if he's asking what I

intended to do *after* I got out of his grip. I hadn't thought that far ahead. Step One: Break the hold. Step Two: To be determined. I'm losing a grip on myself the longer I spend away from the island. I swallow dry air and meet his eyes. "I don't feel safe here."

He looks at me like he knows, of course he knows, that I was going to cut him. He who has done nothing but help me. Who risked his life to remove the tracker from my rib, who dove into the ocean after me so I wouldn't drown, who shared my air tank, my fear, my secrets. I betrayed him. I was planning to slice my way out of his hold, before I even thought of trying to ask him to stop. I am impulsive. I am driven by rage. I am nothing more than the person they believe me to be. Selfish and self-righteous. I am.

I want to apologize, to ask forgiveness, to take it back, as impossible as that seems. But words mean nothing. Action, everything.

I let the pieces fall to the floor in a tiny melody, in surrender, and all he does is bend down to clean them up, making me feel even worse.

"Why didn't you tell?" I ask. It's obvious that Casey wanted any information I had, and it's obvious that he knew about the coordinates. I wonder if Dominic is right, if they really do care about what I say. But I think that was just Dom, twisting words, twisting *me*, to get the information he needed.

"Wasn't mine to tell," he says, still looking at the floor.

"What does she want from me?" I ask.

He pauses, the glass half in his palm, half on the wood floor. "Also not mine to tell," he says.

He continues to pick up the pieces. "Then why are *you* here? What do *you* want?"

He doesn't answer at first, staring at the floor, at the pieces of glass. And then at me. "I'm here because she'd do this anyway. I'm here because I'm scared to lose her." He stands with the glass, and then he shocks me by coming closer. "I'm here because I have nowhere else to go."

Closer still, and I feel a hand on my waist again. "I'm here because I would do anything for my sister," he says, and now he's whispering. "And I'm *still* here because I don't see any other option." I feel his fingers along the side of my pants, and I don't know what to do. His fingers find the pocket, and I'm holding my breath, and I feel the shards of glass drop back inside my pocket. "This really wouldn't have done anything to me. There were two other people in the room. You get that?" I nod, because I'm out of words. "I'd do anything for her. Do you understand?"

He backs away, and his words echo in a pattern in my head.

His sister.

Other option.

Do you understand?

He leaves me in the main room with the glass in my pocket, and he disappears into the bathroom.

Yes, I think. *I understand.*

People do stupid things for the people they love. My parents went to jail for me. Cameron is here, giving up his freedom, a dead man walking, as he said, for Casey. And I don't even know what June did for Liam White, or what he did for her. But I do know it was stupid, since they both ended up dead.

I understand Cameron, and my body thrums with anticipation.

He's handing me a code. Like the lines of DNA: *Hi, Alina Chase.*

I was always looking for messages. For code. I was always sending them out, waiting for someone to respond. So when Cameron tells me these things, with his careful, deliberate words, I understand. When he leaves the glass in my pocket, I understand.

He's saying I may need it—I don't feel safe, and I may need it. He's not sure Dom will let me go after this. Use it wisely, he's saying. Use it *better.*

I'm not sure if I should trust him. But there's a chance that I can. When the time comes, the chance will have to be enough, because it's all I have.

There's a list in my head, a list I start making for when it's time: a GPS, food, water, blankets . . . and then I stop myself. I amend it. *You. Just you. You and* out there, *you will make it.*

Of course you will.

Cameron makes a fire in the wood-burning stove, but it's not for cooking. It's for the heat. The mountains are cold at night, even in the summer. It crackles, and the heat comes off it in waves. I've never been so close to a fire this size, and the smell of it sets my nerves on edge. Everything has changed.

We eat directly from containers—dried, salted meat, trail mix, lukewarm beans. I'm not going to lie: it's disgusting.

"This is gross," Casey mumbles, and even Cameron seems to gag as he chews.

"It's just temporary," Dominic says, yet again.

The temporariness of this situation goes unspoken—it lasts until I lead them to the way to access the information inside the database again, and we each get what we came for.

"I'm just saying it wouldn't have killed you to get some chips or bread or something . . ." She's looking at Cameron when she says it, but Dominic is the one to slam the container he's been eating from onto the ground.

He fixes his eyes on her. "Do you have any idea how many trips the equipment alone took me? Cameron and I had to carry it all in here. Piece by bulky freaking piece. For *weeks*. While you were getting fed in training and on duty, standing around, watching *her*. Did you see a grocery store on the hike in? Excuse me if I picked efficient."

My spoon scrapes against the metal can. This is the first moment we've had to pause and catch our breath. The plan is fluid, and developing as we speak, and it's finally something other than the steps they had laid out in front of them. This is the leap of faith they were taking: that they'd find something in me. And now they have, only it's vague and insubstantial with no end point in sight. The tension crackles through the room along with the fire.

Cameron cracks his knuckles.

"Efficient," Casey says. Then she laughs. "My appetite is efficiently gone," she says, slamming the half-empty can on the ground and heading to the bathroom.

I finish my portion. I finish hers, too.

I'm not used to the sounds in here—the crackle of the fire and the humming of the computers. But the fire dies down and the computers are shut off as we move to the bedroom, and I'm not used to the sounds that remain either. The crickets. The wind. The way you can hear it coming through the trees before it reaches the house, pushing against the door and the mesh-wired windows.

The sleeping arrangements are much like the night before. Except now we're in thick sleeping bags on the hard floor. We're all piled in one room together again—the difference this time is that somebody stays up at all times. I'm not sure what it is they're worried I might do, whether I'll claw my way through the wood walls, whether I'll smother them in their sleep, but it makes me think that this place isn't as secure as the locked basement we were last in. Maybe they're right to be cautious— I already have glass resting in my pocket. I'm unable to move because of it, but I feel safer keeping it there.

I hate June Calahan for what she allowed to happen back then and for what she allowed to happen to me now. This is what June wanted, after all. It's what she believed. A dangerous soul is dangerous. It's funny, I think, that she didn't realize she'd be lumped into that category when all was said and done.

I want to stay up. I want to whisper to Cameron and listen,

I want to watch Dominic and Casey and learn more. But mostly, I want to be ready. And so I sleep.

I wake up once, during Cameron's shift, because I feel a body standing nearby, and my senses are on high alert. But he's not looking at me. He crouches beside Casey, and I can't hear them exactly, but I can tell they're disagreeing. I hear someone say, "This is completely screwed up," and I know it's Cameron, because his shadow clenches its fists at the same time the words carry through the room.

Then Casey pushes herself upright, and she sticks her finger at him, saying, "I need to do it, *we* need to do it."

"No, we don't," he says.

It feels as if they've repeated these words to each other over and over again, because Casey just lies back and says, "We're already doing it."

"It won't change anything," he says.

"It changes *everything*," Casey says. I don't even have to strain to hear her, and Dominic's sleeping bag rustles.

The shadow retreats to the door, Casey rolls over, the conversation is done.

The next time I wake, there's just the faintest color to the sky, so I can see the mesh wires crisscrossing the solitary window. Casey is sitting with her back against the door with her eyes closed. But I can tell from the tension in her jaw that she's not asleep. Light snoring comes from the other two sleeping bags. "Hey," I whisper, and her eyes flutter open, focusing on me. "Can I use the bathroom?"

She checks her watch and stands. Then she looks beyond me. "Dom," she says. "Time to wake up."

She waits for them to stir, then leads me out of the room without touching me. Whatever sort of camaraderie we shared yesterday is gone now. We're all playing our hands. There's no point pretending anymore.

I have decided the most essential item for survival is a pair of shoes that fit. Blisters are the devil. At this point, I'd rather have Cameron cut a tracker out of my rib again. Okay, maybe not. But still. I slide the shoes onto my feet and already feel the chafing on my heel, my ankle. Dominic is packing an insane amount of material into a tiny knapsack, like a magic trick. And Casey makes a trip out back where there's allegedly a well for fresh water.

I stare at the front door, open just a crack, calling to me like a magnet.

"Alina," Cameron says, like he's already said it. I shift my gaze to him, and he shakes his head, just once. "Heads up." He tosses me a roll of beige tape from the first-aid kit on the counter. "Wrap your ankles. It helps."

I do, and he's right. I end up binding the sneakers as well, tightening them even more, securing them in place. "Thank you," I say. Then I take another strip and place it in my pocket, folding the pieces of glass inside.

Casey comes back with several canteens. Dominic can barely keep the smile from his face. Casey is anxious as well, checking the lids, lining everything up in neat rows.

Cameron watches her with his breath held.

"Okay, everyone," Dominic says, scanning all our faces. "Breathe. It's just a hike."

Casey laughs, and Cameron relaxes, and even I feel something unfurl inside me.

Because as much as I would like to think about running—as much as I think about the door open a crack and the glass in my pocket—I hear those numbers whispered into my ear, and I want to know. God, I want to know. They're meant for me, and I want to know what's waiting there.

I feel like June must've felt, in the moments before she got inside the database. All the information, just waiting to be seen. I'm like her after all—truth at any price. No matter what it says about me, about me and June in the same sentence, it's true.

Dom shrugs the largest pack onto his shoulders and waits for us to do the same. We walk in a single-file line out into the sunlight. Dom, then Casey, then me, then Cameron.

I picture June's mouth reciting the coordinates to me, and I want to grab her. I want to shake her, and ask her why, and then I want to see what she has left for me.

I guess we're about to find out.

We're mostly silent for the hike. Mostly, I think we're all lost in our own thoughts, because whenever somebody does speak, it takes the others a moment to catch up. Which is what's happening right now.

"I mean, it's been seventeen years, it's not just going to be sitting somewhere in the middle of the woods, right?" Casey asks like she's been mentally talking to herself. "We're looking for some instructions she's left behind, right? It can't be this easy, can it?" Her voice is breathy and hopeful.

"I wouldn't call this easy," Cameron mumbles.

"You know what I mean," she says. "The Alonzo-Carter Cybersecurity facility hasn't been compromised since June and Liam—not for lack of trying. So either she's leading us to a shadow-database she set up to mirror the original, or to some sort of instruction guide to hack it externally . . ."

"My money's on some sort of code," Dom says.

"I don't know," Casey says. "Security could change a lot in seventeen years, which she must've known. My money's on some sort of shadow-database."

"Funny," Cameron says, "considering neither of you has any money right now." I laugh unexpectedly, but Dominic scowls at him. "Maybe we're just being led to the money," Cameron says, but Dom waves him off.

"June was about more than money," Dominic says.

June. God, he's obsessed with her. "How would *you* know?" I ask. "She's dead. The only thing you know is what other people tell you about her."

"And you," he says. "I know you."

I narrow my eyes at him. "You do realize June wasn't a programmer, right?"

"Oh, we know that," Dominic says. "We know that she used Liam to get in. But after she got him killed, she still had access somehow. The blackmail continued until her death. So either she knew how to get in or she had a shadow-database set up, copying the information remotely. Either way, she was *in*."

"It's just a movie," I mumble, but Dominic stops walking. We all stop walking.

"What did you say?"

"I said, it's just a movie. We've all seen it. But the only people who were *there* are June and Liam, and they're both dead, so how do we know what really happened? Maybe Liam set her up to take the fall. Ever think of that?"

"He had a *recorder*, Alina. When he was shot. *That's* how they know."

The recording was actually released—I heard it in one of the documentaries on her life. There have been several. Some paint June as misguided, or at the very least, a reluctant villain. But this documentary was particularly harsh on her, painting her as borderline sociopathic. This documentary made it seem as if she didn't even have the potential for good.

That's another thing scientists have correlated as best they could with the data they had: sociopathic tendencies. It's not a chance—it's practically a guarantee, like left- and right-handedness.

Anyway, the recording was of June's voice, in the same voice I'd heard a thousand times before, where she said that she was not the threat, not the danger, but the message. The bell. Warning people about the potential criminals among us.

But in *this* recording, her voice was tight and desperate, and her words echoed off the walls. It was recorded in that building where they were surrounded on Christmas Day. It's the message that landed me in a lifetime of prison.

I did not take any money, she claimed. *I did not blackmail or bribe. The truth will not die with me. It will still be here, waiting for me. You cannot end me. I will be back. This is your warning.*

And then they left it recording, as they said their good-byes. *I would know you anywhere*, she says. The voice is hers but strained. Pained.

You can even hear the gunshots at the end of the recording, but then most everything is muffled, the recorder on the ground. Everything static and foggy—even Liam White's very labored breathing, until eventually that, too, fades to nothing.

"It actually makes perfect sense," Dominic says. "We've both tried—we've *been* trying—for a long time. *I* can't figure it out. *Casey* can't figure it out, and she's incredible." Casey looks shocked by the compliment, but I believe it. "We can't even come close enough to see what we're up against. It's impossible to hack. It was *made* to be impossible. June wasn't a hacker. She thought different . . ." He scans me quickly. "And so do you."

They're insane if they think I'll miraculously see how to break into a database, when I know nothing of programming or code. They're insane if they think I'll be able to decipher June's life and find some hidden shadow-database that nobody else has managed to find. It won't be in these woods. Not functioning in the middle of a forest for seventeen years. They're wrong, and I'm terrified because I will not see what they need me to see. "I don't know if you realize this," I say, "but it didn't end well for the people who hacked into it last."

Dominic laughs. He really laughs, like I'm funny. But I was serious. "They were loud," he says. "They were loud when they should've been quiet."

Casey won't look at me. I stare at her, hoping to catch her eye. "You want to be like June, Casey? You want to be the villain and have your soul suffer for it forever? You want to end up like me?" When she doesn't answer I turn to Cameron. "And you would let her do this? So much for *anything*." And he flinches.

"No," Casey says, "I care about only one thing in there. A single thing." I remember the news program. Her twin sister died. Of course. Basic human nature, refusing to let go.

"You want to find who Ava is in the next life?" I ask. "I'll tell you: an infant. An infant who deserves its own life. She won't be the same person," I say, and for a second I think she's going to hit me. Instead she just shakes her head at me, like I'm a fool.

"You know what would be great?" Cameron asks. "If we can get on with it already."

We start moving, and Cameron falls into stride with me for a moment. "It's not what you think," he says. "I promise."

But to take him at his word requires both belief and trust, and I am currently empty of both.

The GPS coordinates aren't specific enough. Dominic says the coordinates cover an area one kilometer in each direction. The area in question all looks the same as the rest of the woods. No particular paths, no cabins, just brush and roots covering the soil, trees like every other tree in the forest. "Keep your eyes out," Dominic says. He puts an orange stake into the ground and keeps walking, marking off the area as we follow.

"For what?" Cameron mumbles.

There's nothing here. I know it as we trace the potential area together, and I feel them know it as their breathing comes in short, desperate pulls. As they walk faster, their bodies become tenser. We finish the loop, and all we've seen are trees and dirt.

"She could've buried it," Casey says, and Dominic nods, but everything's starting to take the tone of desperation.

"Right. Of course she did, otherwise it wouldn't survive seventeen years. I'm just looking for some sort of marker, but again, it's been years. It could be crushed, or eroded, or just . . . gone," Dominic says.

"Check the trees," I say, and they all look at me like I have some unexplainable insight into June's psyche. I roll my eyes and say, "Bark doesn't change as much over time. If she wanted a marker to last, she'd use that." We all know June wasn't stupid. She wasn't going to stick a stake in the middle of the floor and expect it to last until the next generation.

I stop at a tree, running my fingers over the bark, imagining June's pale hand doing the same. "Cameron," Dominic says. "Stay with her. Casey, you're with me."

Why did she leave something? How did she know she would die? That she wouldn't just be put in jail where she could leave letters for real people? That she wouldn't just disappear forever? Dominic made it sound like this was June's blackmail.

A fail-safe. A reason for her not to be killed. So again, I wonder, *How did she know she would die?*

It's like she didn't trust the world. Didn't trust the law, or humanity, any of it. Like she knew what would happen when she left the woods. *God, June, why did you leave the woods?*

"Do you really think there's something?" Cameron asks. He's close. I didn't feel him coming closer, but he's close enough that I can feel his breath on my shoulder as he tries to see what I am seeing.

"Yes," I say, and it's the truth.

"What about this one?" Cameron asks, running his fingers along the bark of a tree. There's a diagonal scar across the trunk, and it's impossible to tell if it was put there on purpose or if it's just a naturally occurring scar.

I shrug. "Mark it," I say, and Cameron ties an orange piece of tape around it. This is our fifth marker, and we're not even one-third of the way through our section. It's painstaking, checking each trunk, around and around, from base to branch level. Looking for discrepancies. At the rate we're moving—or *not* moving— we won't be going back to the cabin tonight, that's for sure.

We back down a row, and Casey and Dominic are coming toward us from the other direction. Cameron calls over to them. "I guess it's too much to hope that you found her initials carved in the side of a trunk inside a heart or something?"

"Ha," Casey says. "So far, let's see, we've found three random lines, three circles, or circularish marks, and one arch, like a horseshoe."

I stop moving. Stop breathing. "Show me the arch," I say, and they look at me like I've lost my mind, and maybe I have. But suddenly I can see June walking this same path, her hair swaying as the wind comes, her steps sure and determined. "The horseshoe. Show me." Dominic shrugs and gestures for us to follow.

He leads us to a thick tree in the middle of a cluster, next to a small clearing. The ends of the orange tape they've tied around the bark flutter in the breeze. I move closer, until I can see the marking. It's faint, and imperfect, but I run my finger-tip through the indentation and close my eyes, and my breath leaves me in a rush. "She did this," I say. I imagine June taking a knife in one hand, holding it steady with the other, and jerk-ing the blade through the trunk, inch by inch, until this was complete.

"It's just an arch," Casey says.

"Or a horseshoe?" Dominic says, coming closer. "Why a horseshoe?"

I shake my head, but my smile grows. "Not a horseshoe. A bell."

I am not the danger. I am not the threat. I am the bell, tolling out its warning.

I am delivering a message.

chapter 12

WE'RE ALL STARING AT the trunk, and then suddenly we're staring at the dirt under our feet. Dominic throws his pack to the ground and pulls out a shovel that's been folded up. But that leaves three extra people to continue staring without purpose. I am the first one on my knees. Something stirs inside me, and my fingers claw at the dirt at the base of the trunk. The earth comes up in tiny chunks, after a generation of weather and water and wind have compressed the dirt into solid ground. There are two pairs of hands beside me, digging into the dirt encircling the trunk now, and Cameron is the first to feel something other than dry earth.

"Rope," he says. "There's rope buried."

He pulls at his end while Casey and I continue to unearth it, scooping the dirt off to the side. The rope is looped through a partially exposed root, and as we free it from the ground, it disappears into a path that takes us farther from the tree. It's braided and fraying and off-color, but I know June's hands were here, seventeen years earlier. We pull at the rope, all four of us, all completely focused on the task of unearthing it, and the ground cracks and disintegrates as the rope emerges. It stops suddenly, and I feel resistance just as I hear a clang of metal.

Dominic uses his shovel to move the dirt off the surrounding area, and a dark-green tarp emerges underneath, the rope disappearing below. I go to pull at the tarp, but Dominic points at me with the shovel. "Wait," he says, and he continues to move the dirt off the top. I use my feet to brush aside the dirt that he has broken and softened, and Cameron and Casey do the same.

Eventually, all that remains is a pine-green tarp with remnants of dirt covering an area of the forest the size of my bathroom floor in the small clearing. My limbs are shaking.

Dominic nods at me and this time I carefully peel back a corner, heavy from the dirt that still remains. I lift it and shake it out, careful not to disturb the area below. I'm still removing the tarp when Casey sucks in a breath and Dominic lets out a laugh.

"Holy shit," Cameron says.

I drop the tarp in a heap, forgotten.

In the middle of the forest floor, in the middle of nowhere, there's a wooden door. The rope attaches to a metal hook in the center of the panel of wood. Dominic pulls on the rope, and the door gives, just a bit. Dominic's hands tremble as he reaches his fingers under the splintered edge and pulls it back.

The hinges moan in protest, and the door scrapes against the wooden sides after decades of resettling. And then there is a dark cavern. I can't see a ladder and I can't tell how deep it goes, and apparently neither can anyone else. "Flashlight," Dominic says.

Casey drops her pack and rifles through it, pulling out two palm-size flashlights. She keeps one for herself and hands the other to Dominic. Both of them lie on their stomachs, leaning over the mouth of the entrance, their beams pointed below. We're all leaning over the opening, casting shadows, but I can make out a dirt floor not too far below and a wooden ladder lying across the ground.

Dominic crouches down, and for a second I think he's going to jump in first, but then he eyes me—eyes us—over his shoulder and says, "Casey, care to do the honors?" It's as if he's constantly holding Casey hostage, as if he doesn't quite trust any of us.

I don't blame him. For that split second, I considered shutting the top over him, of making a run for it, but the pull of finding out what's inside is too great. I wouldn't run right now. He's holding the information hostage. I'm completely in. He doesn't need Casey.

She shines her light around before sitting on the edge and hanging for a second before dropping. "Whoa," her voice echoes from below. Dominic motions for me to go next, and I do. I feel the temperature drop before I hit the ground. It's colder here, under the earth. Mustier. And before I can see anything, I get the premonition that this is a coffin, and I am June, and this is what becomes of us both.

I don't have a flashlight, but my eyes follow Casey's light

everywhere it lands. There are walls—beams of wood that have created a shelter inside the earth. There's only the one large room, but it's much bigger than I originally thought. It covers the space of the clearing above, though the walls join at weird angles, not squared off at all, like someone had to work around the root system of the trees. But the walls are only the beginning.

There are cots, the type I assume are used in medical triage, against the wall. Two of them. And there are boxes stacked in the corners. There are lanterns around the room, requiring a match and not a battery. And thermal blankets, thick sleeping bags, and a huge supply of canned food and water. It's like a bomb shelter, except it's not reinforced to withstand a blast. It's for hiding.

I didn't hear Cameron or Dominic land down here, but Cameron actually has a hand instinctively on my arm. Maybe he doesn't know it's me. Maybe in the semidark he thinks I'm Casey. Except very gradually, and very slowly, he moves his fingers down my arm until his fingers find mine. He gives my hand a quick squeeze before letting go. I think it's meant to reassure me, which only has the opposite effect. Dominic whirls on me with the flashlight, and I pull my hand away even farther, using it instead to shield my eyes. "Do you know what this is?" he asks.

Oh, I can guess.

And so can he.

"This is June's hideaway," he says.

Does he not see the *two* cots? The *two* sleeping bags? The two sets of everything?

"*Liam* and June's hideaway," I correct.

I look at the boxes, and it's as if I can feel June's whisper coming from across the room. *What do you want to show me?* I wonder.

There's nothing personal belonging to June in the entire room, at first glance. No heart-shaped engravings of *June loves Liam* or *Liam loves June*. Guess there was no time for that kind of romanticized love. June was my age when she went to college—a year ahead of her peers. My age when she met Liam White. My age when she broke into the database. They met in college and broke into the database six months later. I imagine they were nearly always on the run after that, and Liam was dead within the year.

There's also nothing at first glance, boxes included, that gives away the fact that this was left by June. It's like she wanted to be extra sure that, if this place was found, it wouldn't be connected to anyone.

There are no trinkets or pictures—nothing to live on that wasn't completely generic. Maybe the boxes are full of her things. I hope so. I imagine her discarding everything that was once hers, that she cared for, that reminded her of someone or something, until all that remained was this. And here she sat for over a year, with nothing but boxes and food. Until she became nothing more than this.

At least my room had a window.

At least my island had electricity and running water, books and computers, TV and people.

Dominic heads straight for the boxes. He's practically ravenous, a hunger I've never seen in him. Casey fidgets, looking over his shoulder. It's meant for me, the information inside, and I feel the anger rising. These boxes are mine.

He takes the top box off the stack and peels back the tape, which has been binding the top closed, and I feel him peeling back my skin.

He unfolds the top, and I feel him staring through me, my soul exposed.

And just when I think of doing something impulsive and reckless, Cameron leans over and says, "You doing okay?" like he knows I am not.

I can't really see him down here, and it almost feels safe to lean into his body for absolutely no reason I can give, other than the fact that I want to.

I feel like a magic trick—that I am both out here and inside the box, and I want to ground myself here. To grab something on this side. I want him to hold me here.

I'm reaching for him, and the flashlight swings at me, exposing me. Cameron looks at my hand, halfway between us, but Dominic is too amped up to notice or say anything. "Come see," he says.

And just like that, I feel June whispering to me, pulling me away. I step back from Cameron. It was a stupid impulse anyway.

The first box is filled with reams of paper, the black ink gone gray, the edges curled and stiff. I try to make sense of what's written there, but they're numbers, just lists of numbers, printed out in rows from a computer. Many digits long, grouped together across the page—some in groups of two or three, some more, some on lines all by themselves. I know what the groupings mean, just like I knew what this place was for. The numbers are records in the database, and they're grouped with their matches. These numbers show groups of lives that have had the same soul. Just a handful of generations—that's all the data we have. Dominic flips through the entire stack with the beam of his flashlight. "I don't see any names," he says.

Just numbers. The numbers aren't coded to anyone. But some have asterisks beside them. This data alone doesn't tell us anything we can use, for which I'm both grateful and disappointed. He drops the box and moves to the next one. Another box of paper, another list of numbers without names.

It's possible for souls to disappear from the database for a generation if parents choose not to get their children screened, though that's rare. Or if they die while out of the country. Or they can appear out of nowhere if someone born in another country comes here. This database is a national system only, not yet tied to other nations. Some countries refuse to screen at all, claiming it's not a real science. It's illegal in some nations. Pointless in others. But here, we're obsessed with the idea of it. Of what it means.

Is that number all we will ever be? Do our actions in one life influence the next, as some people believe? Are we drawn back together? Is there a reason some souls feel grounded, with roots, and others wander restlessly, searching, yearning, as I am now? Or is it all random—another life, another chance, another try—with no consequence? We're not even close to a complete understanding. We've just touched the surface. The information is dangerous enough as it is. Nobody has been given access since June broke in. It's too dangerous in the wrong hands.

I stare at those numbers grouped across the page, of the asterisks that sprinkle the paper, and I wonder what it all means. I'm still flipping through them, meaningless as they appear, when everyone else moves to the next boxes.

Boxes three, four, and five hold electronics. Computer parts, hard drives, circuit boards. "What do you think?" Casey asks.

"I think they're wiped," Dom says, "Or too old to use. But put them in your pack. We'll check them out when we get back to the cabin."

We rifle through the next box, Dominic and Casey pulling out papers and holding up their flashlights while I try to make sense of what I'm seeing. I'm trying to see June here, to see her boxing this up, to see her intention. The rest of the room has been getting darker. Cameron is sitting on a cot, and he's yawning. Seriously. This last box, I can tell right away, is different—full of blank postcards with numbers scrawled across them, in lists. It's not June's handwriting. I've seen it enough times to know that, and I feel that stomach flip of hope.

This isn't her stuff. This is Liam's. *Liam* was in charge. *Liam* printed these lists and wrote these numbers. It was him and him alone, and June was being used like I've always wanted to believe.

And then, underneath, there is a notebook. Dominic

opens it, and I see June's handwriting. I know it's hers in the same way I knew the carving in the tree was a bell—from a lifetime of studying her. Somewhere, I've seen her handwriting before, and it's filed away in my mind under All Things June. And that brief moment of hope—that she had nothing to do with this—bursts, replaced with something sharp and sour.

It's her handwriting, but it's still just numbers. No, it's math. It's equations. It's numbers and not words, and they mean nothing to me. Her lines slant across the pages, one after the other, with parts circled in various stages of the equation. Dominic flips the pages back and forth, the flashlight held between us, the numbers meaning nothing.

"Does this mean anything to you?" Dominic asks. "Because it's sure as hell not computer code."

"No," I say. Other than the fact that every number she's circled is a decimal, such as 0.4 or 0.2. Eventually, there's a 0.32 circled several times. But it's all meaningless. I'm not good at this. I haven't *let* myself be good at this. This was something June was gifted in, and in my childish rebellion to reject everything and anything associated to her, I have rejected this gift as well.

"Look closer," Dominic says, shoving the notebook into my lap, like the answer, the meaning, will suddenly appear in my mind—when a piece of paper flutters out of the back pages.

The writing is words. The first words we've seen in this place full of numbers.

It's written, carefully, methodically, in her handwriting, in black marker. The paper is creased, as if it's been balled up and then flattened out again—now it's wrinkled through the words, like the writing is trying to shift itself into focus, from past to present.

224081 - Ivory Street - Edmond

"It's an address," Dominic says.

It belongs to me.

"The shadow-database location?" Casey asks, ripping it from his hands.

It's meant for me, and no one else. June left me the coordinates to this place—she left me the bell carved into the tree. She left it for me, and nobody else.

I take the paper from Casey, staring at the numbers, feeling June's breath on my cheek as she recites the information to me, committing it to memory before I destroy it.

But Dominic seems to sense something has shifted in me, because he takes it back, ripping it in the process—and all that remains in my hand is a torn corner with -*mond*. Half a town.

I can't see the details of his face in the darkness, but I watch as his shadow folds the paper and stores it in his wallet.

"Do you see anything else here?" Dominic asks.

Casey's trying to talk around the flashlight in her mouth as she moves papers aside in the box, but eventually she spits it out. "Damn it!" she says. "We need more light. Did you pack matches?"

"No," Dominic says. "We'll bring the boxes up to the surface." There's too much to carry back to the cabin. And there's not enough light down here. I feel suddenly claustrophobic, like I can't breathe, like possibly we're running out of air and I'm the only one who's noticing.

I move the ladder myself, lean it up against the entrance, and start moving. Cameron watches me from the cot, but he says nothing.

"Where are you going?" Dominic's hand is on my ankle, like a handcuff shackling me to my past, to the person I'm scared I am.

"Up," I say.

Dominic curses as he looks up. "It's dark," he says.

But it's darker down here. Up there, I see the moon through the tree branches and the stars beyond. I feel the crisp night air—air to breathe. "Okay," he says, "listen. No need to set up tents. We'll stay down here for the night. There's plenty of gear. As soon as it's light, we'll bring this all to the surface."

I don't move off the ladder. "Come on now," Dominic says, and his hands rest lightly on my waist, much gentler than I expected. It's unfamiliar. Unwelcome. I flash back to Genevieve, holding me in her arms while I cried for my mother. It was the last time someone held me like that. I was ten, and I was a child, and children can be held like that. But she's dead. Dead, because of me. Because she felt too much when she held me.

I'm so sorry, Genevieve.

The thought makes something crack inside me. Some anger fighting its way through. The only people who have ever cared for me have been punished. My mother, my father, Genevieve. I have ruined lives, much like June has, just by existing. I push his hands aside before stepping off the ladder. I want to see what else is in those boxes. I want to peel back the tops, like I'm cracking open my own ribs for a look inside. It's self-indulgent, and possibly self-destructive, but I need the truth. God, both June and I did. And look where it's getting us both.

"Can I have a flashlight?" I ask, and Dominic pauses, as if he thinks I might use it to club him over the head. "Please," I add, though it kills me.

He nods and hands it to me, his hand connecting with mine, and I make myself hold my ground, not flinching, not pulling away. And then I shine the light against the dirt walls, while everyone else prepares the food we brought in our bags, even though there's plenty stashed here from Liam and June. But that food belongs to the dead. As does everything else in this place.

I'm looking for words traced into the dirt, her handprint, as she leaned against a wall. I'm looking for what she did for a year and a half down here. And I'm looking for the reason she left. She had been safe here. Safe and hidden, and it wasn't until she left that people caught her trail again. She died while running, trying to get back into the woods before she was caught. Run down in a street, with nothing on her. With no one near her.

My God, June. Why did you leave the woods?

You were safe once.

I was safe once, too. But it wasn't enough.

chapter 13

"TAKE THE COT," DOMINIC says. I'm not sure what's with his change of attitude, but I don't care for it. It's somehow worse. Like I've done something to please him, and I guess I have.

All I did was exactly what they asked of me. I found June. I found what she wanted me to see, though none of us can make any sense of it. And she's not finished with me.

Cameron hasn't spoken to me again, not since Dominic has started being nice, as if I am somehow on his side. Maybe June wasn't ever real to Cameron before—just a story, a legend, a person who never truly existed in his mind—but being here changes all that. Seeing her things, the signs she has left for me, the truth she has sealed inside those boxes . . . she's real, and she's guilty, and she's me.

I grab a sleeping bag and unroll it across the cold ground, ignoring Dominic's gesture. I draw the line at sleeping in her bed, shifting restlessly in her shadow. The material is cold, and definitely dirty, and I try not to imagine June curled up inside here in the winter, her blond curls spilling out as she tucks her chin farther inside, Liam smiling at her from nearby.

Casey takes a cot, and so does Dominic, wedging the ladder between himself and the wall. But he leaves the door over the top open. Maybe he doesn't like the feel of a coffin either. Nobody would find us if we were trapped down here. June was counting on it.

My sleeping bag rustles every time I move. I am restless, living in her place. The outside noises fall away, and all that remains is the steady breathing of the people around me while I stare at the angled walls in front of me. I feel like if I stare at the dark corner for long enough, she will take solid form, emerging from the darkness. I turn away from the corner, and Cameron's sleeping bag rustles nearby.

I feel like I am still on display, even in the dark, the sleeping bag giving me away: *Alina turns to the right. Alina still isn't sleeping. She turns over again. Pulls her legs up. Alina's soul is restless.* Like they can still see everything I'm thinking. Screw it. I kick out of the sleeping bag and stand in the dark, backing toward a wall in the blackness, waiting for my eyes to adjust, but they never do. The only thing I see is the square of moonlight shining through the entrance. I sit inside the square of light, and eventually I lie back against the ground, and I picture my mother.

I picture her looking exactly like she did in the article after she was arrested, saying to my father, "I cannot be responsible for the soul of June Calahan." I picture a baby crying in a bassinet, all alone. And when she gets out of jail she changes her name and thinks, *Finally I am free of her*. And she disappears into the world that is so, so big, like Dominic says.

I feel the dirt taking root under my fingernails. I hope she's happy. I really do.

I dream that someone is holding me underwater. I do not fight it.

I wake up gasping for breath, water dripping down my face, falling into my mouth, my open eyes—mud forming in the ground beneath me. I sit up and refocus, grasping for my bearings. Rain. It's raining, and I'm in a cave. June's cave. My hand rests over my heart as I try to slow my breathing. Cameron is up, or I have woken him with the gasping for breath, and it takes him a moment to realize what's happening, dripping wet as I am in the middle of a dark cave.

He's beside me then, pulling me up, and says, "We need the tarp before it spreads." But the tarp is up above and we are down below and the ladder is behind Dominic. And I am covered in mud and dirt and grime. So I take a breath and I stand under the rain, already coming down lighter than a minute ago, like it's a shower. And I feel the clothes sticking to my skin, and Cameron's eyes taking me in, and the mud and dirt and grime trailing down my body to the earth.

He comes closer, takes my hand, like he's going to pull me out of the rain. He tries, tugging me toward him, but he's not expecting me to resist so much—I do not want anyone touching me, and I do not want to go back to the dark shadows, where June lingers—and when I pull back, he falls toward me, suddenly wet. He steps back, but then his face shifts, and instead he steps closer, underneath the hole with me, and he laughs silently as the rain soaks him as well. He wraps his arms around my back, like it's the most natural thing in the world, and the rain and his arms feel so good I can't even think about why, *why* he'd possibly do such a thing, before I'm resting my head against his chest and trying to pretend that I'm laughing instead of crying, until the rain lets up.

He steps away first, without any warning, as if he had been in a trance and someone has suddenly freed him. I don't understand at first, and then I see Casey sitting upright, flashlight in hand, watching us. "Dominic," she says. "The tarp." They go to work, climbing to the surface, securing the top, making sure nothing is damaged. And after, she climbs back into her bed, flashlight still on. She looks at me once more, like I am responsible. Like he was under a spell, and I am the witch.

We bring the boxes to the surface in the morning, even though the ground is wet, the water still dripping periodically from the leaves, or maybe the sky—it's impossible to tell. Dominic puts the green tarp over the other boxes when we're not looking through them.

They are full of everything. Full of nothing. They are the random assortment of thoughts and things that June decided to keep. We cannot tell her motive or her intentions. Whether this wooden box with wet matches inside means something besides *This is the box I kept matches in, but they got wet*. Whether the engraving on the bottom, the RGB, are initials—whether they have meaning behind them, or whether they're the generic branding of the manufacturer.

There are more printouts, too. Lists of names in order by time stamp, not birth date—with a long code assigned. I guess the file number of their soul in the database. But there's only one set, one generation. I take Liam's postcards and try to match the numbers he's written to the printouts. But the truth is, the data is endless, and we need a computer to sort it.

Casey and Dominic are looking for something specific. They are looking for information about this alleged second shadow-database, or some sort of instructions. We have the address, but that could be anything. Maybe where the money is.

They're looking for something in their own language—something written in a programming language—something they could understand. I don't bother telling them, *yet again*, that June was not a programmer. *That* was Liam. They know this, and yet they believe June is the key.

It's what others believe, too. That it was the two of them together, two different ways of seeing things, that got them inside. Liam with the coding. June with the patterns—like she could break a code that nobody else could see.

I don't know if I really want to follow her trail any farther, because the closer I get to her, the farther I feel from myself. But I also know there's no way to be free until I see this through. Because I have this feeling that she's telling me something—that her math means something—and if there's the slightest possibility that she's not at the center of this all, if she was telling the truth in that recording she left with Liam White, then I need to prove it, for the both of us. So while they look for code, I look for the trinkets, the things that give me insight to her motive. God, I want her to have a motive. I want her to have been wronged and misguided. I want there to be a *reason*. I want there to be a chance it is not in her makeup, or mine, but a thing that veered her life off course, off its intended trajectory. I want *her* to be the anomaly.

She lived here alone for over a year. What must it have been like, with no one but herself to talk to? I see no diary. And then I start laughing. I know exactly what it's like. Who am I kidding? I spent seventeen years contained on an island. I spent the last several with people who had no sincerity.

Do they not realize that they have made me in her likeness?

I think of what June is trying to lead me toward.

What do they think I will do with it when I have no other options?

Sometime after lunch, Dominic has all but given up finding anything else. "Pack up everything worth taking," he says. I take that notebook with June's equations, the one the note fell out of, and I slide it into Casey's bag along with the hard drives.

Dominic has his GPS out—the paper with June's handwriting sticking out from his open wallet as he looks from one to the other, plugging in the numbers, the street, the city. "It doesn't exist," he says. "Not in Edmond. But there are, like, fifteen other places with this address . . ."

I grab for the paper, knocking his wallet to the ground. Not that it will change anything, but it's mine. If June wanted someone to see it, that person is me.

I hear June's voice, reciting the information in my ear. *224081 - Ivory Street.*

I picture the reams of paper with the numbers. Six or seven or eight digits long.

224081 Ivory Street.

"What the hell, Alina?" he asks, grasping for my arm.

He's got a hold on my right arm, and the paper is balled up in my fist, but like a child making a last stand with a piece of candy, I refuse to unfurl my fingers. "What do you want with June?" I ask. "What's the obsession?"

He looks away. "Don't you see? The database is power. It's money. It's whatever you want it to be."

"It's blackmail. And death," I say.

"It's knowledge," he says, like he's trying to appeal to my desires. "It's fate," he adds, so low I barely hear it. His eyes are staring into mine, but I won't be the first to look away.

He gives in first, glancing at his shoulder. At Cameron's hand on his shoulder. "Let go," Cameron says, but he doesn't.

Except then Casey says, "Edmonton? Edgington? Maybe there's a mistake?" She's typing away at the GPS, completely ignoring us, and Dominic finally releases my arm.

"Let me see," he says, leaning his head toward Casey's.

The paper is still in my hand. Dom is focused on the list of addresses on the screen as Cameron bends for the wallet.

"224081," I whisper to Cameron. "224081. Dash. Ivory Street."

"Oh," he says, holding Dom's partially open wallet. "*Oh*," he says again.

I nod—the knowledge, the excitement, pulling my lips into a smile.

The numbers before the name. The file name. It's not a place. It's a designation. It's a soul. A person. Ivory Street is a name. A name that June wrote in permanent marker and stuffed in the back of a notebook full of equations.

"Try Edmont," Casey mumbles to Dominic.

Holy shit, Cameron mouths.

I glance at the wallet in his hand. "Is he telling the truth?" I ask.

Cameron examines Dominic's license and holds it toward me. "Looks like it." And it does. His picture. The name "Dominic Ellis." The official state seal. His birth date.

His birth date.

I tear the wallet from Cameron's fingers, bringing it closer to my face, and feel the earth start to move, though I know it's not the earth at all, but me. My world, shifting again.

"Dominic!" I yell, and he slowly turns around. He stares at the wallet in my hand. Everything seems to hum—the trees, the air, the truth.

"You were born the day after Christmas?" I say a little too loudly. My voice comes out high and tight. I look to him to confirm, and it's like he's mentally debating something, and so I say, louder, "Your birthday. It's the day after Christmas?"

His gaze moves from his wallet to my eyes. "Yes," he says,

and he waits for my next question, because he knows it's coming. I see the year. I know the facts.

It's Christmas Day, and it's starting to snow, and there are lights strung up in the windows behind him.

"Where were you born?" I say, but I can't seem to make my teeth separate as I talk. They're clenched together. The edges of my vision clouds, so Cameron disappears, Casey disappears, and he is the only one in my sights.

He runs for the barricade lined with police cars as she sneaks onto the roof and down the fire ladder.

Dominic shakes his head.

"Answer me," I say.

He pulls a weapon at the last minute, and the sound of gunfire accompanies June as she races frantically through the woods, as tears run down her cheeks.

"Cut to the chase," he says, and he says it so faintly that at first I'm not sure if he meant to speak it at all.

But I don't even want to say it. "Did you find out who your soul belonged to? When you turned eighteen?"

"Yes," he says.

His blood seeps into the thin blanket of snow surrounding him, beside the weapon that turned out not to be a weapon at all but a metal recorder.

I know the answer, but I ask anyway. "Is it Liam White?"

"Yes," he says, and everything that has happened—last year in my room and now in the woods—takes on new meaning.

Liam White, the goddamn martyr.

"Did you know?" I ask Cameron, I ask Casey. "Did you?"

They look at each other, at him, at me. They did not know. God, what the hell are they doing here?

Now. I have to go now. There is only one reason Liam White comes back for me, if not for revenge for his death, and that's to get inside the database and continue what they started. Power and money. The belief that it's rightfully his. June and Liam. Me and Dominic.

I drop the wallet, and my hand moves instinctively to my pocket, the one with the glass. I cannot be here. Not with him. *Not with him*. On the one hand, I'm furious. On the other, I am responsible for his death somehow. He is the thing on the tightrope that must be balanced, and for once, I must do the balancing. This is my test.

He wants me. He wants June. He needs us both.

He's walking closer, but carefully, as if I'm a skittish animal that could bolt at any moment. I stay perfectly still, waiting. Waiting. "Guess you were wrong, huh?" And I don't understand what the hell he's talking about. "Turns out you wouldn't know me anywhere, after all."

But I'm not sure. Because the first time I saw him, the first time he smiled at me, *I don't know*. I don't know what really happened back then, and I don't know what's happening now. Is it possible? I really don't know.

I think of what Cameron said to me. About that chance.

I would do anything for my sister.

I hope this is true.

Because I'm not stronger than Dominic. And I'm not stronger than Cameron. But I think I'm stronger than Casey.

I circle to the side, away from Cameron, away from Dominic, so we have to switch places—like I'm scared of him. I mean, I am. I really am. But that's not the only reason I'm moving. I circle slowly, with nervous eyes, taking in everything around me as I move closer to Casey and farther from Dominic and Cameron.

He reaches for me but doesn't come any closer. "Okay, calm down, you're shocked. You're in shock."

I am not.

"You don't have to be afraid. Don't be afraid."

But I am.

"Casey," he says, like a warning. To grab me? What?

I close my eyes and breathe steadily. I'm not sure, to be honest, if I'm stronger than Casey. But I believe I want to escape more than she wants to hold me, and that must count for something. I need the distraction, and I have to trust that Cameron will let me go.

I want it more, I want it more, I want it more . . .

She's moving closer, I guess because Dominic told her to, and I count. One step. Two. And then I move.

I lunge behind her, catching her by surprise, and bring an arm around her neck, my other hand gripping the longest shard of glass, pointed at her neck. I feel her heartbeat through her skin. I see the artery in her neck, pulsing, right under the glass. I hear the catch of her breath each time she breathes in, the rest of her body completely rigid.

I stare at Dominic, who looks surprised. I can't look at Cameron. I can't.

"Whoa, whoa," says Dominic. "No need to get violent." He steps closer, his hand out, and something in my face must make him stop. "Alina, be real. I'm not going to hurt you. I *need* you."

"You need June. I'm not her."

"You're making a mistake," he says.

"What was your plan, huh? Let's say you got in. What happens to me, then?" I'm backing away, and my hand starts to shake. Casey moans, and Dominic holds his hands up for a moment.

"Whatever you want, Alina. Okay? So what is it that you want right now?" Like he knows, of course, I would only do something for a trade. For a purpose.

I don't want to be part of this. I don't want to become June.

"I want to leave. I want to be done with everything related to her." I want to stop chasing the last life and live this one instead. "I'm leaving," I say, and I take a step back. Casey follows my lead. I want to tell her I don't mean it, that I won't hurt her, that I would never, but now is not the time. I will drag her to the tree line, and then I will run. I will find my way out, because I have to. It's the best I can do.

Dominic runs his teeth across his bottom lip, moves his hands to his hips, and says, "No, Alina, you're not." And before I can register what's happening, his hands have slipped behind him and under his shirt, and he pulls a gun out. He points it at my head. Why the hell does he have a gun?

What good will the glass do if he pulls the trigger? I am outmaneuvered and he knows it.

"Stop," Cameron says, but I don't know who he's talking to.

Dominic grins, just the slightest bit, and begins to lower the gun. It drifts from my head downward, to Casey's chest, where it remains. Casey shudders, or maybe it's me.

Here I am trying to get redemption from my past life, and I haven't even bothered to realize who I've been harming in this one. Like a vicious cycle, here I am again.

Here I am again, with another person about to die in my place.

chapter 14

I AM GOING TO get her killed. I am killing her right now. It's me with the gun. It's my action. Her life on the tightrope. He doesn't care about her. He's going to shoot my leverage.

I listen for June, for a moment, with the insane hope that she will know how to get me out of here. But there is nothing. The only one standing here is me.

And so I throw her. I glance at Cameron for the briefest moment the instant before I do it, and it's like we communicate by instinct. I twist my arms out and to the side so she falls to the ground, out from under my grip, just as Cameron runs at Dominic. Dominic pulls the trigger once, and I feel the hot sting on the side of my waist where Casey was once standing, an instant before I hear the sound of the bullet firing. I turn back around and he moves his gun toward Casey again, but Cameron tackles him to the ground as the shot goes off.

I don't have time to look. I can move, so I must be okay. Casey is moving, so she must be okay.

She scrambles along the ground for her pack of electronics. She's barely got a grip on one of the green arm straps when I pull her to standing, and I drag her. She's screaming. She's screaming for her brother, and he needs our help, but I am not that brave. Not when there's a gun and it was pointed at my head. Not when faced with my suddenly very real mortality. Not anymore. I keep dragging her, as her feet kick up dirt, her heels digging in, until we are at the tree line. I turn, for a heartbeat, and I see Cameron pull himself to standing. The gun is in his hand and he points it at Dominic, who is facedown on the dirt but pushing himself up.

Cameron plants his feet. Holds his arm to steady himself. He waits. I wait. There's a tremor that runs through him. And in the moment when he's paused, a thousand thoughts run through my head: *Do it. Don't do it. Run. Runrunrun.*

He drops his arm and runs toward us.

I pull at Casey's shirt, and she's on her feet again. I start running before he reaches us, because he's faster and I'm hurt. I can feel it now, not as a sharp pain, but as a dull ache, like I am racing myself. How far can I get before it slows me, until I am caught? I feel the stitch in my side, the muscle tensing, and I bend over and run with my hand pressed into my side. It slows me down, but I keep moving.

Cameron catches up, the gun still swinging in his hand as he runs, and he grabs my elbow and pulls me along, following Casey. We run at a full-out sprint, tearing through the brush, until the seconds become minutes, and the minutes become a tangible distance. Eventually I hear a faint rumbling, and at first

I think it's thunder, but then I think my mind is playing tricks on me, because it doesn't stop. Instead, it gets louder. Casey skids to a stop at the edge of something. I fear we're trapped. But then the rumbling in my ears grows even louder, and Casey gestures to what waits before her: a river. It leads somewhere. It has to.

I tell my feet to keep moving, but my breath hitches as I run toward her, and I hate that I need to be dragged again. Cameron lets go of me when we get to the river because the path is too narrow along the edge, but at least it's mostly hidden, mostly protected, our sounds muffled by the moving water.

It occurs to me they could leave me here. I am nothing to them. I held Casey hostage and lost them God knows what, and Cameron has the gun. I am the weak link. I'm slowing them down. Casey nods at us and hits the path, moving fast, and Cameron pushes me in front of him. "Just keep moving," he says. "Don't think. Move."

So I stop thinking.

I move.

I keep moving.

Without speaking, we forge a path along this ledge, the three of us, heading downstream with the water.

I don't stop until the river stops, catapulting over the edge of a cliff into a waterfall, a lake stretching endlessly into the distance.

And then I can't start again. My legs are weak and spent and useless. I imagine being thrown off a cliff again, but that doesn't seem to be the plan. Cameron grabs my arm and we climb down the side, rock by rock, inch by inch, clinging to the slick rocks and the jutting roots and each other, word-lessly. It's slow going. It's even slower because of me.

I am weak, because as I cling to the rocks, or to Casey's arm, or to Cameron's leg, I wish for the island. I wish for my bed and the four walls and the window with the perfect angle to the sky. I wish for safety and routine and predictability. I wish for a shot of pain medicine when I'm hurt and my hot shower and my computer full of information. I wish for cliffs and restricted air-space where no one can reach me. Where no one can hurt me.

I wish all these things until we are at the bottom, at the lake, and I sit with my forehead pressed to the rough bark of a tree, and Casey is pacing with her hands on top of her head, staring out at the water. I wish all these things until Cameron settles in next to me, and one of his arms circles behind my back, and he says, "Hey. You did it."

And then I am weak because I want him to stay with me, with an arm around me, indefinitely. And I almost ask him not to go when he disentangles from my pathetic grip to go check on his sister. Instead I say, "I think he shot me," which is true, but it also makes him stay.

"Casey," he calls, gesturing to the hand I have pressed into my side.

Casey is not entirely gentle when she lifts the bottom of my shirt to check. She pokes at me, runs my shirt across the blood in a harsh swipe, and I bite back the yelp. "Just grazed you," she says, dropping it back down. "Burns worse than it really is. Nothing that can't wait."

"Case," Cameron says.

"What?" She's got her hands on her hips. "What is possibly okay about this situation right now? We are so screwed!"

"He's a freaking psychopath. He had a *gun*," he says.

"It wasn't safe with him. He was going to shoot you," I add. "I didn't think he would do that. I just wanted to leave."

She points at me as she leans toward Cameron. "She backed him into a corner." And then she subconsciously rubs her hand against her neck, where there's a tiny prick of blood, from me.

"I told her to do it," he says, which isn't entirely the truth, but it makes me feel like I am suddenly not completely alone for the first time ever.

"You're an idiot," she says. "Ever think of talking to me about this first? God." She rubs at her neck again, and he grabs her arm.

"Tell me you didn't know," he says.

"That he's Liam White? Are you kidding me?" she continues.

"You promised me you checked him out," Cameron says, but he's not yelling. He's eerily calm. He's doing that thing that I do when I want to hide how I feel. Hiding everything under a sedate indifference.

"I *did*," she says. "He was exactly who he said he was. A past guard, removed after an incident with the assignment, but somehow still in contact with her. He said she was the only way in. The rest—who he was?—that's privacy law, national security, and you know I can't hack that. It's the whole reason we're here. He didn't tell me. I didn't know. I swear."

My identity was the only one sought. I am their only mistake.

Something twitches in his jaw, and then his face is calm again. "What's done is done," he says.

"What now?" she whispers, resting her forehead on his shoulder. I wish I had this type of comfort with anyone. That you can take comfort in a beat from the contact, draw strength from it, even when you're fighting. "What the hell do we do now?"

"Hey," he says. "I'm sorry. You're okay. We made it."

She pulls her head up, ruffles Cameron's hair once, even though he's taller than she is, and takes a step back. "Of course we made it."

There's no sign of Dominic. I think this is good news, but Casey thinks it's bad. Very, very bad.

"He could turn us in," she says. "He could call that number and there'll be helicopters searching the area in no time."

"No, he wouldn't do that, right? Not after everything he's done. We'd turn him in too," I say.

She shakes her head. "I don't know what he wants. Whether it's the information in the database or just the money associated with you . . ."

"You don't know? Then how did you end up working together?"

"I didn't even know him," she says adamantly, like a defense. "Not in person, anyway. Just online. He . . . saw me, I guess you could say. Where I shouldn't be."

"Hackers," Cameron whispers. "They were both hackers."

Casey looks around, searching for something. A solution, possibly. Dominic, maybe. "Anyway, we were both trying—and failing—to get into the database. There are a lot of people who try. But it's safe to say we were the most . . . determined. He came to me with a deal I couldn't turn down. But I didn't realize . . ."

"That he was a freaking psychopath?" Cameron cuts in.

She narrows her eyes but doesn't disagree. "Does it really hurt?" she asks, glancing down at my waist.

"Nothing that can't wait," I respond. She grins an apology.

"Anyway, he had the resources. And all the information on you. He was much, *much* closer than I'd ever get alone. And it was obvious he was extremely dedicated. He was playing the long game. I only met him in person right before I joined the guard."

"And you still did it?" I say. "You still went along with it, even after you met him?"

"God, Alina, don't you see? The things I was doing . . . they're not exactly legal. He had evidence I had hacked into the security surrounding *you*. He could've turned me in. He was in the system . . ." I think of his hands over my keyboard, and wonder what he was up to back then. "He kind of . . . trapped me there," she says.

"Me? Why were you looking at *me*? What the hell did I have to do with anything?"

But she doesn't answer. She continues, "I joined the guard on a false identity. I hacked into government files. For me *and* for my brother. And Dom knew. He knew who I was. And . . ."

Her eyes watered. "I still wanted it. So bad. I just didn't realize . . . everything that came with it."

She didn't realize he was Liam White and we were replaying history, and now they were a part of it. That whatever they wanted came at the price of their identity. Forever.

"I'm sorry," Cameron says, and I can't figure out why he's apologizing for anything. I'm the one who held glass to his sister's neck, I'm the reason they're in this situation at all. But he's not talking to me. "I couldn't do it," he says—his arms are shaking, and maybe not from the adrenaline. He still has a death grip on the gun, like he's still debating, still at war with himself.

He couldn't go through with it. He said he would do anything for his sister, but that's not exactly true. She doesn't know what he's talking about, but I do.

He couldn't shoot Dominic, couldn't kill him so that we'd be free of danger, and he thinks that makes him weak. But I think it makes him perfect.

"It was the right choice," I say.

He shakes his head. "He could tell them where we are. Right now. For the money. It's better than nothing. And you're right, we'll never make it out in time."

I smile because he's wrong. "No. No, he's coming for me."

"How do you know?" he asks.

Because I am the missing puzzle piece of his past, and he is mine. And there's something there—some answer, something unfinished. The puzzle pieces are in motion, spread across the surface of a table, and every one of them is in play now, leading us to something. Because he's playing the long game, and now, so am I. "Because it's what I would do," I whisper.

"He doesn't have a phone," Casey says. "Or a gun now."

"Just a GPS," Cameron says. "And the car waiting in the woods."

We're armed with the same information right now. But there's only one car.

We must all realize this at the same time, because we start pacing, even though we're exhausted. "We need to get out of here," I say.

I think back to everything I learned about the mountains—that they formed when the tectonic plates pushed together, that they span the coast from north to south, that if we keep heading east—if we manage to hold a straight course—we'll eventually reach civilization.

I'm thinking too big, because Casey says, "This lake stretches around to the other side, that's where we came in." And I am in awe of her again. So is Cameron. We stare at her.

"What? I didn't come into this blind," Casey says. "I did my research, too. I knew there was a river, and that it would lead us back. And I know that right now we're less than a mile from the road."

I want to hug her. I do. "He knows we're going for the car, right?" I say.

"It would be stupid not to," Cameron says. "We have nothing to live off of out here. So it's either the cabin or the car."

"Shit, I can't believe we left everything just sitting out in the open. I've got the computer stuff," she rifles around in her pack, "and June's notebook . . . but he still got the address, and all that information." Casey says. "This notebook means something to you?" she asks.

"It doesn't mean anything to me," I say. "I was telling the truth. I hate math."

They look at me like I am a stranger, which I guess I am.

"You can't suck at math," Casey says.

I don't. I just don't spend much time with it. "I never wanted to learn it. The name that looked like an address, on the other hand, with the numbers? That I remember."

"The name?" Casey asks.

"224081. Dash. Ivory Street. Dash. Edmond. Ivory Street is a person."

Casey lets out a surprised laugh. "What about Edmond? Is that where she lives?"

"Maybe," I say. I clear my throat. "How fast is Dominic?"

"Faster than us," Cameron says, and I know he's referring to the fact that I am injured and possibly slowing them down, once again.

But we're already moving as we discuss whether we have a shot. It's the only option. We have to do it.

Dominic isn't at the car. Not that we can tell. We're still hiding in the trees, trying to get a clear look without revealing ourselves. My heart is beating so hard I'm sure it will give us away.

"Do you have the key?" I ask.

Casey presses her lips together. "We have Cameron," she says.

Something in his jaw twitches, but he doesn't acknowledge her. He's still watching the spot where the car sits, just off the road. "I wish it was in the clearing," he says. "So we could see anything coming."

"We go together," Casey says.

"No. I'll check it out first." He puts the gun in Casey's hands. "Don't give it up."

"Right. Okay," she says, and she crouches down next to me, aiming the gun in the direction of the car. She keeps her eyes on the trees surrounding him, and I do the same. "Alina," she whispers, "please tell me you know how to use this gun."

I have absolutely no idea how to use a gun. "Point and shoot?" I whisper back.

Her arm is shaking, and she uses her other hand to steady the gun. "I guess that'll have to work."

Cameron moves silently. Perfectly. He's there in no time at all, pulling on the handle once, but the door doesn't give. He looks around the ground, picks up a rock, and hurls it into the back passenger window. The sound makes me jump. Or maybe it's the speed at which his arm moves—the damage he created with his bare hands.

He swipes the glass away with his elbow and unlocks the door. He disappears inside, and a few moments later, I hear the engine start to catch.

Casey lets out a small laugh, then refocuses on the trees.

"He's never going to let me live this down. The thing I gave him hell about is the thing that's about to get us out of this place."

"He's done this before?" I ask.

Her jaw tenses. "Allegedly."

"Did he get in trouble?"

A pause. "You could say that."

I try to amend this picture of Cameron in my head: not a kid casually walking down the halls of school, his backpack slung over his shoulder. Not the image of him running out the door with half a bagel in his mouth. Instead I imagine a boy who lurks in the shadow of a building, waiting for his opportunity to take something that does not belong to him. I imagine deliberate steps, determined eyes, his elbow in a car window with the alarm going off, sirens in the distance as he callously drives away.

"Is he dangerous?" I ask, even though I don't believe he is. I turn my head to find Casey staring at me.

"Funny," she says, "he asked the same thing about you."

The leaves rustle behind us, and Casey spins around, pointing the gun at the trees. She moves it side to side, but we see nothing. I hold my breath, like that might help her.

She puts her arm out, pushing me back by the shoulder. "Come on," she says, and she starts walking backward, slowly.

The engine catches, and the car rumbles to life, but we hear a sound in the brush to our left and we spin in that direction, as Casey points the gun.

A hand grabs my arm, and I scream at the same time

Casey jumps, but then we hear Cameron. "Get in the car," he says, and the three of us scramble backward together.

I'm at the car, stepping in the glass, when I hear my name. I can't see Dom, but he's out there. Casey's trying to push me into the car, but I'm searching for a view of him. "Alina," he calls again. "You're never going to be free like this and you know it. June and Liam left this for us. They left us a way in for a *reason*. It's worth a lot. You could use that information, you know, to make people help you. You could use it to start a new life."

I don't even know what I would do with one now. I don't even know what that means. If maybe freedom isn't a place at all, or even a state of being to achieve, but something else altogether.

Cameron takes the gun from Casey and holds his arm out, moving the gun across the perimeter. But Dom's voice keeps moving, keeping its distance.

"Why are you doing this?" I ask. "You don't have to do this," I yell. "We can all walk away. Right now." The words sound like lies, even to me.

I see him then—through the trees. He's crouched between two trunks, but he lets me see. I'm staring right at him. "They would die for each other," he says. "That's a bond that doesn't end with one life."

And for the first time, I wonder. I wonder if he did fall for me, in that room, the moment before I hurt him. If he planned to one day come back for me, after he accessed June's money.

"*Get in*," Casey says from the driver's seat.

"We're not them," I say, as I start backing into the open door.

"We paid the price in one life," he says, and he stands upright, steps around one trunk. "Don't you think we're owed this?" he calls.

I'm at the car, and Cameron's hand is on my waist, pulling me inside the back door. The gun is positioned over my shoulder, but I don't think Cameron has a view of him.

But Dominic must see, because he shrinks behind the nearest trunk. "Don't you think *you* owe me that, Alina?"

I back up into the seat, but still Cameron stays in the open door, gun positioned. He waits until the last second, until Casey has the car in gear, before sliding in behind me.

She tears out of the woods, onto the dirt road that I didn't see on the way in, and Cameron has the gun pointed out the window the whole time. Even minutes later, when we all know there's no way Dom could've kept up, he won't let go.

I put my hand on his shoulder, but it's like he doesn't register me. I move it to his arm, his hand, and I pry his fingers back gently.

He turns to face me, his lips parted, his pupils wide. He lets me take the gun from him. Every muscle is tense, and I don't know how to make him relax. And I don't know what to do with this gun. So I do what he did for me when we were in June's hideaway. I lace my fingers with his for a second and squeeze before I let them drop.

Cameron looks down at the gun between us, and he starts to breathe again.

This gun is our protection, I know that. I know we didn't escape without it. But I also don't want to have the power to take anyone's life. And I don't want anyone else to have that power over me. I press the lever at the bottom of the gun, the bottom falling out, the bullets stacked inside in deceptive simplicity.

I feel Cameron watching me, but I pretend I don't notice because I don't want him to tell me to stop. I roll down my window, holding the part of the gun with the bullets. And then I tip it over, letting them scatter across the road.

And then it's just me and Cameron and Casey, nothing between us but an empty gun, and I feel a calm settle over me—like when they used to administer the needle to me on the island. I settle back into my seat, but I can feel Cameron watching me still.

His hand rests on the seat between us, where the empty gun remains.

He stares at me as the trees blur behind him. "Who are you?" he whispers.

I don't know. *I don't know.* But I'm finding out.

I bring my hand down to his, and he doesn't weave his fingers with mine, like he did earlier. But he doesn't pull away either.

"Cameron," Casey says, in that secret language of theirs.

His hand slides out from under mine. "Yeah?"

"What . . . what do we do?" she asks. "Where do we go?"

Casey keeps driving, her knuckles white on the wheel.

"How do we stay hidden?" I add. I know they were counting on the money. That we needed it.

Her eyes flick up in the rearview mirror, but she's looking at her brother. Something passes silently between them.

"What?" I ask, as he looks away. "*What* are you guys saying with your random eye-contact code?"

He smiles at me, and I don't think either of us expects it. He looks out the window again. "Casey's saying, with her random eye-contact code, that this part would probably be my strength."

"Finding a place?" I ask.

"Hiding," he says.

chapter 15

CASEY KEEPS GLANCING AT us in the rearview mirror, but Cameron is still staring out the window. "Can you think of anyone who would take us in? Keep quiet? Do you trust anyone?" Casey asks.

"Casey, even if I did trust any of them—which I don't—there's not a single person who wouldn't turn me in for a million dollars."

"Your parents?" I ask, and by the way Cameron's mouth twists, I quickly realize that was the wrong thing to say.

"Don't think of people," Cameron says. "They're unpredictable." He looks at me quickly, like it's a bad thing.

"Don't lump all humanity into the category of Ella," Casey says, ignoring him.

But Cameron gives her a look. He leans his head back on the seat cushion. "The way to stay hidden is to not go anywhere you'd be expected. And to keep moving. Which means don't think. Tell me, what do we need?"

"Internet access," Casey says without hesitation.

"Who's Ella?" I ask.

"Ex-girlfriend. Spawn of Satan," Casey says, but Cameron makes no indication that he's heard either of us.

"We also need food," Cameron adds.

"Running water would be awesome," Casey says.

And since I guess he's not going to answer my Ella question, I switch gears. "Someplace deserted."

"It's the summer," Cameron says, and he's nodding to himself. "We need," he says, "a school."

I've never seen a school, other than on TV. My school has always been held remotely, on a television. I watch lectures streamed from colleges. I have a room full of textbooks. I take online tests and complete practice work with answers I can check against a key afterward. Technically, I'm homeschooled. Technically, I earned my high school diploma two years ago. Technically, I'm a sophomore in college.

Not that I've ever been to one of those, either.

"Keep to the back roads," Cameron says as we approach an intersection.

We pass a few stores as we keep to said back roads: country shops with small areas out front or to the side for parking—and I wonder if these, too, have video feed. "Head down, Alina," he says, and I quickly listen, staring at the floor. "Just in case."

I don't know if the periodic sound of helicopter blades in the distance is a normal occurrence, but it keeps my nerves on edge. From the way Cameron has his fists clenched in his lap, I'm guessing it's doing the same to him.

Casey turns the radio on, flipping from station to station, bypassing every song. After seven random turns on the road and what feels like an eternity of flipping stations, Casey lands on a news report.

". . . three days since the elaborate escape of Alina Chase from her protection detail. To recap, she is believed to be traveling with nineteen-year-old Casey London. It is not yet known how they are connected. Photos taken at the scene also show a media intern registered under an alias. Authorities believe that he is the eighteen-year-old brother of Casey, Cameron London, who has previously served time in a juvenile correction facility for auto theft and is currently wanted for questioning in the presumed death—" Cameron lunges forward between the front seats and jams the power button on the radio with the side of his fist.

"Shit," Cameron says, leaning back and resting his head on the seat.

"*What*?" My throat constricts. "Questioning in a *death*?" My shoulder presses against the window, and he sighs, shaking his head, his eyes squeezed shut.

"Presumed," Casey mumbles.

How can anyone trust anyone out here? I amend the picture of Cameron in my head. I imagine him walking down the hall of a jail, his wrists shackled in front of him as he keeps his head down. I imagine him stepping out into the sunshine and squinting against the glare, rubbing at his wrists, now free of handcuffs. I see Casey picking him up in her car. And then I imagine him taking a gun from the glove compartment and sliding it into the waistband of his pants, telling Casey to drop him at the corner . . .

"Listen," he says, "I didn't. It's just for questioning. But the fact that I was already locked up for three months *really* doesn't look good. And now I'm eighteen. Sorry, not gonna risk it."

I remember his arm, shaky with the gun. Unable to kill.

"You wouldn't . . . ," I say, and he tenses. I know he believes this is a weakness, but it's not.

"It doesn't matter if I *would* or not," he says. "The point is that I *didn't*."

"Which you could've cleared up by heading in for questioning—" Casey says.

"Don't," he says. "They've already made up their minds, what they think of me."

I stare at him, trying to see through him, trying to understand all the different versions of the boy in the seat beside me. The person who saved me but spent time locked up for crimes he does not deny. The person who couldn't kill but who's wanted for questioning in a presumed death.

He frowns at me. "The way you're looking at me pretty much says it all."

I have forgotten to hide my thoughts, and I'm scared at what he sees on my face. "I know what it's like to be locked up," I say. "To have people assume things about you. I wouldn't risk it either."

His face relaxes, and so do his shoulders, his breathing, his posture. "So you see," he says, "it's not just the past life that can come back to haunt you. It's the past in *this* life, too."

I cannot reconcile the two different Camerons in my imagination. Which version of him is the real one? What is the nature of his soul?

I have aligned myself with people with their own questionable pasts. Is there anyone normal out there? Though I guess people wouldn't feel the need to risk anything, let alone their lives, if they had something worth losing.

I'm starting to feel nauseated, but I'm not sure whether it's the unpredictability of the people around me, if it's the feeling that I'll never know them—which version of my imagination is the true one standing before me?—or whether it's the motion sickness.

"Pick a point in the distance," Cameron says as I feel my skin turn clammy. He's pointing through the front window. "Something stationary. Keep your eyes fixed on it. It'll help."

I do. I watch the end of the road, the place where the dirt meets the sky, always somewhere out of our reach. And the world steadies. My stomach steadies. I close my eyes, and I hear my mother's voice: *Duérmete, mi niña, duérmete, mi amor* . . .

"Turn!" Cameron yells, and I jump. I lose the horizon, and my stomach lurches, instead noticing the white lines across the road, marking a school zone. "Drive past it," he says. He's leaning forward, between the front seats. "Don't stare."

Casey drives past the long brick building way under the speed limit. "Looks deserted," she says.

"Yeah, well, it's Sunday," Cameron says.

Casey turns down the next street, but it's residential and there are kids playing in the front yard of two of the homes. We drive past, and the smallest boy stops jumping rope for a moment, following our path with his eyes. I keep my head down.

"Do you hear that?" Casey asks. But all I hear are bells. *I am not the danger. I am not the threat. I am the bell, tolling out its warning.*

"Yeah," Cameron says. "Go right."

The bells sound like they're getting closer, and then we pull into a packed church parking lot. And I am confused, because it's currently full of cars and I remember reading about how the discovery of soul science conflicted with so many long-held religious beliefs. "What's this used for now?" I ask.

"Um, a church?" Cameron says. Casey turns off the engine, and we sit still, our breathing the only sound, watching for people in the parking lot before exiting the vehicle.

"But there's no . . ." I have Cameron's full attention now. Casey turns to look at me, her head tilted to the side. "Heaven," I finish. "Afterlife. Anything."

"Maybe not," Cameron says, and he motions for us to duck down as someone walks across the lot, taking the steps up to the entrance two at a time, obviously running late. We rise when Cameron does.

"How many generations are in the database, Alina?" Casey asks.

I think about the computer printouts in June's hideaway. The number of lives grouped together. "Three, four tops."

"And is every soul there?" she asks, but she obviously already knows the answer, because she answers it herself. "No. People could die out of the country." Their souls reborn elsewhere. I wonder if one day, out of the blue, they will pack their bags and hop a plane, unsure why. I wonder if they will find a way back home.

"And some parents never register their children," she continues.

"I know that," I say. But the absence of one thing does not prove the existence of something else.

"And do you know for a fact that the *soul* is what's supposed to move on to heaven? That there's not some other essence to you? Is what we know now everything we'll ever know?" Casey asks.

I hate feeling like I'm a step behind. Like there was something missing inside my mind, and now it's struggling to make room for its possibility.

"Is it possible there's a heaven? Nirvana? An afterlife, besides on earth?" She shakes her head at me. "Faith doesn't disappear, Alina. It just shifts. It adjusts to make room for the things we know, and the things we believe. Faith isn't just something you have or don't have."

This is easy for her to say, as someone who obviously has it.

"Our grandmother went to church," Cameron mumbles. He grins. "I've heard that speech more times than I can count."

"What about you?" I ask Cameron, who remained silent during Casey's speech.

He pauses before saying, "Can't say I have faith in the same things my grandmother did."

They talk about her in the past tense, and I never hear him speak about their parents.

"Your parents?" I ask, and from the look on his face, I immediately wish I could take it back.

"Let's go," he says, before I can say anything else. Casey grabs the bag, and I hand her the useless gun, which she tosses inside with the computer equipment and June's note-book. Once we're out of the car, Cameron strips off his shirt and starts wiping down the inside of the doors, the steering wheel, the radio dial. Casey and I wait in the trees, tucked out of sight. Then he shuts each door and wipes the outside as well. He puts his shirt back on as he joins us in the trees on the edge of the lot, but not before I see the raised scar across the back of his shoulder. It's whiter and rougher than the rest of his skin, and it still looks slightly pink down the center when the shad-ows shift and the sun hits it straight on.

"Keep in the trees," he whispers. The roads are lined with trees, but they back to more streets. We're not in the safety of the woods any longer. We're in a neighborhood, completely exposed.

We stand out. We make people look. We're still in hunting gear. And I'm bleeding. And we're sweaty and gross. We even-tually have to leave the protection of the trees to cross several streets, and Cameron sends us one at a time, waiting a few moments between each of us. I watch for cars and people, and I listen for the sound of helicopter blades, but we have very few options if someone stumbles upon us. Mostly, I stay low to the ground and hope for the best. It's all I can do.

Eventually we find ourselves behind the school, and I let myself relax for the moment. It's less than a mile away from where we've left the car, and the parking lot is completely empty, from what we can see. The lights are off, and the doors are shut.

Cameron tells us to wait behind the school, that he's going to look for the easiest way inside. "There are probably security cameras in the halls," he says. "And the doors will have alarms. But if we can get into the gym, we'll have a lot of different exit strategies."

He stands, ready to leave, and says to Casey, "I need the gun."

"It's empty," I say.

He holds his hands out, presses his lips together, and doesn't meet my eyes. "It's *almost* empty," he says. "There should be one left in the chamber."

Casey hands it to him, and I don't like the fact that he either needs it or intends to use it. I don't like the fact that he knows how guns work, and that he didn't tell me I was missing a bullet when I emptied it.

I imagine Cameron holding a gun steady as he approaches a car on the street and telling a man to get out of the driver's seat. I imagine him tossing the driver to the ground. Stealing his car. Racing as the police sirens follow him.

"Don't look at me like that." He's talking to me, but I don't know what he means.

"Like what?"

"Like I'm a criminal."

Except he is. He's wanted. We all are. "We're all criminals," I say. Casey laughs and Cameron kind of grunts before turning around and heading toward the building, gun in hand.

While he's gone, Casey says, "It's not his fault. He and Ava kind of got sucked into a shitty group."

It still sounds kind of like his fault. A shitty group does not equal blackmail or coercion. A shitty group does not dictate your entire fate.

"But you didn't?" I ask.

"I got accepted to a high-tech boarding school across town. The whole programming thing. I didn't go to school with the same people. Not since middle school, anyway. I was only home on weekends, and in summers I'd take any internship I could find, just to get away from that house. It only got worse after our grandma died. God, I couldn't wait to leave." She pauses for a moment, lowers her voice. "When Ava disappeared . . . at first the cops didn't even look too hard. 'Oh, she ran away,' they'd say. Or 'She fell in with the wrong crowd.'" She turns to face me, her eyes wide and piercing. "But she was so close to getting out of there. We were going to get a place where we could go to school together after graduation, take Cameron with us. We had a plan—"

The sound of a gunshot cuts her off, and we jump. My hand is on Casey's arm. Her muscles are tense and frozen.

I picture a thousand different possibilities: Cameron stumbling upon security and firing the gun into the air—or worse, firing the gun at him; Cameron stumbling upon security and the guard firing the gun into the air—or worse, firing the gun at Cameron.

Casey grabs my hand, and I make a thousand silent pleas in my head. And then I hear footsteps.

I see him, through the trees. Not bleeding, not even running. Just strolling toward us. "Your entrance is ready," he says.

"Tell me you did not shoot out a window," Casey says, but I'm hoping that's exactly what he has done. That seems the best possible outcome of the gunshot.

His silence is the answer, because Casey pulls him down to crouching. "Are you stupid? How quickly, do you think, will the cops show up?"

Cameron shakes his head. "You can always get away with one shot. People don't give it a second thought. An engine backfiring, a firecracker. If there's not a reason to think it's a gun, they don't think it's a gun."

But Casey makes us wait, not trusting this information. We wait a long time, maybe thirty minutes, and still nobody comes. "I hate that you know that," Casey says, standing up.

Cameron only smiles, leading the way to the school. I hate that he knows that, too.

chapter 16

THE WINDOW HE SHOT out belongs to the gym office, he says, and it's just out of our reach. It's wider than it is high, and honestly I'm concerned about Cameron's ability to squeeze through. Cameron laces his fingers together and crouches down, and Casey steps into his hand. "Watch the glass," he says. He pushes her up until her elbows are wedged at the base of the window, and her feet scramble against the brick for a moment before her upper body disappears inside. Her legs follow a second later. "All good," she calls.

"Incoming," he says, tossing her backpack inside.

"Ready?" Cameron asks, lacing his hands together again.

I place my hands on his shoulders as I step into his grip. "Thank you," I say, as our eyes meet. I am thanking him for this, and for everything before, and everything to come. I am thanking him in spite of who he was, and who he might still be. And in that moment I believe in telepathy, because he freezes—his shoulders frozen beneath my hands, his hands frozen beneath my foot, his eyes frozen on mine.

"You're welcome," he says. And then the words jar us out of the moment, and he lifts me up, my elbows wedging into the sides of the open window. I let out a noise of weakness as my waist rests against the ledge, the rawness of the skin that was grazed by the bullet rubbing against the windowsill, and then I am through. Casey half catches me as I land on the carpeted floor, my arms bracing my fall. She has a cut on her hand—I imagine from the glass as she tried to brace her own fall.

She sees me looking. "It's not deep," she says. But she balls up her fist, and I wonder if she's telling the truth.

She laughs as blood drips out the bottom of her fist, staining the carpet, a permanent trail of us. "God, we're a mess."

Cameron lands on his feet behind us. "Seriously, how do you do that?" she asks.

"Trade secrets," he says. And then he focuses on her hand.

"No worries," she says. "I'm sure there's a first-aid kit. It's the school gym. Band-Aids are sure to abound."

Casey assesses the room. A computer, a desk, a phone, her backpack. She opens the drawers to find pens, some coins, and a few wires. "This could work," she says.

Cameron pushes open the office door leading to the school gymnasium, which is dark despite the daylight. The doors to the outside are sealed, and the windows are high up, which is why we had to come through the office. Every step we take echoes. Doors labeled for locker rooms line the same wall as the office, and there are blue mats stacked up and pushed against the far wall.

"I doubt there's anyone watching the security cameras, but they're probably still running. So let's keep out of the hallways," Cameron says.

Cameron flips a switch, and a few panels of the ceiling move aside, revealing skylights. "Safer than turning on the lights," he says.

There's a basketball hoop directly over my head, and when I look through it, up to the skylights—at the clouds moving beyond them—it gives me the feeling of motion. When I look back, Casey has her hand in the water fountain, watching the watery blood circle down the drain. She wipes her hand on the side of her shirt, then guzzles the water from the fountain. She runs the back of her hand across her mouth, then puts her hands on her hips. "Okay, well, guess I'll get started." She strides back into the office, leaving the door open, so I can see her opening the bag of hard drives we found in June and Liam's hideaway.

Cameron motions for me to follow him, and we check out the closets and storage areas attached to the gym—we find a bunch of team uniforms and a box of lost and found items, which we drag into the open gymnasium.

There's a tall toolbox on wheels behind a net full of basketballs and a stack of cones, and Cameron rifles through it. He pulls out a screwdriver and something that looks like a set of pliers but smaller. "Casey!" he calls, and her name echoes loudly across the gym. I cringe.

"Yeah?" she calls back, and nothing happens. No alarms sound. Nobody comes. It's just us.

"Tools in the closet if you need anything."

"Okay," she says.

He points out a map—a labeled fire-evacuation plan—hanging on the open closet door, and we see a layout of the school with an *X* marking our location. His finger traces the rooms. "Looks like the cafeteria should be attached somehow, through whatever's on the other side of the locker rooms." Then he grins. "Hungry?"

"Starving," I admit.

I follow him through the boys' locker room, passing the bathroom stalls, the lockers, the showers, and I think, *Thank God.* If there's food, I might stay here forever. I want to stop running. How long until school starts again? One month? Two? What I wouldn't give to pause here, stay hidden for that month or two, until interest dies down, until the conjectures begin—that I've died, that I've disappeared, that I'm gone. And then maybe I'll dye my hair and put in colored contacts and walk out of the school, and nobody would know who I am—nobody would be looking for me any longer.

Cameron tests the handle on the unmarked door beyond the second alcove of lockers, but it doesn't budge. He takes the tools from the cargo pocket—the screwdriver, the thing that looks like pliers—and crouches in front of the lock. It doesn't take him long.

"Oh," I say.

His hair drops in his eyes, and when he looks up at me I

cannot read his expression. "I'm very good at what I do," he says.

"I know you are," I say, suddenly feeling entirely inadequate. Because the thing I'm supposed to be good at, I have avoided. And the things I *am* good at are not coming in useful right now.

"Okay." He pushes the door open, and we find ourselves inside a storage closet that must be used by the janitors. There are mops and buckets and cleaning supplies, and the room smells faintly like bleach. There's also a door on the other side, and Cameron starts working on the lock again.

"Cameron," I say. "What is it, exactly, that you do?"

He pauses, pretending to concentrate on the door in front of him. He's thinking of what to say, how much to say, how to say it. Eventually he says, "I get things for people."

"Is that why you did this?" And by *this* I mean *me*. "You got me for Dominic?"

"No, Alina," he says, opening the door. "You're not a thing."

Finishing that lock, he continues into the next room, and he doesn't notice that I have frozen. Because it's the first time someone has acknowledged that maybe I am my own person, someone other than June. "I'm Nobody, who are you?" I mumble, following him. We're inside a large room with tables, but the tables have all been stacked against the walls for the summer. There's a long metal counter set up with a plastic shield, separating the cafeteria from the kitchen.

"You're Alina Chase," he says, which is what everyone calls me. Full name. Because I am a thing. A thing in a history book. Nothing around me has ever been real. People speak with me because they are supposed to, and they don't speak with me if they're not supposed to.

I weigh my words before I say them. They're one thing I do have control over. And so I am purposeful with them. Deliberate. I decide what to give and what to hide. I watch for reactions. I study their impact.

I remember Dom saying that everyone was scared of me on the island. And I can't say he's wrong.

I have become the very thing they feared.

"Okay, *Cameron London*. See? Even you talk about me like I'm a thing on the news."

He looks at me from the side of his eye. "Or maybe I just really like your full name. It's got a good ring to it." He grins. "And it sets you apart from all the other Alinas in the world. I know you just fine."

I'm not sure what he means by that—what he thinks he knows of me. That I am weak, that I don't know how to swim, that I had to be dragged to safety, that I made an impulsive decision that got us all into this mess.

"I'm good at what I do, too," I say. "But those skills are really not useful right now. A lot of the things June was good at, I ignored. I should be better."

Cameron runs his hand across the metal counter, walking toward the kitchen, as he says, "You escaped an island, let me cut the tracker from your rib, swam when you couldn't swim, figured out where the hideaway was when no one else could, threw my sister out of the way of a bullet—yes, don't look so surprised, I noticed that. Honestly, helping you escape will probably turn out to be the one good thing I do with my life. You're incredible."

My heart is beating too fast, and I'm hoping he doesn't turn around again, because he will see the heat creeping up my neck. My face feels as if it's on fire. I make myself look busy, prying open a box left in the corner.

Except he pauses.

Because he knows.

I've noticed that Cameron doesn't always weigh his words. He speaks them, whatever he's thinking. He doesn't study their impact, or wonder how they'll be received, or what he can gain. He says them, and they're out there now, and I don't know what to do with them other than to continue rifling through this container filled with boxes of dried cereal like I haven't heard him.

"Well, if you ever decide to start getting people," I say, "I think you're pretty good at that, too."

"Inanimate objects are a lot more predictable," he says. But since I'm avoiding eye contact, I can't tell if he's being serious or trying to make a joke. The conversation stops, but it still lives, replaying inside my mind. I am imagining the twenty different possible things I could've said back to him, and how everything could've changed from a sentence. If I told him I thought he was incredible, too, or if I'd told him I've spent the last four days in a state of total fear—that I did those things because there was no other way. No going back, only forward. I am imagining each of these things, and in every scenario,

Cameron comes closer. But imagination is not the same as a memory, and I make myself stop. I see the scenario for what it is: I am ignoring him, and he is pretending not to notice.

In the end, we decide to bring back the cereal and a bunch of snacks that Cameron has miraculously retrieved from the vending machine without money.

We avoid eye contact as we carry everything back, and we remain silent as we enter the gymnasium. Casey is standing in the middle of the empty room. "God, you guys scared me to death. I had no idea where you went." Then she punches Cameron in the arm. "Next time, tell me, asshole."

"Casey, we're going to look for food. Be back in a few." He smiles.

She punches him again. But then seeing a sealed chocolate bar, she smiles. "My favorite," she says.

"I know," he says.

She opens it on the spot, talking while chewing. "I hit a roadblock. Those hard drives are at least seventeen years old, and I don't have the right cables. I need to check out the computer room or media center or whatever."

Cameron mumbles something and grabs a team uniform from the box and disappears into the locker room. When he comes out, he looks hilarious in basketball shorts that come past his knees and a navy-blue jersey with the number twelve on the front. "Don't laugh," he says, but Casey giggles anyway.

He has a ball cap pulled down low over his face, and his hair is tucked behind his ears. He grins at me and says, "Welcome to high school. This is what we look like."

"So basically I haven't been missing anything?" Except as ridiculous as he looks, I am ridiculously drawn to him.

"I'm in disguise," he says with a smile. "Okay, seriously." He moves his jaw around, as if he's trying to keep from smiling. "I'm assuming the cameras aren't on a live feed, because what's the point? So I'm gonna go turn them off. If they look back through the tapes later, hopefully they'll just see a kid in a basketball uniform. Not *us*, just some kid up to no good."

"Just some punk," Casey says, but she grabs his upper arm as he passes. "Hey, punk?"

"Hmm?"

"Don't trip anything," she says.

"I won't. But if I do, do me a favor and run."

"Not a chance," I say. And I'm not sure where that came from. They're both looking at me.

"Like she says," Casey says, "not a chance. So just don't trip anything. Got it?"

"It's a school," he says, rolling his eyes as he backs away, "not a bank vault."

He decides to leave through the locker room, explaining that if he's on film, he wants them to think he came from the cafeteria instead of the gym, which I think is for our benefit. He seems completely unworried, and Casey smiles, like she's not nervous either, except she's pacing. Pacing and pacing and pacing. She doesn't speak to me.

"Casey?" I say, and she grunts at me but keeps moving. "What are you hoping is on the hard drives? Could it be the shadow-database?"

There's a long moment where I think she won't answer me, but then she does. "No," she says. "It's not nearly big enough. If there is a shadow-database that June managed to set up and hide somewhere, it's got to be bigger than this, to store all that data. But maybe . . . maybe this is some of the data she copied. Or maybe this will show us the way to get back inside," she says, still moving across the room.

"So you just mentioned that the hard drive is seventeen years old, and that's a problem. Don't you think security has changed over the course of seventeen years? Don't you think June would've known that?"

She stops pacing. "Maybe they left themselves some sort of password access. Maybe they do have everything mirroring to a second device somewhere. The point is, nobody knows. The point is, she left something. June didn't do it alone. She had Liam. And you have me. I'm as good as Dominic, I promise." Then she pauses. "I'm better, I think."

"I think so, too," I say.

The locker room door flies open, and we both jump. "Cameras off. Computer lab unlocked." Cameron bows.

"You're so cocky it pains me," Casey says. "Also, you're the best."

"Remember that next time you're trying to pull the big-sister act, okay?" She rolls her eyes. "Turn left out of the cafeteria; go to the end of the hall, turn right." She starts to move. "And Casey? Nothing stupid."

"Ha," she says. And Cameron laughs, too. Because we all

know, this thing they've already done? They can't possibly do anything stupider.

And then we're alone in this big empty room that echoes. Cameron clears his throat. "How's the side?" he asks, his gaze just over my hip.

It stings. "It's fine," I say.

He's looking at my shirt. At the spot where he stitched me up. At the other spot, lower and to the left, where the bullet grazed my skin. But then his gaze moves to my eyes, and there's a danger to his honesty—now it's reflected in his eyes. I read his look. I've never seen it before—never directed at me, anyway. But I understand it completely, and I can't move forward.

I should show him. It's what I would do—what I would've done—yesterday, or a few hours ago, even. But something very sudden has shifted. Something I don't know what to do with. "Let me see," he says. I'm searching for that girl who pulled her shirt over her head so he could take out the tracker. I'm searching for the girl who took a shower with him on the other side of the distorted glass. And I'm searching for the girl who doesn't understand the need to keep things hidden like that. But all I can think of are the words he has said to me, and there's a feeling in the pit of my stomach like the churning ocean, like the horizon shifting.

I lift my shirt, but only a little, and only on the left side. He comes closer and kneels beside me, examining the mark. His hand is on my stomach, and I can't breathe. His fingers trace the edge of the mark, and I don't know what to do, other than to continue not breathing. "Yeah, it's just gonna sting. I'll see if I can find some antibiotic cream around. Let me check the stitches. Make sure there's no sign of infection."

He starts lifting my shirt higher, his knuckles trailing inside, and I push him away. "I want Casey to do it," I say.

He freezes and drops my shirt. "I'm sorry. Okay." He cringes and looks down. "I'm sorry," he says again.

I'm cringing, too, and not doing a very good job of masking it. "No, it's fine. Don't apologize." I try to backpedal, because he hasn't done anything wrong. It's me, it's the situation. It's him too close and the words he's said and the way he looks at me. It's a wave of nerves where there should be none. I've had Dominic in my room, and I knew what to say, how to say it. I kissed him, even, but the only nerves I felt then were for the weapon in my hand I was about to use. "You didn't do anything, I just . . ."

"Okay," he says. "We're fine." And I think that maybe he doesn't understand why I acted like that. He clears his throat and stands up. Backs away. He runs his hand through his hair, turns to say something to me. Stops himself. No, I was wrong, he understands.

"I'm going to see if Casey needs help," he says, staring at the locker room door. "Do you want to come?"

"You go," I say. "I want a shower. I want to put on a ridiculous uniform."

He smiles, and my heart stops. "Okay," he says, and then he leaves me. He leaves, and I am frozen. He didn't even pause, didn't ask me not to leave, didn't warn me or threaten me. He just left me, with an open window, alone. He left me, with the cameras off and at least twenty different exit possibilities. He left me, trusting me to be here when he returns.

I walk to the showers. And after I'm clean, I find the stash of uniforms, and I change into a softball uniform—long shorts, short-sleeved, soft shirt, a hat I tuck my hair through, creating a ponytail. I'm barefoot, and I stay that way. No need for more blisters.

I catch a glimpse of myself in the mirror—how common I look. This is the life I didn't have. The girl with no past, with the normal life, going through high school.

I think of Casey and Cameron somewhere far away in the building. I check the gym office, and I see Casey's blood on the carpet. I take my time scrubbing it out. I look up at the open window and check the floor for any pieces of glass left behind, but it appears that someone has already cleared them up.

I wipe down the computer and anything else I have touched with another shirt, like Cameron has taught me.

And after, I go to find them.

chapter 17

I REMEMBER CAMERON'S DIRECTIONS—left out of the cafeteria, right at the end of the hall. School is not how I pictured, or maybe it's different when it's completely empty. It's more like how I imagine an empty jail, or some asylum, and everything about me echoes still. Lockers line the walls, and the wooden classroom doors are shut and closed off. There's a window in the center of each door, and the classrooms beyond look sterile and dusty. I can hear my own breathing, my own heartbeat. There's no one watching me. No one following my signal from a tracker. No one balancing me on a tightrope. I don't hear Cameron or Casey. I don't hear anything. I move faster, anxious to not be alone anymore.

I see them through the window of the door, which they've kept closed. But it's the only classroom with a light on right now. Casey's hands fly across the keyboard, and she pauses to adjust the cables she has running from the hard drives, in some sort of maze, to the computer. Cameron sits at the desk beside her, leaning forward with his head resting in his hand, his eyes skimming his own computer screen.

It's so silent, I'm scared to break it.

I raise my finger and tap gently on the glass. They both still jump, startled to see me there. I raise my hand, and their faces relax. Casey tilts her head to the side and grins. I know what I look like—someone unlike myself. Casey waves me in.

She looks at Cameron as I enter the room. "You left her just wandering the school?"

"No, I was taking a shower. Now I'm done taking a shower," I say.

I see his eyes flick over me quickly and go back to his computer. He keeps his gaze fixed on the screen. I walk behind Cameron and look over his shoulder as Casey goes back to her work. He's reading articles about me. About us. "What do they say?" I ask.

He closes the article before I have a chance to read further. "They can say anything they want. You know that, right?"

"I know that."

"Doesn't mean it's true."

"I know." God, what must they be saying about me?

But he doesn't show me that article. Instead, he clicks on another tab, pulling up a different article, this one detailing the events of our escape—as much as they've figured out, at least.

He pushes the chair beside him out with his foot, and when I sit down, he hooks his ankle around the chair leg and drags it closer, so we're sharing the same space.

The article has a lot of the escape details right, though

they're missing Dominic completely. But they've found the sets of breathing equipment. They know there was a fourth person, but if they have any guesses, they're not being reported. Honestly, I'm not sure whether it's better or worse that they don't know. They've traced us as far as the sewer, and then after that we all but disappear. There've been reported sightings all along the East Coast, and at bus stops and gas stations all throughout the country. If Dominic has managed to reach civilization by now, it doesn't appear he has turned us in. "We're like ghosts," Cameron says.

"Except ghosts that have to stay hidden," I say.

The article also details the increased police presence, the helicopters perpetually scanning any region with reported sightings. I haven't heard any helicopters flying overhead recently—maybe we're really safe here. Or maybe it's just the insulation of the building. Part of me doesn't want to find out.

The other articles we read are about what I might potentially do once I'm out. Whether June has left me instructions somehow. Whether there's a second shadow-database. Whether I will continue what June and Liam started. Even if the only thing June left for me is the information she might've copied seventeen years ago, that's a lot I could still do damage with. The article is open for comments at the bottom, and the first commenter manages to sum this all up with the following rather ominous line: *What she might do, one can only guess; where she might go, one can only dream.* About as vague and factless as the article itself.

A-plus reporting right there.

"Cameron, come here," Casey says. He leaves me at the screen, and I quickly pull up the recent Internet history, searching for the article he didn't want me to see. I want to know what they're saying about me. All of it. I pull up the article and quickly scan the words, but it's not about me at all. It's about him and Casey and their missing sister, Ava. It's about how Casey attended a specialized school—how promising she was—while Cameron and Ava remained home, raised primarily by their grandmother until she passed away, and then by the mother he never speaks about. It mentions that Cameron spent time in a juvenile detention center for auto theft.

The article paints Cameron as a criminal, and Casey as a genius, and Ava as absolutely nothing—a figment of our imagination. A girl who is gone, and is therefore irrelevant now.

According to the article, Cameron got out after serving three months, and he reported Ava missing soon after. At which point Casey dropped out of school, and I guess that's when Cameron went into hiding, taking Casey with him this time. And for what? For this?

"Come see, Alina," Cameron says, and I close the window and plaster a blank look across my face as I approach.

Numbers scroll across the screen, in lines grouped in three or four, like the printouts in the hideaway underground. Some are starred, just like in the printouts. "Spreadsheets of numbers, that's the only thing on this one." She switches hard drives and pulls up the next files. She selects the first one, and it's a science journal, dated over twenty years ago: "Generational Linkage of Violent Criminal History in Souls."

My eyes skim the article. I recognize the material, though I've never read the original article. It's the data, and the statistical analysis, the grant funding, the science. I take in as much as I can before Casey closes the document. She opens the next, and it's an unrelated paper: "Genetic Influences versus Soul Influences: A Study of DNA and the Soul."

Every file here is a scientific article: "The Role of the Soul in Sociopaths; Correlation of Areas of Extreme Giftedness and the Soul." Casey opens each article, quickly scans it, and moves on to the next. On the last one, my eyes skim the authors, and I see: Ivory Street.

I grip the edge of the table. "Go back," I say. "Open the last article again." She opens the file before, and there she is, right under the title. I point out her name in the list of authors.

"Holy shit," Cameron says. "Ivory Street."

We scan through every one, and her name is in every author list. "Why did June have this?" Casey asks. "Do you think that because this Ivory Street person conducted this study, she had access to the database?" Casey gets so excited, she pushes her chair back from the desk. She starts talking with her hands. "Someone had to have access, right? To do the study, somebody needs access. Do you think June got access from her? Maybe she didn't just break in."

I look at the name on the screen, and I wonder. Maybe it's easier to break a person than to break a code.

I don't know, but Casey's eyes are wide and hopeful. There's a pattern here, and I need to find it. There are similarities within the documents that my mind trips over as I skim through them. "Give me some paper," I say, nudging Casey out of her seat.

"Um," she says, but she doesn't object. She pulls a ream from the nearby printer. I don't know what I'm doing exactly, but something's taken over me. Like June, stumbling upon this herself. I picture her doing this very same thing. I'm closer. I'm close. I can feel it.

"Okay, I guess, um, you do whatever it is you're doing . . . and I'm going to find this Ivory Street."

Cameron pulls up a chair and props his feet on the bottom of my own. "What are we looking for?" he asks, his voice low, like he's in on a secret.

"Honestly? I don't know," I say. "Get me a pen. Or a pencil. I need one."

He pulls out the drawer beside me and shows me the collection. "Oh." I pull one off the top and get back to work.

I'm scanning the documents, jotting down notes for myself—author names, funding sources, data analysis programs, population samples—when Cameron taps the brim of my hat with his finger.

I'm jarred back to reality, but at first my eyes don't leave the screen.

"So, question," he says. "And it's kind of important. You're left-handed?"

I stop writing. I put the pen in my left hand down. "Not exactly."

"I'm confused. I thought these papers"—he gestured toward the screen—"I thought that science proved that left- and right-handedness were almost completely tied to the soul. And June was right-handed, if I'm remembering correctly."

"Just because I'm right-handed doesn't mean I have to use my right hand." I flex my fingers, transfer the pen to the other side, where it does feel easier, and say, "When I was ten, I started pretending that I didn't have a right hand. Now it's habit."

"When you were ten?"

"Yeah. When I realized my whole life was bullshit. That I was stuck. That it was . . . a prison. So I thought if I could convince them I wasn't June, that they were wrong, they'd let me out. To my ten-year-old brain, this made sense. If science says it's passed down, and if I'm not right-handed, then I can't be her, right?"

He grins and taps the brim of my hat again, and I look away, back to the screen. "It's pathetic, I know. I was ten."

He's silent for a long time, and I've gone back to working by the time he responds. "It's not pathetic," he says. Cameron pushes his chair back, the legs squeaking against the linoleum. "I'm going back to the gym. Hungry."

Casey raises her hand as he passes but doesn't make eye contact.

Eventually, I decide to print out the articles and bring them back to the gym, where I can spread them out and analyze them a little better. And eat at the same time.

"Hey," Casey says, as I'm leaving the room. "Save me dinner."

"If by dinner you mean cereal, that won't be a problem."

"By the way," she says, the door half-closed. "Nice outfit."

I don't see Cameron anywhere when I get back to the gym, so I pull one of the blue mats onto the floor and spread the articles around, lying on my stomach, propped up on my elbows between them. I should've printed off the other hard drive, the one with the information June kept in the hideaway, with all the numbers, but that would've taken far too long. Besides, sorting all of that . . . that's the kind of stuff you use a computer for. I'll ask Casey to help with that later. But *this* is the kind of stuff you need your own brain for.

I don't like being in this empty gym, I don't like this feeling of being alone, that anything can happen to me and nobody would know, but this information is like a comfort to me. Like June is here with me, sharing it. Pointing things out. Her ideas, her thoughts, twisting their way into mine.

I read the articles in full. The famous study, reduced to numbers and math. To get the right data—a sample of uninfluenced *human* data—they used markers for other aspects correlated to criminal activity. For instance, they only studied souls that remained the same sex from generation to generation, because most violent crime was committed by men. They didn't want the fact that a man's soul later became a woman's soul to influence the data, since one had a higher chance of violent criminal activity to begin with. They also grouped by souls born from generation to generation with similar socioeconomic backgrounds, living in areas with similar crime statistics. So all that was left was a subset of souls with little variation from generation to generation, as controlled an experiment as a human soul could be, I suppose.

The resulting evidence was purely empirical, but it's presented with graphs and equations and a concluding statement about the calculated correlation between violent criminal activity and the soul in the samples they studied: 0.8.

Damning.

When I'm done reading several of the other articles in detail, I flip onto my back with my eyes closed and let June's voice tell me what we know: the data subsets, the publishing journal, the grants received, the tagged markers, which must correlate with the starred data on the spreadsheets. Her words fill my head until they start to make sense, coming together as something I can almost grasp on to. Like I can see the connection, but not what it's connecting.

I hear steps, and I know it's Cameron the same way I know things belong to June. I've been studying him without realizing it. I know his walk. His pace. His looks. The mat underneath me shifts with his weight, but I don't know what will happen when it's just the two of us here on the blue mat and I open my eyes. I'm not sure what I'll say. What I'll do. I have not had time to think it all through.

"You up?" he asks, but he asks it so softly, I'm not sure if he expects me to answer, to have heard.

I am thinking of all the different incarnations of Cameron I have been imagining, wondering which one is the closest to the truth. But maybe this is the only one that matters. Right now, *this* is the real one.

I open my eyes, turning my head toward him, but his eyes are drifting over my shirt, down my arms, down my legs, to my toes. And I feel a rush of something—like I am more naked, fully clothed, than when he cut the tracker from my rib. I wiggle my toes, and his gaze drifts back up quickly, and he sees me looking.

He stands abruptly and says, "Casey's probably on her way back by now." Like that's a legitimate reason for him to stand. To move away.

"It's not a crime to sit here," I say. "I mean, not that that would stop you . . ."

He sits back down. "Are you making criminal jokes now? Is that what's happening here?"

I meet his eyes, and I summon every ounce of bravery I possess to the surface. "I don't know what's happening here."

He nods so subtly I only see it because I am currently hyperfocused on everything Cameron. "About earlier," he says. "I'm sorry. I'm sorry I made you uncomfortable. I thought you were used to people seeing you. Looking at you. You told me that once, and I just thought . . ."

"I'm not used to people looking at me *like that*," I say, pushing myself up on my elbows. It comes out accusing, but I don't mean it to.

He winces, but he doesn't deny it. "I'm sorry," he says.

God, it's impossible to say what I mean, to even put it into words. I feel like we're having a conversation with the things we don't say instead, and the only thing he's capable of saying is *I'm sorry*.

But I don't want to forgive him for it. It's not something I want him to take back. "I just said I'm not *used* to it. That's all." It made me feel out of control again. Out of my element. Like I wasn't in charge, didn't have time to weigh everything and think about what to say, what to do.

He plays with the back of my ponytail for a second, as if he's testing something, and I stay perfectly still until he lets it drop.

I don't know whether it's normal for my heart to beat so fast it feels like it's tripping over itself.

I don't know whether it's normal to both want and fear a kiss. For the anticipation to be both crippling and thrilling. He's close enough to do it, but he hasn't moved. Like he's waiting for some sign from me.

I think back to every movie I've seen, every television show, every book I've read. I turn to look at him, I drop my head slightly to the side, I lean, just an inch, toward him. But he doesn't do anything. Doesn't come closer or bring his hand to my face or *anything*. I know my face is red now, which makes me even more embarrassed, which makes me ever redder, I'm sure. I lean back that one inch, and I straighten my head. I look away.

"Can I ask you something?" he asks. But he doesn't wait for me to answer. He puts a hand gently under my chin, guiding me to look at him. "What Dominic said out in the woods—about June and Liam, and how they would die for each other, and how that kind of love lasts beyond just one life. Do you think that's true?"

"No," I say. "Remember the whole 'he's a psychopath' thing?"

"Yeah, but what if you'd met him somewhere else. If you weren't locked up. If he wasn't trying to use you for something." He drops his hand from my face and looks away. "You're drawn to him, aren't you? You were at one point, anyway. And I've seen the way he looks at you sometimes. I think it would be easier for him if he didn't care, but he does. And so do you."

I shake my head even before he finishes speaking. "Stop. I don't want to have anything to do with him. I won't."

"But if you knew him in some other setting . . . if he was a guy in a coffee shop and you were a girl in school . . ." His words trail off as his eyes drift to the side—to nothing.

At first, I thought he was accusing me. But part of me thinks that maybe he's jealous. That maybe I'm not defending myself here, but reassuring him instead.

"But I'm not," I say, mirroring Cameron's own words. He wouldn't even check to see if his last life had left him something. All the hypotheticals in the world can't change who we are right now.

"There are things about your personalities that must make you compatible," he says.

He's right, of course. There's *something*. But it's not enough, on its own. "You're right," I say. "There must be. But only on paper. Human beings aren't quantifiable," I say, thinking of those scientific studies. What I wouldn't give for just one life. Just this one.

His eyes meet mine. "You kissed him," he says. It's a statement, but it's also a question.

"Yes," I say. I'm incapable of lying to him, apparently. Consequences be damned.

He pauses. "Why?"

"To buy myself some time. To catch him off guard." I don't pause. The words pour out of me, and I don't know what he'll do with them.

He nods to himself, like yes, that seems like me, and my heart sinks. "Dominic said you don't do things without a reason."

"Seems like a good idea to have a reason for things."

"You want me to kiss you?" he asks. Cameron kills me with his honesty. With the way he challenges me to be honest with him, as well.

I squeeze me eyes shut and almost deny it, but stop myself. "Yes."

"Why?"

"I thought you wanted to," I say, evading the question.

He half laughs. "Yeah, which is why I'm asking. The thing is, I have a terrible history with girls I like betraying me. So I'm feeling just the slightest bit cautious." I assume he's talking about this Ella person, but the only thing I notice is the whole "girls I like" part, and that I'm included in this category.

I look away, trying not to smile, then face him again. "I have no idea why I'm doing this."

"That really doesn't sound anything like you. Do better than that, Alina." He leans back on his arms, and he watches my face as I answer.

I shrug with one shoulder. And I tell him the thing I was thinking, but didn't say, back in the cafeteria. "Because I think you're incredible. Because I want you to."

And that's all it takes. He leans forward and pulls my hat off, my ponytail now undone. He puts both hands on each side of my face, and his kiss is soft—softer than I expected. I don't know what to do exactly, as my only experience before this was a fake kiss and I wasn't thinking so much about the kiss as I was about the next step. But now I am lost in this moment, and this one only. He's breathing me in, somehow, but he's going slow, like he's waiting for a sign from me, but I can't move. And I can't get him to move any closer.

I'm resting on my elbows and I have no idea how to move without us both toppling over, without ruining this. So I stay perfectly still, with his hands on my face, and his lips barely pressing on my own. I should probably do something. But I'm frozen, because there are a thousand different possibilities suddenly before me.

Like that moment when we left the underground for the rest of the world, that new and terrifying possibility of something *more*. It's all I wanted, and now it's right here, right in front of me. Suddenly, I have it: somebody who doesn't see me as June—I am free of her. And now I'm just Alina Chase, and I don't know if that's good enough. How frightening that big expanse of freedom can be when you finally get there.

He pulls back, resting his forehead against mine, and it leaves me wanting and wanting and pushing up on my hands and leaning closer for more. He puts a hand on the back of my head then, and he gives me exactly what I'm asking for, coming closer.

I stop thinking. I know nothing.

Except this: with his hands tangled in my hair, and his weight on top of mine, I have never felt so free.

And then the door opens.

"Oh, ick."

chapter 18

"STOP." CASEY HOLDS A hand out. "Rewind. Undo. Cameron, a word?"

Cameron pulls back in record speed, his hand dropping from my hair, his body shifting to the other side of the mat.

"Find anything?" he asks, acting like nothing has happened, nothing has changed. Like the whole world hasn't shifted in some way.

My body still feels charged—I can't shift back like Cameron has just done. I feel like the room is moving.

Casey stands with her hands on her hips. "This"—she points at Cameron, then me, then him again—"isn't happening."

"Like I said," he says, shrugging with one shoulder, "find anything?" I can't tell whether his shrug means *okay sure, nothing will happen* or *hey, that was nothing anyway* or *I'm ignoring you*. There's so much I don't know about him still. The last moment has made me feel like I know both everything and nothing about him. That he's telling me something and yet showing me how much more there's still to know. The world balancing on a point, and he is at the center.

"Cameron," she says.

"Casey," he says.

She gestures to the doors behind her.

He sighs and shrugs again, but he follows her out into the hallway. Great. I flip onto my back again, and I try to switch my mind like Cameron has done. I think of the data, the names, the science, the starred numbers. But they float through my mind with no purpose, deemed unimportant by the current state of events.

I can hear them arguing, because as one voice raises, the other raises higher, until they're almost yelling. "Casey, get a grip!"

"No, you get a grip!"

Ugh.

And then the door flies open, and someone sounds out of breath. I don't dare move. They pace around the room, and finally, when I can't stand it anymore, I ask, "Did you find anything about Ivory Street?"

Casey huffs, and I can't tell whether she's mad at me or him or the entire situation we're stuck in. "As a matter of fact, yes," she says. "I've found out she's unlisted. But her name was on a paper published two years ago, which is promising."

"How is that promising?"

"Well I was hoping she's not dead, seeing as this was seventeen years ago . . . but no worries, she's fifty-five and alive and well." She pulls out a folded-up sheet of paper. "Here she is. At some political fund-raiser." The picture is grainy and black-and-white, and from the distance, I can't make out her features. "And while I don't have a contact for her personally, I *do* have the location for her lab."

I walk toward them, focusing on Casey, trying to ignore Cameron standing there completely perfect in my peripheral vision.

"So we just show up?" I ask.

"No," Cameron says. "We go there to find her. And then we follow. Where is it?"

"Five- or six-hour drive, maybe more. I don't know," Casey says.

"Okay. Should we leave tonight?" I ask.

"No," he says. "I need to get a car first."

"We have a car," I say.

"A different one," he says.

I feel like I'm keeping a mental tally of crimes, but I don't have any better options. We don't have any money—or access to any money without someone noticing. I hope the end justifies the means. I hope I am forgiven. I hope there's something at the end of all this that makes these wrongs worth the price.

June, I hope you're worth it.

And I swear I can hear her, as she whispers in my ear like an echo: *I hope* you're *worth it.*

Cameron is tasked with creating some sort of meal from the things we've found in the cafeteria, and Casey picks a uniform from the pile and heads toward the girls' locker room. I start to help him, but Casey stops at the door and calls to me. "Come with me, Alina." I glance at Cameron, but he's ignoring me. "Cameron says I need to check your stitches, anyway." I start blushing again, remembering how I blushed back then. His hand on my stomach. His knuckles trailing against my skin. His kiss.

Casey walks into a shower and pulls the curtain shut behind her. She hands me her clothes through the side of the curtain, and I stand there, completely useless. The water turns on, and the steam drifts from her stall. "Oh, my God, this feels so good," she says. Maybe she does want to check out my stitches, but it's obvious that mostly she wants to keep me from Cameron.

"So listen, Alina," she says, over the sound of running water. "We need to have a talk." Okay, so I was wrong. Not only does she want to keep me from him, apparently we need to talk about it. I think about slinking away. I wonder if she'll even notice. But in the end, I stand there holding her clothes, because I do owe her this. I do.

"Okay," I say.

"I think you're . . . Well, you're you. And I like you. And obviously *he* likes you. And I think you like us?"

I'm not sure if I'm supposed to respond to that, but she doesn't give me the chance anyway.

"But I'm not sure. And that uncertainty, I can't deal with it right now. You understand? I can't stay up worrying about whether you're playing him for something."

"I'm not," I cut in.

"I hope you're not, I really do. So if you mean that, stop playing."

I'm not sure what part of this she thinks is me playing anything. It didn't feel like playing at all. It felt like something bigger than the moment we were in. Bigger than the situation. Bigger than the goal. Something that had both nothing and everything to do with it. "But I'm not playing."

She turns the water off and extends her hand through the curtain, and I place the uniform in her open palm. "This. Just stop this. Please," she says. When she's dressed, she pulls the curtain open, wringing out the ends of her hair. "His last girlfriend—Ella? It's the whole reason he was locked up. She got him into the mess, and then she flipped on him to save her own ass. So please. You held a piece of glass to my throat. We risked our lives for you. The only thing I'm asking is for you to keep your distance. No distractions. This isn't the time. You can see that, I'm sure. This *isn't the time.*"

I nod. It's all I can manage.

"Now let's see the damage," she says, like everything's normal again.

I pull off my shirt. She leans closer. "He did a really good job," she whispers. "No signs of infection, either." Then she checks out my side. "Still sting?" she asks.

"Not too much," I say.

She smiles. "I do like you, Alina. But we're so entirely screwed right now. The only way to make it out of this is to get into that database and hope like hell there's something we can use."

I hate the idea that I must be like June, using what we might find for selfish reasons. I hate it, and yet I don't have any better ideas.

Like the terrifying ocean. The only way past it is through it.

Dinner turns out to be cereal and soda with a side of chocolate bars.

And distance turns out to be the length of one blue gym mat, separated by one watchful sister.

Even in the dark, I see her staring at me. "See?" she says, "I already can't sleep. This is ridiculous."

Cameron, on the other side, is already breathing slowly and steadily, apparently unworried and unaffected by the whole situation.

"Don't worry, Casey," I say.

And then I spend the night trying not to think of him. Instead, I see the starred numbers on the printouts, boxes and boxes of paper in the hideaway. I try to focus, but instead my mind keeps replaying Cameron's face the second before he kissed me. And then the kiss. And I can't unfocus from it. I have decided it's really unfair. I should get to decide what my mind thinks about, and not the other way around . . .

I bolt upright, my head swimming with Cameron and numbers and stars and data. I grab June's notebook, flipping through the pages in the dark. Not that it would suddenly make sense to me now, even if I could see it. I need to see what's on the hard drives again. I need to see the starred data and the data in the articles.

"Casey," I say, shaking her shoulder.

"What?" she asks.

"I need to see the data again."

"I'm actually sleeping here. In the morning, Alina."

But I can't sleep again. I can't stop thinking of June, of what she must've felt. Because I realize, this path we're on, I'm no longer following clues left behind for me. It's me stepping in June's footprints. It's me reliving her life. It's me seeing things exactly as she saw them. She hasn't left me anything more. Now I'm discovering, just as she did. And so this feeling—this feeling that there's something in that data—I know it's not just my feeling. It's June's.

And the answer, I know, even though it pains me to think it—the answer is inside the database.

Cameron wakes before Casey. He sees me sitting in a ball on the mat, and he pushes himself to standing. He grins and disappears into the boys' locker room for less than five minutes and comes out looking completely put together. He has on the uniform again, and for a moment I can picture him like this, walking out of the high school locker room, onto the court to play a game. I see him smile at some girl, like he's doing to me, an acknowledgment of some secret they share. I see that he has had a life, and he won't have it again. And maybe it's not the same—from hiding to free, from free to hiding—but that difference, the distance from what we *were* to what we *are*, is the same. And if we really are so similar—people, I mean—then I think I understand him. I think he understands me, even.

"Off to get a car," he says, jogging toward the office with the open window. I remember how he said that freeing me might turn out to be the one good thing he does with his life. How much we all need this. How much we all need each other.

I want to tell him to be careful, but I decide that makes me seem needy or nervous or both. He's halfway toward the office, but I whisper it anyway.

Casey wakes almost as soon as he leaves. "Where's Cameron?"

"Committing auto theft," I say. "Ready?" I grab June's notebook and hope I can make sense of it—if I can at least figure out what she was looking for.

"Ready for what?" she asks.

"The data. I need to see it again. You said in the morning. And it's morning."

"Right," she says. She gropes around for the bag with the hard drives and stands up. "You're a little intense in the morning, you know that?"

I think I'm probably a little intense all of the time. I'm realizing I don't even care to hide it.

Casey walks with me down to the computer lab and sets up the cables, loading the files for me. As I sit down, she groans. "Give me five minutes. I would kill for some caffeine right now."

She leaves me in the room, her footsteps quickly disappearing as I pull up the files of starred numbers. I do a search for the data, for the amount of asterisks. And I do a search for the total number of lines in the spreadsheet. I write down the answers, and I'm reading through the science article again when I hear the footsteps returning. They pause in front of the open door. "This has to mean something," I say. "They don't match up."

And when the footsteps don't continue, don't respond, I look up, and I freeze.

There's a boy in the doorway. Or a man. That in-between, indeterminate period. Probably my age. "Oh," I say. "Hi." I wish I had the ball cap on, so I could hide behind the brim. But at least I'm wearing the uniform.

He's holding a mop and has a ring of keys attached to a belt loop. "Do you work here?" I ask. Trying to make it seem like I belong here, too. *Smile*, I remind myself.

"Yeah," he says slowly. "In the summer."

I lean back in my seat and pretend to refocus on the screen. "I'll see you around, then," I say, trying to convince him that I belong here, that I am meant to be here in this room, that he's mistaken if he thinks otherwise. I am good at pretending. I am good at hiding the truth.

He takes a step back, then says, "You play for our team?"

"Uh-huh," I say, because what else can I say when I'm wearing the school uniform and I'm in the school computer lab and he knows my face from somewhere. This school is probably small. He probably goes here. I'm probably screwed.

"Hey, Melissa!" I hear Casey yell from down the hall.

"In here," I call back. *Thank God*, I think. Casey is better at people. She'll know what to do. She already does.

"I was looking for you." She skids to a stop in front of the room, pushing past the guy without making eye contact, like he's in our way and his presence is inconsequential. "You done yet? We need to get back to the gym."

I take the hint and start packing the cables away, disconnecting the hard drives, putting everything back in Casey's bag.

But the guy just stands there. "What's going on at the gym?" he asks.

Casey places a hand on her hip and still doesn't look at him, but she puts on this condescending air, which makes her seem younger, instead of the other way around. "We're volunteering," she says. "Come on." She pulls my arm, and I follow. We're walking down the hall, ignoring him, when I hear it.

The click of a camera.

Casey hears it, too.

She spins around, and the guy gets off one more shot before sprinting in the other direction. "Shit," she says, and she starts to run.

"Stop!" I say. "What are you going to do when you catch him?" I ask.

She stops, staring back at me, her eyes full of desperation.

"It's too late," I say. We're not going to hurt some kid. Someone who's here by accident. Someone whose only crime is the circumstances of his location. I was a victim of circumstance, a victim of my life—there's never a good enough justification for the things they have done to me because of it.

She stands in the middle of the hall, still debating. And then she turns in my direction.

"Damn it," she says. "We need to hurry."

"Cameron . . . ," I say.

We race into the gym, and I throw everything I can into Casey's bag. My papers, the articles, whatever food my hands grab in the minutes we have. I slide my feet into the sneakers that don't fit right, the laces still undone. We're already heading for the office when Cameron comes racing through the office door.

"There's a car here," he says, out of breath. "Someone's here."

"Too late," Casey says, and Cameron's eyes go wide, seeing us and the chaos we're leaving behind.

"Go," he says, boosting me up through the broken window first. "To the church."

Casey's on the ground a moment behind me, and we're both racing toward the church, and I'm listening for sirens, but my breath is catching in a way that makes it seem like I'm crying.

Maybe I'm out of shape.

Maybe I'm tired.

Maybe I'm panicking.

The grass is slick beneath my feet, and there's a light, cool rain coming down around us. Cameron catches up to us, catches my hand, pulls me to a brown car with deep, tinted windows. I dive into the backseat, and Casey and Cameron sit up front. Cameron starts the car, and we drive just over the speed limit through residential streets when I realize that I am actually crying. This is my life. I am not free. I am running. I have to keep running. I can't stay in one place for any length of time. I cannot have human contact. I cannot be free.

Casey turns around and says, "We're okay, we're fine."

But we're not. I can hear it in the quiver of her voice. It's shaking, uncertain. Desperate. She's supposed to be good at people, and the fact that she can't even hold it together breaks the last thread within me.

It's drizzling outside, and Cameron turns on the headlights. The wipers cut through the rain in a pattern like a metronome.

I hear the inevitability of my life, and the one before, heading our way.

Cameron and Casey tense when they hear it, too. In the distance, but coming closer.

The sirens. They've started.

chapter 19

EVENTUALLY WE STOP HEARING the sirens. Eventually we hear helicopters instead. I look up from the corner of the window and see a news station symbol on the side of the nearest helicopter. But there are others in the distance—black and sleek with no visible designation. I instinctively back away from the window, but I keep watching. They circle the area over the school, possibly believing we're still holed up inside. That kid took our picture. They will find our prints. They will know, for a fact, we were there. I don't think they see our car. If they do, I don't think they know we're in it. I keep my face covered, just in case.

"Tell me you wiped the search history," Cameron says.

"Of course I wiped the search history," Casey says. "Who do you think I am?"

Search history. Right. That's how I pulled up the article Cameron was reading.

"Of course, if they bring in someone who actually knows

what they're doing, that won't really matter." Cameron tenses behind the wheel. "But that will take time," she says.

"I didn't," I say. "I didn't wipe anything from the computer I was using."

"Did you search for Ivory Street at all?" Casey asks, spinning around.

I shake my head. "No, just looking at the data on the hard drives."

Cameron taps his fingers against the steering wheel in a frantic rhythm. "Can we disappear?" he asks Casey in a low voice. "Can you work up some identities?"

"And then this is all for nothing?" Casey asks.

"Not for nothing," he says. I know what he means. I am out, and that counts for something. The idea of freedom would be nice, but we have limited options.

"There's no turning back," I whisper. "You'll be fugitives forever. Dominic was right—we have to play the hand we've been dealt."

It's quiet inside the car, but outside, the helicopters circle. The sound is physically painful—I wince every time they come closer.

"Something doesn't add up, about June, about me," I say. I'm stuck thinking about the past life, but everyone else is focused on this one, like always. "I think June knew something . . . I think she and Liam stumbled upon something in there . . ."

"I want to find Ava," Casey whispers. And again, I think of Ava in that database somewhere, and the fact that she will not be the same person, which Casey must know.

There's a beat of silence as Casey rifles through the bag, checking on the safe keeping of the hard drives, when Cameron says, "I don't want to lose you, too."

"You won't. I promise. But we're out of options, Cameron. I'm so sorry. I'm sorry I got you into this mess," she says, pulling out the stacks of paper taking up space in the overstuffed bag. "But we have nothing right now. No answers, no money . . . Oh, God," she says. She squints at the articles I've printed out.

"What?" I ask.

"I forgot. The printer has a memory. It can reprint."

I'm picturing our secrets dispensing from the base of the printer, eyes reading what I've just read—I wonder what, if anything, they will see.

"Why would they even check?" I ask.

She turns around in the front seat, her eyes wide. "That kid is going to say he saw Alina Chase in the computer lab. Of course they're going to check!" Casey says.

"Well, I'm sorry, I never knew that a printer had a memory. And you didn't tell me. And they're just science articles! What does it matter?"

"It matters because they'll know what we're after. It matters because they'll eventually find what we were searching for. I printed off her picture. I can't believe it. It matters because they'll be able to find us, Alina. God!"

"*We* don't even know what we're after! We have no plan! Don't you get it? My entire life is riding on this, right now!"

"Don't *you* get it?" she yells back. "So are ours!"

"Stop!" Cameron says. "We're in a car, we're not caught,

we've got some time. We need to stay a step ahead, is all. Get there first."

I'm panicking, and the words are flowing from my mouth, unchecked. I have no control over the situation, and I can't see beyond the four doors of this car. I can't even imagine a place where I will be safe.

"Get where?" I ask, but I know the answer. Cameron catches my eye in the mirror, because we all know the options on the table. If we're going forward, if we're not throwing in the towel and trying to disappear with absolutely nothing, we're going to find Ivory Street. I have no idea what June wanted her for, but I know she saw the same thing I did—her name on all these articles. Maybe Casey is right—maybe this is how they got into the database. Maybe Ivory Street will have the answers we need. June went to her, I'm sure of it. And now, so will we.

And then what? I want to ask. But I know the plan. There is none.

I can't let myself think past the next step. There's nowhere else to go.

Our main problem comes not in the form of a search helicopter, which apparently stayed near the school, but three hours later in the form of a nearly empty gas tank. "It's safer to just get another car," Cameron says.

"Of course, because we're on a goddamn crime spree! It's like the Cameron London show—how many crimes can you commit in five days?" Casey responds, her hands flailing in the air as she speaks.

"Casey, what do you want me to do? Pull up to the gas

station with no money, fill up the tank in view of the cameras, and drive away, leaving them a map of where we've been? What the hell are we supposed to do?" He pulls the car off the highway, and we take the ramp.

"It makes us look bad," she says. "Like we're just a bunch of criminals. That we didn't do it for a good reason."

"We didn't," he says, and he calmly puts the blinker on at the stoplight.

"I did it for Ava. And for you," she says, but he spins on her.

"You did it for me? Are you sure? Did you really? Or did you just . . . want an excuse? Because this, what we're doing, doesn't make me seem like anything other than what everyone already thinks. That I'm a criminal. It's just an excuse and you know it."

She leans back but doesn't respond.

"Maybe you're wrong to have so much faith in me, Casey," he says. "Maybe I'm nothing more than what everyone already assumes."

"You're not," she says. And I silently agree.

True to his word, Cameron is good at staying hidden. He drives the car far off the main roads. There doesn't seem to be much off the exit other than a truck stop, a gas station, and a convenience store. He bypasses all of these and takes a few turns until the straight roads turn curvy. We idle for a moment in front of a sign announcing a community with home sites available. He rolls down the windows, and I hear the sound of construction, of vehicles. "What time is it?" he asks.

Casey checks her watch. "Just after three."

He starts driving again, turning into the neighborhood, but we don't go far. The gas gauge hovers dangerously close to zero. "We'll never make it to Ivory Street's office before it closes for the day anyway. And this is as perfect as it gets."

There's a dirt road off to the side that leads to a dead end, around the bend of the road. There are home sites listed on signs stuck into packed dirt with the number to call for more information. But the sites are still filled with trees for now, backing into the woods. He pulls the car off the dirt road around the bend, hidden from the street unless someone turns down this dead-end road. "Now what?" I ask.

"Cross your fingers that nobody comes down here," he says. "And cross your fingers they don't see us when they leave in a few hours."

Casey quickly exits the car and walks a few paces into the woods. She leans back against a tree, leans her head against the bark as well. I go to follow, but Cameron says, "Leave her. Give her a few minutes." So I close the door again, and I crack my knuckles against my legs.

The car is off, and the heat automatically starts to settle in, like a thickness to the air, but it's more than the heat. It's the tension of being alone with him again. Of not knowing where we stand. "We're going to asphyxiate in here," I say.

He unbuckles his seat belt and stretches, smiling at me in the rearview mirror. "Imagine the headlines. 'Alina Chase Found Dead in Hot Car.' Watch how I can spin this." Then he holds up a pointer finger. "'Wanted Criminal Holds Hostage in Car in Apparent Murder-Suicide.'" Another finger: "'Accidental Death while Hiding from Authorities: Alina Chase and Accomplice Fall Asleep and Forget to Crack the Window.'"

"I don't like that one," I say. "We sound stupid."

He puts up a third finger. "'Foul Play Suspected in Hot-Car Death. Bodies Moved Postmortem.'" He turns to face me. "I mean, technically, we could suffocate anywhere . . ."

I grin. "I'm suffocating *now*," I say.

"I'm just getting started. That's just the news reports on the first day. Soon we can get into conspiracies. The government found us, staged our deaths, and is currently holding the soul of Alina Chase in an undisclosed location. Or a horde of angry citizens takes their revenge." I cringe, because it feels a little too close to the justification for keeping me on the island. Cameron's smile stretches wider. "Or aliens."

I laugh. "That one will never hold up. Nothing to back it up."

He shrugs. "You can do anything you want with facts, make up any story to fit. Truth is in the eye of the beholder."

"I thought that was beauty," I say.

"Both. People see you a certain way, and it's so easy to believe it. To believe that's all of you."

I imagine he's talking about his own past, but it could also be mine. And I hate that his smile is gone. I want it back.

"Or," I say, "this was all an elaborate ruse by Alina Chase. The body isn't even hers. Whereabouts unknown." I lean my head back.

"Alina Chase, you continue to surprise me. Who knew you were such a sucker for the happy ending?"

Our eyes meet in the mirror. "This was all part of my plan, you see," I say. "Didn't you get my subliminal messages, leading us to this very spot?"

He actually laughs, and in some corner of my brain, I know that this is not a normal conversation. That talking about methods of death and our own inevitable demise is not typically a reason for laughter. And yet, here we are. "Do I survive the ruse?"

"Of course," I say.

"How generous of you. Where do you go then?"

And this is when the conversation turns dangerous, because suddenly it's straddling that line between fiction and hope, and hope is something I cannot afford right now. Something clamps down on my heart. "To the land of dreams," I say, trying to be ironic. But Cameron frowns, and Casey knocks on the window.

"You guys are going to asphyxiate."

And then the moment is broken. I laugh as Casey walks away.

When we exit the car, we follow Casey into the woods. The sound of the construction vehicles makes me nervous—there are people too close, or *we* are too close. But nobody seems aware of our existence. I ask for Casey's bag, putting aside the empty gun and hard drives to get to the articles and June's notebook again. Cameron and Casey talk strategy for tonight, in hushed voices that still carry on the wind. Cameron needs to figure out directions, and he's sure there will be Internet access somewhere on the premises. He's also convinced there will be a place for us to sleep. Casey wants to know where he'll get another car, but he says she worries too much about the details.

Meanwhile, I am drowning in details. I have nothing to write with anymore, so I've taken to carving numbers in a space of dirt I've cleared of leaves.

I've got rocks holding down pages of a few articles, and June's notebook is open in the middle of the area, and I'm standing over them all, writing numbers that jump out at me in the dirt with a long stick. I use June's equations as a guide, plugging in the data from the study. I'm so engrossed in this, the numbers ordering themselves in my head, and not quite aligning how I expect them to. It's this unsettled feeling I'm trying to grab on to. It's not the numbers I have. It's the thing that's missing.

"What are you looking for?" Cameron asks. He's right behind me, and when I turn around, I see Casey not too far away, leaning against a tree, watching me work. I don't know how long they've been standing there, watching me this way.

"I don't know. But something is wrong. Something is missing."

They look at me very carefully, with heads tilting toward me, toward the numbers on the ground. "What's missing?" Casey asks.

I shake my head. "I don't know how the data was selected

and sorted, but I can't make it fit. And I *won't* know unless I can get in the database and see what she used."

I know who I sound like: June. Convincing people her motives were altruistic. But they led to chaos, to death, to *this*.

Casey eyes the dirt. "This means something to you?"

I feel Cameron looking at me, and I get the meaning in Casey's words. This was June's thing. I'm just a shadow of her, but I can feel it in me, this talent. I've wasted it, but it's there.

I use my feet to dig into the dirt, swiping it back and forth, reducing it all to nothing again.

We hear the trucks rumbling up the hill when the sun is still in the sky, and Cameron motions for us to stay very still. I hold my breath, begging them not to turn down this road, but they rumble past us. A steady stream of vehicles moves by over the next thirty minutes, and we wait another hour still, until the sun is low and the shadows are long and the mosquitoes come out for blood.

Cameron takes his shirt off to wipe the car down again, and I get a better look at his back this time. The scar is long and white and raised, and I wonder if maybe the cut on my rib cage will eventually turn itself into the same.

Casey is packing up her bag and checking our site when Cameron turns back around, catches me staring. And I don't want him to think it's for any other reason. "Looks like it hurt," I say.

He puts his shirt back on quickly. "Do me a favor, Alina. If you ever decide to stab me, don't do it in the back."

"Deal," I whisper, and I quickly look away.

We walk with everything we currently own—that is, everything that fits in Casey's bag and the school uniforms we're still wearing—down the dirt road, and eventually Cameron points out what he calls "the main office," which to me looks like more of a trailer than an office. It sits in the middle of the construction site, between four partially built homes—skeletons with roofs, in various degrees of completion.

Cameron unlocks the trailer door for us, though I'm sure we could've gotten inside in countless other ways. And the first thing I'm met with is the scent of cigarettes and sweat. Casey flicks a light switch, and a fluorescent rectangle on the ceiling buzzes to life. The carpeting is covered in muddy orange footprints. There's a desk with chairs on either side and a small table near a smaller refrigerator. I opt to stay outside. I wonder what my first foster home was like—if it was full of scents and dirt and the remainders of real people—or if it was more like my island. I can't remember. But I've seen the envelopes, the letters, that led to my removal from that place. I've read about the lives that June had ruined; I've felt their need for revenge. It wasn't safe for me out there, within reach. If they left me there and something happened, they'd be at fault. I see it now, the fine line of my imprisonment. That perhaps we are all victims of circumstance. Products of both chaos and fate.

There's a monitor on the desk, and Casey walks straight for it, seemingly unaffected by the odor.

"If you're going to stand out there," Casey says, "at least keep an eye out for anyone coming."

I turn around, my back to the room now lit by the unnatural white glow, and I stare out at the twilight. We're not in the mountains anymore, but possibly we're at the edge of them—the roads rose and dipped on our drive, the trees became denser the farther we got from the highway. Cameron and Casey talk behind me, but not to me, and I imagine myself disappearing—walking straight into the distance, nobody to stop me; or standing right here, fading to nothing. They'd look up, and I'd be gone.

I could do it, if I wanted. I've earned their trust, and I could run. It's becoming more and more clear that I will never shake her skin—that I will always be seen as June Calahan living inside the shell of Alina Chase to everyone else.

But not right here. Right here, when I look over my shoulder and Cameron catches my eye and smiles, when Casey barks a command in my direction—*listen for cars*—it's only to me.

The world is big, and we are small.

But maybe this is enough.

I'm lost in a daydream—me in a yard somewhere, standing like this, and laughter from the cabin behind me, and a deep voice calling my name—it's so real I can feel it taking shape inside me, and I know how dangerous this is, I know. How hope can spread, how it multiplies when you linger in it. How it works its way into your life, before you remember that it's not real. How insidious hope can become if you let it.

I'm deep within this dream, so I must not hear Cameron the first time. Because his hand is suddenly on my shoulder and his voice is in my ear. "Alina," he says, and the vision is gone, replaced by the sound of Casey's fingers typing on the keyboard, the floor that creaks below us, the smell of the cigarettes and sweat. "Check out the home sites with me?"

He doesn't grab my hand, but his passing body has the same effect, pulling me along.

We walk toward the half-built homes. One, with a door and green paper covering the roof and walls. One, just a foundation and the start of a wooden frame. The other two completely framed, but without windows, without drywall. I can see through the beams of the houses in sections—a hallway from this perspective, but step to the left and the wood lines up, and I can see into another room. Cameron steps through the doorway of the closest one onto the solid, wooden floor.

The whole place smells like sawdust, with the scent of something faintly burning.

"Do you smell that? Like a fire?" I ask.

"Left behind from a saw on wood, probably. The heat from the friction almost makes it burn," he says.

The scent sets my heart on edge. Like the candles on my birthday cake—like something changing, a passage of time. It's been only five days, but it feels like a lifetime we've spent running.

Cameron heads down the hall, but I check out the rooms

off to the sides. Perfect squares, empty and exposed. The walls will go here and be painted, and the wood floor will be hidden. I can picture a couch here, against the wall, maybe blue. And a black-and-white picture hanging on the wall behind it. And me, sitting there with a book, legs crossed at the ankle . . . light footsteps down the hall, the sound of my mother humming before she comes into view . . .

I've got to stop this. This dreaming of possibilities that can never be.

I open my eyes, and the room is bare, the night visible through the slats of wood. And the footsteps are Cameron's hiking boots. "Hey," he says, "I was worried you got lost." He leans against the wooden beam at the entrance to this room, and there's nowhere to go but closer to him. Casey asked me to keep away, and it's the least I can do for her, but there's nowhere else to go. There's no other choice, and he's walking closer.

"This will work," he says, looking around the space, and I'm trying to see what he sees. What version of this house he's talking about.

"Work for what?" I ask.

"For tonight." He smiles, and he stands maybe three feet from me, keeping his voice low. "I know it's not completely protected or anything, but it's a shelter, and there's a computer nearby. Oh, and there's a ton of food in the minifridge back at the trailer, in case you missed it."

"I did," I say. "I missed it." Stuck in my daydream instead of reality.

"Yeah, I thought so. Where were you back there?" He taps the side of my head.

I shake the thought away. "Just imagining things. Got lost for a minute."

"Good things?" he asks.

I remember the voice I heard behind me, the deep voice from inside, and I fear he can see it all on my face. "Things that won't happen."

He tilts his head to the side. "I hope you're wrong," he says, but it's the word he uses, that he knows how unrealistic that is, too, but the room starts to shift on me, and I can see both at once. The empty room, the full one. Me at the center.

"Whoever lives here better realize how lucky they are," I say.

He shakes his head. "A house doesn't make people lucky."

"But the people in it," I say, "the people you live with."

He cringes and then gestures to me. "Some people never know their parents and wish they did." His lower jaw shifts. "But some people do know their parents and wish they didn't. No house in the world would've changed that," he says.

I wish, for a moment, that the world was simple and predictable. That a family meant safety and unconditional love, and all the things I read about in children's books.

This is my fear, too—the one I keep buried. That maybe the reason my mother does not speak out, does not fight, is because I no longer matter to her. That I am but a distant memory that resurfaces when she hears a crying baby, or reads an article in the paper, or realizes it's my birthday. That when she said I could visit her in my dreams, in that song, that was her way of saying: *nowhere else.* That maybe she is scared of me, too.

"Do I scare you?" I ask.

"No. You surprise me, Alina," he says, pulling me toward him effortlessly.

And that's the change I was sensing in the air, not the scent of something burning, but this. One moment I'm sinking, and then I'm floating. Like being in the ocean with him.

But I put my hands on his chest and push back. "I promised Casey," I say. And then, when he frowns, "She's your sister." That must count for something.

"She *is* my sister," he says, but he's not backing away. "Not my dad, not my mom, and not in charge of me." And then he adds, "Or you."

He is the spell. He's the spell, not me, and I need to break it. "It's not the time," I say, repeating Casey's words, because they make sense, they have logic and a purpose.

He looks around the empty house, and I know he's seeing a thing none of us will ever have. Not anymore. He leans his forehead against mine. "I'm scared," he whispers, "that this is the *only* time."

I hear Casey in the distance, the door to the trailer, and I know she's coming.

Cameron presses his lips quickly to my forehead.

I feel him slipping away, feel time doing the same.

"I hope it's not," I say.

Imagination is not the same as a memory, and hope is not the same as reality, but still, I am filled with hope for everyone in that moment. For my mother and father, for Cameron and Casey, for June's soul, and I guess for my own, too. I hope there's something more than what we were and what we've been. I hope that life surprises me.

So I change my mind and pull him toward me, and I'm the one to kiss him this time. I do it even though I hear Casey's feet just outside, and even though it's reckless and this isn't the time. I do it because I realize that life *did* surprise me, and it comes in the form of the guy in a ridiculous-looking basketball uniform in a half-built house. And it comes in the form of the girl walking down the hall, too. And it comes in the form of me, standing on my toes to reach him, and this moment I can steal, even here, even now.

chapter 20

I'VE PULLED BACK FROM Cameron, but the moment must still be obvious on both our faces because Casey dumps a bag of food on the floor in the entrance to the room, drops her bag beside it, and says, "Wow, I'm so glad I just spent the last twenty minutes finding food for everyone and getting directions and checking the news. So glad to know you were doing something useful."

He ignores her but grabs a can of soda and takes a bite out of a bagel that he's found in a brown paper bag. Casey is staring at me, obviously trying to catch my eye, but I keep my gaze focused on the food while I rifle through and decide what to eat. How can I explain to her that I don't have hope that there will be a right time, but that I want to? That I'm trying to create it out of absolutely nothing? That every choice is a betrayal to one side or the other?

I sit back against a wooden beam, next to Cameron, and I take a bite out of a slightly stale bagel.

A beam of light cuts through the night, and I drop the food, heart racing, ready to run. "Headlights," Cameron says. We're hidden, but only partly. I press myself, stomach first, against the floor, and hear them doing the same. The car engine idles near the end of the road, the headlights still breaking up the dark.

"What are they doing?" Casey asks. But the beams shift as the wheels move over the gravel, driving away.

We wait in silence, flat against the floor, for a good ten minutes before rising. "Probably just someone checking out the home sites," Cameron says. But he doesn't look at us when he says it. And neither of us responds.

We eat in silence, and then we rest against the wooden beams in silence. When at least another hour has passed since the car turned down this road, Cameron dusts his shorts off and says, "If anything happens while I'm gone, head down the road toward the highway, and I'll find you."

"While you're *gone*?" Casey asks, and my food is stuck somewhere halfway down my esophagus.

"I need to get us a car," he says.

"We'll all go. What would've happened at the school if you weren't back in time? If that car didn't leave? No. No way. We'll stay hidden while you get it," Casey says.

"Seriously, it's a lot easier for one person to sneak around a neighborhood than three people."

"And what if you get caught?" I ask. "What then? There's nobody to help you."

"I won't get caught," he says.

I'm on my feet now. "How can you say—"

"Have a little faith, Alina," he says, but he smiles when he says it. "I'm good at what I do, remember?"

But he cannot possibly know all the different potential outcomes. What might happen between now and then. He cannot promise that he'll be okay. Oh, God, he has to be okay.

Casey has her arms folded across her chest, blocking the exit, which is ridiculous because he can just as easily slip between the wooden beams all around us. "Casey, I'll be okay. I'm coming back."

She nods, like she's trying not to cry.

He turns to me, puts my face in his hands. "I'm coming back," he says to me, too. And I feel it, those words, a promise down to my soul.

Casey gives me her best attempt at the cold shoulder, but it's obviously not something she does a lot, because she could use some more practice. She's cleaning up the wrappers and cans, and I'm helping her carry the leftover food back to the trailer when I say, "I do care about him."

"Right," she says.

"I do, Casey, and I'm not asking you to understand, but I want you to know that it's true. I won't turn on him, won't turn him in, nothing. If I'm taken, I won't tell them anything." She keeps walking, pushing the door open with her hip. "For you, either," I say.

"You expect me to trust you after you held me hostage? After I asked you to stay away from Cameron and you didn't?"

"I don't expect you to, just like I don't expect you to understand—"

She laughs, and it sounds cold and mean. "You're just a kid, Alina. A kid who doesn't think about anything but herself. A kid with absolutely no responsibility, who hasn't had to make tough decisions . . ."

She dumps everything into the trash container outside the trailer and folds her arms across her chest.

"I went!" I say. "That was a choice. You think that was so easy? To leave everything I've ever known?" The way I ache for the island, sometimes I think it's a sickness, but other times I think it's the most natural thing in the world. It belonged to me, I belonged to it—I knew my place there. I was treated kindly, if distantly. I was cared for, though not cared about. I had safety there. I could've stayed another year, rolled the dice to see what eighteen got me. I could've waited it out and crossed my fingers, but I didn't. I took the risk, with people I didn't know, with a plan I didn't understand. I took a leap.

I'm shaking as I stand before Casey, and I don't understand why.

"I'm sorry," she says. "I'm scared, and I'm taking it out on you."

She takes me in her arms then. We're about the same size, and my arms hook all the way around her back, and hers around mine. And this time, I don't flinch.

"Casey," I say, when my chin is on her shoulder. "I think it's time to tell me what you're after. When we get there, I can't help unless I know."

I feel her body stiffen, but she doesn't pull away.

"My sister," she says. Her chin is still resting on my shoulder, and her breath brushes my ear as she speaks.

There's nothing we will find in the database that will make her happy. Nothing. "She won't be the same person," I say.

Casey pulls back, her chin off my shoulder, her hands off my back. But she's still so close—I can see my reflection in her eyes. "No, you don't get it. Before she disappeared, she got a message. I was home over break, and it was accidentally given to me—the curse of being a twin. A man hand-delivered it, and the only thing he said was, 'What a lovely soul you are,' which I really didn't think anything about at the time. Inside was some website address with a really long password . . . I gave it to her, thinking it was for school or something. That's when everything changed."

"She disappeared?"

"Not at first, but she started acting different—not sleeping, constantly on edge. I confronted her, but she wouldn't say anything. Just blew me off. I went back to school, because it was *so important* to me at the time, you know? *Then* she disappeared."

"What does this have to do with me?"

"The message. I couldn't find the paper again, and Ava's computer went to sites that just . . . didn't exist anymore. Someone went through a lot of trouble to set that up. And the message. About the soul. Don't you see? June blackmailed—"

"Allegedly," I mumble, thinking of her message on that recorder.

"Whatever," Casey says. "Someone sent Ava that note, and then she disappeared. I thought you were in the database again. I thought you were blackmailing her for something. I wanted to find out what Ava saw. So first I went after security where you're held, thinking you'd still managed to get through it. But it was obvious you weren't doing anything—nothing was sent from your location. But that's how Dominic found me. I guess he watched what I was up to after that, too—how I started going after the database. He tracked me down and sent me a note. Told me I wasn't so good at covering my tracks. Asked me what, exactly, I was after. So, yeah, Dominic kind of forced my hand, but I want in that database to see what happened to Ava. Which is what Cameron doesn't understand. And I need . . . I need to prove she's not in there again. Not reborn. Because if she hasn't been reborn, she hasn't died, just disappeared."

It's like proving the negative. "And what will that prove? What if she just doesn't want to be found?" I ask.

"Alina, seriously? Cameron is wanted for questioning in her alleged death."

And the bottom falls out of my world.

"He wouldn't," I say.

"I know that. But the evidence is . . . unfortunate. They were out with friends, and they left in a car together, and he's the last person who saw her. They got in a fight, she was scared of something, he said. Jumpy and taking it out on him. Everyone saw them fighting. There's evidence of blood in the car, but come on, that could've come from any time. Doesn't matter, though, it all adds up to a case against Cameron. She had a lot of money in her bank account, which I guess would've gone partly to Cameron eventually . . . I seriously have no idea where that money came from. And there's the problem of his past criminal record."

"He's not a killer," I say. And now I want in the database to prove it for him. This. This is something I can give him. "Someone's still in the database," I say.

"Yes," she says. "Either there really is a shadow-database somewhere that someone still has access to, or someone else has hacked it."

That letter to Ava came from somewhere, and it wasn't me. And if it's not me now, there's the possibility that it wasn't June back then, either.

June was in that database, that's a fact. She released the information, that's a fact. But there's something more going on, and the proof—for all of us—is inside.

Casey and I return to our skeleton house and sit across the room from each other, our backs against the wooden beams.

How long have we been waiting for Cameron? He hasn't come back yet. And the possibility creeps in that maybe he won't.

I don't know. June left Liam. Just left him there to take the fall, and she supposedly loved him.

Casey must see something in my face. "He's coming back," she says.

The wait is as endless as the ocean. Where everything falls away but the voice I long to hear, whispering through my head. Only this time, it's not my mother, or even Genevieve, singing a song. It's Cameron, laughing. Telling me that I'm a surprise.

It's long past midnight, and we haven't slept. It's probably halfway to dawn. Neither of us has spoken, because then we'd have to acknowledge that he's not back yet, and maybe something happened, and then what will we do? Neither of us wants to think it, and so we do not speak.

Casey hears it first. It's completely dark, no lights anywhere nearby, and we should probably be trying to sleep, but we're listening for everything, for anything. She turns onto her hands and knees, crouched low, face pressed between wooden beams, and then I hear the slow sound of tires over gravel. Casey has one foot pressed onto the ground, as if she's at the starting line of a race, waiting for the sound of the gun. And I understand. If this is not Cameron, we run. Run for the highway, and he will find us.

If he's okay.

There are no headlights. But a dark van turns the corner and pulls directly in front of this house, the engine still idling. There are no windows in the back, and the ones up front are still dark. A window rolls down, and I hold my breath. "Is there some secret code word?" Cameron calls.

I'm smiling so big as Casey and I run for the back doors and pull them open. The overhead light turns on, and I see that the van is a dark shade of blue, and inside, there are old blankets and no seats and it smells like smoke in here, too. Like something burning, something changing.

Casey smacks him lightly on the arm from the back of the van. "Took you long enough."

He grins at her, then catches my eye in the rearview mirror, and says, "Told you."

The windows up front are tinted. And I think, *He has found us the perfect car, because he is perfect.* And I wonder if people do this all the time: fall for people because of their ability to pick getaway cars; or fall for people because of the way they look when they think nobody is watching; or fall for people because of the things they say, or the way they look at them, or the things they give up, or the things they cannot do.

I thought it was because of hair and eyes and a sense of humor, or similar personalities and common interests—but it's not. It's the ability to pick getaway cars. To weigh crimes. To take the risk on someone again, even when he's been betrayed once before. To have faith in himself and in me. To see me.

He pulls a knit hat down over his ears, his hair curling out the bottom, and he turns to us for a second as he shifts the van into gear. "Full tank. Tinted windows. No complaining."

"Good job, little brother," Casey says.

He looks at me, to check my reaction, and I say, "Blue is my favorite color."

He smiles.

I smile.

We are not even faking it.

Cameron pauses at the end of the road. "Which way?" he

asks, but I know what he's really asking. Are we going to disappear? Or are we going to take the risk and track down this lead?

Casey is silent, which means that for some reason they're waiting for me. "If someone's in the database, and that someone isn't me," I say, "then maybe it wasn't June back then, either."

Casey stares at Cameron. "I told her about Ava," she says, and he nods.

I pause, thinking of how to put into words what I'm just barely understanding. "The study. I think it's wrong."

"What study? What are you talking about?" Casey asks.

"The big one. The only one that matters! The one June and Liam used. I think, once June got into the database, she saw something. Something that didn't match. The souls are tagged, but I don't know how they're tagged." I close my eyes, because I know what I'm about to sound like. "I need to get into the database. I need to prove it."

"That's . . . that's something bigger than us. That's huge."

It's bigger than us, but it's everything. It's the force behind all of this. "I can clear June's name," I say. And then I think, *And yours. And mine.*

"Okay," Cameron says. "Okay. We keep going."

Dawn is approaching when we make it back onto the highway, me and Casey in the back, no seat belts and viewless, Cameron up front, hoping the tinted windows do their job. I get nauseated, but I don't get sick. Maybe I'm getting used to it. Maybe motion is just another thing I was deprived of, that I wasn't accustomed to, and now I'm part of this world, always moving.

Casey hands him the directions. "We should get there before noon," she says.

"Oh, there's food under the gray blanket," he says, and I pull it back to find *real* food. Fruit in a plastic container and packets of sliced cheese and bottles of water.

"Clothes!" Casey says, grabbing the stash from beside the food. She pulls out two T-shirts and shorts that probably won't fit right, but at least the shirts cover the uniform. Then I notice that Cameron has changed as well. Khaki shorts, a black T-shirt, like he could fit in anywhere.

"How did you get this?" I ask.

"You don't want to know," he says. And then I see the key dangling from the ignition, and I realize he must've broken into a home, taken their food, their clothes, and then their car. Maybe while they slept nearby. I feel a twinge of regret, but I still can't think of a better option.

Casey digs in while looking at some of the figures on the articles. "Was Ava good at computers, too?" I ask.

The van is silent, except for the periodic grooves in the highway that we drive over. Eventually Casey says, "She wasn't *bad* at computers, but it wasn't really her thing. She'd help me if I asked, but she didn't love it. Not enough to get to my level." She smiles at me. "People were always surprised by that—that just because we're twins doesn't mean we like the same thing. We're not the same person."

"Not the same soul," I add.

"Art," Cameron says. "She likes art." His face changes as he thinks about it. "You should've seen what she managed to do to the side of our old school with just a few bottles of spray paint," he says with pride.

"So," I say, "she was more like you?"

"Ouch," says Casey.

My face burns, because I didn't mean it as an insult. "I just meant . . ."

"I know what you meant. Yes, Alina. Same friends. Same neighborhood. I don't even have a reason for doing the things I did, I really don't."

"Like you ever had a choice," Casey says. "Come on, your friends practically roped you into it. Guilt by association. You never stood a chance. If I lived there full time, I'd be right there with you both."

Cameron grimaces. "Nah, I doubt it. The thing is, it was just . . . effortless. It's so easy to take the path of least resistance," he says. "To be exactly who people think you are. To not fight it." He looks at me then, and says, "And then you're so deep in it, you figure, this is who I am. And then your girlfriend strikes a deal to save her own ass," he mumbles.

"Ella?" I ask, and he nods, just the slightest. Then I imagine him with a girlfriend, and I don't like the way it makes my stomach churn, and I realize I am jealous of even that. *Nice, Alina.*

"And then," he says, "because seventeen is considered an adult, and it's on your record, your name is worthless."

And maybe you are, too. I can imagine him thinking it, believing it. But he is not.

"It's just a name," I say, knowing Casey can make us new identities with time, and maybe money. Not that I'd be able to show my face now. Not that any of us could now. But he could have. Before.

"Do *you* want to pick a new one?" he asks, one eyebrow raised.

Alina Chase. It comes with a lifetime full of baggage. And yet, here's the thing: I do not.

Some people believe in karma—that what you do in one life affects the next. But it's too hard to study, to quantify. Too many variables. What makes one life better than another? Nobody really agrees. Maybe I was terrible in a past life, and that's why I'm stuck in a prison this time around. But then I look at the people sharing this journey with me and I think, *How lucky I am.* Does hope count for something?

Maybe there will be a consequence for my choices in the next life. But right now, this is the only one that matters.

I know we're close when we begin stopping more frequently, turning every few minutes. We've moved from the highway into a city, the horns blaring as soon as the lights turn from red to green. I've been reading the science articles again, after Casey looked at them sideways, upside down, and backward. "The only thing in common is her name," she says. Ivory Street. She's the only thing that stands out.

I think of June's math, and these papers, and the math in these papers. The formulas are similar. The answers are different.

"Stop," I say.

Cameron stops. In the middle of the street. A car honks and weaves around us.

"Go," I say. "Sorry. Just listen. June died. She knew she was going to die. She was scared of it. We need to remember that."

The mood changes inside the van as we remember. We're running not only from the people who would punish us but from those who would stop us.

"It's the three of us," Cameron says, and I'm not sure what he means. "That's it. That's the only people we trust. The three of us."

I don't know what to do with the fact that I'm included in this. What have I done to earn it? I'm not sure. But now that I have his trust, I don't want to break it. I want to use it for something right. I want to save us all.

We park in front of a long building, curving in on itself in something between a *U* and a straight line, three stories high, with an artificial green area in the middle. There's a fountain beside the sign.

"Here's what I could dig up on Ivory Street," Casey says. "Her lab received several grants based on proposals from the NSF—a government-run agency that funds proposed projects—and those papers are the result of that research. She published a lot of papers over a span of five years, and then it mostly stopped. There was an announcement about her stepping down from her position about eighteen years ago, which fits in with the time frame—that June managed to break her somehow. Her picture shows up at a lot of political fund-raisers, but she disappears from science journals until this recent one—as the contact for the grant foundation."

"So what's she doing here?"

"She's got an office here, as part of the grant decision-making process. But she doesn't conduct her own research anymore."

"So this is a government agency?" Cameron asks, shrinking in his seat. "No way we're getting close. No way."

"No, we call and lure her out," Casey says.

"With what phone?" I ask.

"Any phone," Cameron whispers, and I know this is yet another crime that will be added to our list. I think how hard it is to disappear with no money: no car, no food, no phone, no place to sleep.

Where the hell did June keep that money? What happened to it? We could use it. We really could. How else are we going to disappear?

And then I think how easy it is to disappear with no money. It's doable. We've been doing it. We've made it this far. It doesn't take money to cease to exist. The world is big. We just need to leave.

One more day, I think. I hope. We meet Ivory Street, we figure out how to access the information in the database, we see what June knew, and we find what Ava saw. After that, we can leave. I have to hope that will be enough.

But right now, we need to borrow a phone.

Cameron looks for a phone in a crowded park nearby. Kids are on swings, with fathers or mothers pushing them, and I picture my own. I wonder if she imagined doing this when I was growing inside her. If she pictured what I would look like, what I would sound like—my high-pitched squeal as I tipped my head back toward the sun at the apex of the swing's arc. It's a thought that suddenly feels like a memory. Her laughter a shadow of my own. And I am overcome with a wave of grief that the memory isn't real. That it doesn't exist.

Cameron's hand slides into a purse left abandoned on a bench. He doesn't take the wallet. Just the phone. Casey and I watch from the van. I look at Casey, but she's staring at the same scene, seeing something in her own memory. "What?" I ask.

"When we were little," she whispers, "we had a park in our neighborhood. And Cameron couldn't pump yet. Me and Ava used to take turns pushing him, because he used to bitch and complain until we did. I pushed him so hard once, he fell off the swing and dislocated his elbow. I was going to get in so much trouble."

"I can imagine," I say. Cameron heads back toward us. There's a man in uniform at the other end of the park, and my heart beats wildly. But Cameron is perfect. He pretends not to notice. Not to care.

"We were all kind of terrified of our father, not that he ever did anything to make us fear him. He was mostly all talk, but the *talk* . . . ," she says. "Anyway, he said he fell off by himself. I don't know why. He was just a kid. We were all just kids.

Even then he was protecting me, when it should've been the other way around."

Cameron opens the door just then and hands the borrowed phone to Casey as he climbs in beside us. "Did you see the cop?" I ask.

"Yeah, I saw," he says.

Casey dials information, asks to be connected to the NSF headquarters, and after a moment, she speaks into the receiver. "Ivory Street's extension, please," she says in a very official and bossy tone of voice.

Her face lights up when someone who must be Ivory Street picks up the line. "There's been a break-in at your residence," she says. "Someone out walking their dog called it in. We'll need you to see what's missing in order to make a statement." A pause. "Sure. 555-4439." Then she hangs up.

"Is that the phone number?" I ask.

"I have no idea."

We watch the front double doors beside the fountain and the sign, and a few people trickle out, but they are too young, or too old, to be her. Casey has the printout of her photo spread between us. And then we see her. A woman in her mid-fifties, a blouse tucked into a narrow skirt that hits below her knees, moving quickly and deliberately toward a black car across the street.

"Bingo," Cameron says. He climbs into the front seat, tosses the phone out the window in the general direction of the park, and eases into traffic behind one Ivory Street.

chapter 21

WE FOLLOW IVORY'S BLACK, expensive-looking car through all of downtown. Eventually, we hit a tunnel, and we're going to have to pay a toll. Or not pay a toll, as it were. "Get down," Cameron says, because there are cameras, and we're going to be reported for failing to pay a toll, and they're going to see our faces, along with the license plates. He lowers his head, but he's probably captured. They will be able to trace our route, in reverse, like I am tracing June's. But we also know, at this point, we're so close.

We just have to stay a day ahead. We are almost there, I can taste it. I know they can feel it, too, with the way we're not talking, but the air seems almost charged, and I can feel it humming against my skin.

We don't even listen to the radio at first, but then Cameron says we need to, to make sure there's not something we're missing. And so we do. We listen to other people talk about us. Casey shrinks into herself when she hears her name—I guess she's not used to hearing others report on her, make things up, twist her life into a two-dimensional, ten-second sound bite.

These are the things being reported: three teens, last spotted in a school, taking shelter. Eating from the vending machine, using the school computers. Last seen wearing school uniforms.

These are the things left behind: evidence of June's crimes. Evidence that I'm looking to repeat them, or complete them.

This is the trail they're on: the first car, reported missing from around the school. They have not found where we ditched it. They have not pinned us to the second, to this perfect van. But it won't be long. They will find the first missing car abandoned somewhere, they will look for the second, and they will see us in the tunnel. They will know our general direction. I don't know whether they've seen the printouts, whether they know we've gone to see Ivory Street.

We have to stay a step ahead.

Casey and I rise back up after we're through the tunnel. Ivory Street is driving recklessly, in a hurry, and my guess is she's not checking her rearview mirror that often. If she were, I'd imagine she could see the blue van, still behind her, turning off the highway, down the ramp, left at the light, into the more residential areas. She'd see us just a block behind her as she turns into a subdivision with a waterfall at the front, and ancient, gorgeous trees that seem to belie the age of the homes. She'd see us follow her to the end of the road, see us stop at the corner as she continued into the cul-de-sac and pulled into the driveway of the first house on the right. She'd see us before

Cameron puts the car in reverse and parks at the edge of a perfectly manicured lawn in front of a house that we aren't here to visit.

Cameron turns off the car, cracks the front window, and climbs across the console into the windowless back with us. Casey is tying and retying her shoes, and Cameron sits extra close to her, taking a deep breath.

"We're here," he says.

His legs are bent, and he looks too young for this. I imagine we all do. "Ready?" he asks. And I laugh, because none of us look ready. None of us look as if we want to leave the back of this van ever again. They both looked so self-confident when we were on the island, so sure of themselves. But then I remember the way Casey's hand trembled as she placed the dish on the table, how the muscles in Cameron's arm twitched as he gripped the edge of the doorway. And the way I contorted my face to look calm and brave, when inside I was full of fear and panic.

We were all faking.

And now, we are letting each other see.

We're all scared. We've made it, and we're about to come face to face with some sort of truth. And nothing I do will change that truth. Whatever June was leading me toward, we're here. And now I don't want to know what she wanted with Ivory Street. Whether she bribed or tricked or bullied her into giving her access to the database. Whether she offered something in return. Whether Ivory Street was a willing participant.

Or if Ivory can give me the answers I want: Who else was in the database? And if June found out there was a mistake in the study, did she have the chance to tell her?

We hear a car rumble down the street, pausing for a moment nearby—I hold my breath and count to four before it continues on its way.

I can sit here all day and think about these questions, or I can get the answers. "I'm ready," I say.

Cameron smiles at me, climbs back into the front, and motions for us to do the same. "Let's go," he says.

I'm already in the front seat beside him, but Casey hasn't moved. "It's way too light out," she says.

Cameron looks over his shoulder. "There's a reason why most break-ins happen in the middle of the day. Everyone's at work, or camp, or daycare. Just act like you belong."

"This car does *not* belong," Casey says, and she's right. The car was perfect for blending in on the highway, or off, in the mountains. Perfect and nondescript for the congested streets of the city. But it's not even close to perfect for an upscale community with high-end everything. The yards are manicured to perfection. The homes rise up behind them in varying patterns of brick and stone. Anyone can see this van does not belong.

"So we're painting, or doing maintenance," Cameron says.

"We should wait," Casey says.

"Wait for someone to find us?" Cameron asks.

But I understand Casey. She sees it, too. We're here. The truth will be unchangeable. We can never go back to not knowing.

But right now, my sympathy will be useless to her. "We're wasting time," I say. Ivory Street will quickly realize that nobody has been in her house, that nothing is missing, that something is amiss. "We either do this now," I say, and I fix my eyes on Casey, "or we do this never."

I reach my hand back for her, and she shuffles toward the front. The three of us are crammed together in the front seat, Casey running her fingers through her tangled hair as she checks the mirror. I'm too scared to check to see what I look like at the moment.

"Let's go," Cameron says, and he exits the driver's side while Casey and I slide out of the passenger side.

We leave the car in front of that house, where it doesn't belong but might just pass, and we follow Cameron.

At least we're out of our uniforms. Now we look like door-to-door salespeople. Maybe we would have better luck carrying cookies.

Cameron quickly slips between the yards of the nearest houses and walks straight to the backyards, like we have every right to be here. We walk along the outside edge of the back fences, and Cameron makes sure to stand tall and walk with purpose, so we do the same. *Just here to check the gas meter. Just assessing the drainage in the backyard. Just visiting a friend.* I can see how people manage to break in to homes in the daytime. Act like you belong, and people believe it. We quickly reach the backyards of the homes in the cul-de-sac, and then we're standing with our backs against the brick wall of her backyard. We sneak around the side—my God, her house is gorgeous. I don't know if others live here, but there's more than enough room. It's been landscaped and there are fancy-looking window treatments visible through the glass. This whole neighborhood looks too formal, too perfect, too planned.

Her backyard has a black metal gate in the center of the brick wall, like the house we first stayed in after I escaped. There's no easy access—nothing that won't push us into full view—so it forces us to the front, and that seems right. We're standing in broad daylight, a few feet from the person we need. We're forced out into the light as we try to uncover the truth. We can't get one without the other.

I want to gain the upper hand, though. I want to know who she is before we face her. And so I crouch down inside her fancy landscaping and watch as Casey and Cameron do the same. There's really nothing we could do to talk our way out of this situation. If someone across the street sees us—three teenagers, hiding in the bushes—we're so screwed. If they find us now, and if they manage to catch us, I don't know what will happen to me. I assume I will not go back to an island—that's not a punishment, that's a containment. This time, I'm sure, I will be punished.

Jail, like my mother. Like my father. A cage with no window past the tree with the perfect angle to the sky. Land that I am not free to roam but that is scheduled as part of my daily routine. No comforts, no computer, no people taking care of my needs. I feel like my heart is being squeezed into a vise, and for a moment, I cannot take in air. And I understand June running when Liam was captured. I do. I don't want to be taken in. My soul was not meant to be in a cage. Not then, and not now.

But then Cameron puts a hand on my back and whispers, "You okay?"

I nod. I am closest to the window, and I motion toward it, because I hear movement.

We must be outside the kitchen, because I hear cabinets banging open and closed. I ease onto my knees, my hands pushing off the mulch and soil, and I rise up until I can peer, just slightly, over the ledge into her home. But it's not a kitchen. It's an office, and the slamming of doors are filing cabinets and desk drawers. Ivory stands facing the open doorway, her back to the grand oak desk and to us. She is assessing things, and she must be confused. She has a paper in her hand, and she picks up the phone—it must be the number Casey left her, because she hangs up after a few moments, looking perplexed.

She takes the phone with her as she leaves the room, and I sink back into the soil behind the bushes. "What now?" Casey asks. And the truth is, I have no idea. I don't want to walk in to this blind, but we can't stay here all day, either.

I hear her voice again, coming closer, but I keep below the window. ". . . not a coincidence. Alina Chase escapes and then someone calls claiming my house was broken into? I'm not being paranoid."

There's a pause, while I guess the person on the other end is talking, but I can hear her as her fingers fly across the keyboard. "I know it makes no sense," she says, "I have no clue why she'd call my office—" The typing stops. And then a string of expletives fly from Ivory's mouth. She laughs, but it's short and cold. "She didn't know where I lived," she says. And she laughs again. "I have to go. You better come. She's here."

My arms, my legs, the back of my neck are covered in a rush of goose bumps. She's talking about me, and she knows. She's told someone else. I have no cards left, except the present. Except the words I have inside me. I have no time to discuss this with Casey and Cameron, but I know they've heard as well. I stand up, in view of the window, even though Cameron grabs my arm, trying to pull me back down.

"Trust me," I ask him, even though I'm not sure what I'm asking him to trust me to do. To get us through this, I guess. God, I don't know if I can do that, either. I'm not only fighting for myself right now, not just for my own freedom, but for theirs. Because if people are coming, they're coming for all of us.

He lets go as I walk up the steps to the front door. They're watching me from the corner of the house, but I don't let on that there's anyone else. Just me.

I ring the bell, and Ivory Street opens the door like she was expecting me. Her eyes behind her wire-rimmed glasses are the deepest shade of blue, and her hair is dyed a shade of red just this side of copper—but her roots show a mousy brown. There's a fine map of lines around her eyes and mouth, and for a second I think she doesn't recognize me. Then she steps back, gestures inside, and says, "I can't believe she actually did it." But then she smiles, and it's all ice, as the door shuts behind me. The lines around her eyes and mouth deepen, and, at the sound of the latch catching, so does my fear. "You are one driven soul, child."

chapter 22

THERE'S A LONG TABLE along the entryway wall—lamps and a phone and mail stacked neatly. An old wedding photo, in a silver frame, with the engraving: *Ivory & Edmond.*

Edmond.

She sees me looking. "I assume it was you who called me in my office?"

I nod, but I don't speak, just in case it triggers a memory of the phone call and the fact that Casey's voice is not my own. I also need to figure out what's happening. I need to weigh her words, her actions, before using my own.

This is what I'm good at. I'm so good at it.

"You must be exhausted," she says. "Thirsty?"

I nod. I need a moment to take her in, figure her out. So, it seems, does she, because she sways into the kitchen, as if this is a normal house visit and I'm nothing but a long-lost friend. There are no windows here—just cabinets going round and round the room, and a long island in the middle. The light comes down through skylights above us. Behind me is a door, slightly ajar, and I can just make out the top of a wooden staircase leading into the darkness. There's a deadbolt on the outside, and I'm imagining all the thousands of things that one might keep in there. I strain to listen for the hum of computers, but I can make out nothing behind the walls. I wonder if that could hold the shadow-database. The wonder starts to veer to hope, and I pull myself out of the daydream.

She takes a glass out of a tall, dark cabinet and holds it under the water dispenser, handing it to me after. I watch her as I drink, then place it on the dark granite counter, and the noise breaks the trance.

"Tell me, my dear, how did she do it? The whole world wants to know. How did June get you to me?"

I pick up the glass again and drink the entire thing, letting her questions, and the silence, linger in the air.

"On second thought," she says, "I think I'll have a drink as well." She walks to the refrigerator and speaks as her glass fills with water. "That was quite the escape," she says. She turns around, assessing me slowly from bottom to top and back again. I feel too small in these clothes that don't fit, too exposed in this room with no windows. "I think even June would be impressed."

"I think so, too," I say.

I put the glass back on the counter, but it shakes as it settles, and she grins, walking closer. "Is she like a ghost for you, too? She is for me. Sometimes, just as I'm waking, I swear I can hear her."

We were right. She knew June. She saw her. Heard her voice. My heart beats twice as fast, imagining June standing before her, just as I am.

Ivory places her glass beside mine on the counter and gestures to the corner of the room, where nobody stands. "I'll be cooking here alone, just me and an empty room, and then . . . poof. Sometimes I see her here, standing in the corner of my kitchen . . . Can she be both your ghost and mine? Can she be in both places at once?" She shrugs. "Or maybe I'm just getting old." She takes her glasses off, makes a show of wiping the lenses slowly with the edge of her shirt. Buying time. Buying seconds, minutes, because someone's coming. But I have to wait. I don't want her to know that June didn't leave this for me, she made me work for it. She left herself for me, and the path she was taking, and I followed her footsteps here, learning less about her than I am about myself. I still don't know what this woman has to do with the database.

"Did you come for the money, sweetheart? I do suppose you're owed it."

Money? What money?

"It will take me some time to get it for you, dear. How much do you need? I assume it's a lot. I assume you want to disappear. I assume you need enough to live on. I can do that for you, sure."

Something isn't right. It's not as we thought—this woman wasn't broken by June. She wasn't used by her. She *did* something. This woman is toying with me as if I haven't spent years studying people. She doesn't know who I am at all. I don't know her either. But I'm learning.

June didn't break this woman. This woman broke June.

And now I'm walking the same path, with the same strengths—the same strengths she can flip around and use to hurt me.

I look to that corner, to the door with the dark stairwell stretching behind, and Ivory smiles. "It's a wine cellar, dear. No dead bodies, I promise."

Still, it makes me nervous.

"The money would be nice," I say noncommittally.

"*Nice*," she says, her hands stilling. "What is it that you want exactly, Alina? What brings you to my doorstep now? I'm not sure what you think I can do for you at this point, other than the money."

This is what I want to know: Why did June lead me here? "Who did you just call?" I ask.

"Ah. Eavesdropping, were we?"

This is a dance. A tightrope. And I have spent years on it.

Actions here will mean nothing. Words, everything.

I think June was trying to find Ivory Street, too—but after. After she got into the database with Liam, after she realized something didn't add up. After they released the names, after Liam died and she spent over a year holed up underground with nothing to do but think. I believe she wanted to ask Ivory Street. To see if there was a mistake with the study. Though if there was, if June used this study that was so wrong, then *she* was so wrong, acting on that information. I wonder what she would've done, if she realized that.

"I've read your papers," I say. "Fascinating stuff, really. I couldn't follow it as well as June. She was much better at that stuff."

"Is that so," she says.

"You know what?" I say, switching gears, "I do want the money. How much would you say seventeen years is worth?"

She pauses like she's mentally calculating the answer. Then she nods. "That's a lifetime, isn't it? For me, it's just a sliver of one. But for you, that's everything, isn't it? A lifetime, then. I can get you one more." As if lifetimes can be bartered and weighed and assigned a value.

"I assume you'll need your computer for this. Office?" I point my thumb in the direction that I watched through the front window, and I know I have unnerved her by the look on her face. Let her think I've been in here before. Let her think June gave me more information than I truly have.

I follow her into the office. Her stride doesn't falter, but she's slow and deliberate. A second here. Another there. Seconds adding to minutes becoming stretches of time. Someone is coming. She's counting on it.

She logs onto her computer but stops. "We'll have to go to a bank," she says. "It's not like you have a bank account."

"You're wrong," I say. "I have an account." Well, Casey has an account. She's got something set up under a false ID, and I realize there's no way one person gets through this alone. June couldn't. She didn't. But maybe—with Casey, with Cameron—maybe I have a chance.

"How resourceful of you," she says, cutting her eyes to me for a second. Her hands pause over the keys. "Tell me, is Dominic Ellis helping you?"

I try to keep my face still, to keep her from seeing that she has unnerved me, too. Instead, I think of the information Ivory is giving me. She has just admitted that she knows who Liam White is in this life. She *knows*. Casey was right. She has a way to access information in the database. *She has a goddamn way in*.

I laugh—I can't control it from bubbling up and escaping. "No," I say. "Dominic would love to be here with me, but he's not."

"Of course he's not," she says, her hands falling momentarily under her desk. "By the time June showed up here, she'd left Liam White behind as well. He sacrificed himself, he really did, because he thought it was his fault. Can you imagine?"

She watches my face, but I keep it still, focusing on her arm, still under the table.

"No, I suppose you can't," she says. "Not quite capable of love, my dear? Throw them to the wolves to get ahead?"

There's movement at the window, and I smile.

I'm focusing on her arm, and not her words, so when she pulls it out from under the desk, I'm ready. A gun. She has a gun. And now I see Ivory for what she is—not just a name on the paper, not just someone who might've made a mistake with that study, but someone who did something on purpose.

And just as I'm seeing Ivory, I see June, standing exactly where I am, as she confronts Ivory about those studies. What did Ivory do when June asked about the data?

I put my hands in the air without her asking.

"Hey, Ivory, tell me. What are the chances of me committing violence? What did you learn from that study?"

She tips the gun to the side. "I think you know," she says, buying seconds again. She doesn't realize I've been buying them as well until they become minutes—until they become something solid and real.

"A likelihood of 0.8, or 0.32?" I ask. "Which is it, Ivory? And if I wasn't violent before, is that good news or bad news for you right now? Am I predictable?"

She scoffs. "You are so predictable. You showed up here, just like June threatened to. You demanded answers, like June. You showed up alone, with no one. You showed up thinking you had the power to do anything at all. But I'm the one with the gun right now, Alina. I'm the one with the power. Now back away, slowly, toward the door."

"No, I'm not alone," I say. I close my eyes, and I imagine Cameron at the window, with a gun pointed at Ivory's head. And it's in that moment—when all the seconds have added to minutes, and the minutes to this moment—that Casey waltzes into the office.

"Hey, Alina," she says, pretending not to notice that Ivory has a gun pointed at my chest.

She waves to the window, and I can't stop the warmth from spreading through me as I see him there: Cameron, behind the glass, the empty gun pointed at Ivory, just as I imagined him.

I smile. "I'm not June," I say.

Her hand falters as she glances quickly over her shoulder. "What do you think?" I ask. "Will I tell him to shoot?" I see her debating, and I wonder myself, if that gun was full, if it had been in my pocket instead of Casey's bag—what would I do? "Put down the gun, Ivory," I say. "We didn't come to hurt you. We came for answers."

She lowers her gun and moves away from the window. Casey walks across the room, lifts the window, and Cameron climbs inside, the empty gun still in his hand.

"Hi," I say.

"Hey," he says, smiling.

"Nice to meet you, Ivory Street," Casey says.

"Who are you?" Ivory asks.

"Casey," she says. "Don't you watch the news?"

I smile at her, but Ivory says, "That's not what I meant."

Ivory eyes the gun but gestures toward me all the same, speaking directly to Cameron. "This is a highly unstable person. You don't know what you're dealing with."

"She's not so bad, once you get to know her," Cameron says, and Casey laughs. God, I love them.

"We have a few questions," I say. "You answer, we go, the end. Got it?"

"I love how simple you assume this will be. Sure. Got it," Ivory says.

"I found June's notes," I say. "I saw her work. She realized there was a mistake."

Ivory is silent, then leans forward. "I'm sorry, was that a question?"

I hear June's voice, whispering into my ear.

224081 - Ivory Street - Edmond

June was sorting through human data. Important facts she was listing for herself as she figured things out. No part of this was a location. These are people. "Edmond is your husband?" I ask, and Ivory flinches.

She leans back in her chair, folds her hands on top of her desk, and says, "He *was*, many years ago. A brilliant PhD candidate, too, if you must know. And he was senselessly attacked while walking home from his lab late at night. He was killed by someone else who worked in the lab. Someone who was not right. So very not right. But nobody knew it, until it was too late."

She stands from her desk then, ignoring the gun. "You know who was the first person I looked for in that database? Not Edmond. His killer. And you know what I discovered? He spent twenty years in prison in his past life. For manslaughter. You don't need a science paper for me to explain that to you. Edmond's death was preventable."

"224081," I say. "Was that him?"

She tilts her head at me in acknowledgment. And I am in awe of June. Of what she uncovered. Of what she risked to come here, knowing what she knew.

June's math comes to my mind, the numbers across the page, so different from the study. The starred IDs, not matching up.

There was no mistake in the research papers. "You did it on purpose," I say. "You self-selected the data. You've done it on all these papers."

"Data," she flings her hand, "can be used however one sees fit to twist it. The truth can be anything. We are dealing with human beings here. There's no control for a human being. Way too many variables. It *could* be the truth. Evil is evil, Alina, there's really no other explanation."

"Do you really believe that?"

"Well, it doesn't really matter, does it? It matters what everyone else believes," she says. "But this much is true: 224081 was a killer in two lifetimes."

"What about the third?" I ask. "Has he died?"

"224081 owes me a lifetime," she says, as a chill runs down my spine. "And he's serving it now, in prison. Do you know what prisoners looking down a life in jail do? They die. They stop eating or find something to hang themselves with when the guards aren't looking. It's a twenty-four-hour job, keeping those people alive. Not letting their souls have a fresh start. But soul number 224081 is still living, still rotting. I've seen to that." She sighs, laughs to herself. "Sometimes I think I should've done a study on suicides. Maybe showing that their souls disappear. Some sort of incentive. Well, hindsight."

Casey and Cameron are shooting looks at each other and

at me, but I am riveted by Ivory Street. At the person she is, and the person June must've uncovered. Of what Ivory Street must've done to June.

Ivory fixes her eyes on me. "But look at you, dear. A lifetime contained and yet still you try. What a hopeful and beautiful thing you are. Waiting seven years after that failed escape. And still going on. Did you think she might come back for you? Is that what kept you going? I've spent a lifetime studying humans. I'm fascinated, really."

"Genevieve died. She wasn't coming back," I say.

The lines in Ivory's forehead deepen as she looks at me, tilting her head to one side. "No, not her. Your *mother*. Did you think she'd try again?"

"What? My mother had nothing to do with that."

She waves her hand. "Of course she did. Seems she lost her nerve a bit after Genevieve's death. Or maybe she was scared off by how it could've been you, dying in that van. I don't think she has it in her, dealing in lives. Being able to make those decisions isn't easy."

She has succeeded in unraveling me. Because now I'm picturing that bridge, rising up. And I'm wondering if we were supposed to go over the ledge, if that was the plan. If we were supposed to end in the water, if the material across my chest was not for the tracker, but to help me float. If there was someone waiting in the water for us, even then. How close we were, how close we were . . . And my mother, planning, biding her time, and waiting.

"I don't . . ." I don't understand, and I look to Cameron to ground me. He is circling closer to me, the gun still pointed at Ivory, like he knows I need him to. I want to linger in this new understanding, let it seep inside and fill me up.

"Alina," Cameron says, like he can sense me drifting away, letting Ivory Street distract me, disarm me. She could be lying. She deals in nothing but lies. *Focus, Alina. Focus.*

"June's warnings," I whisper, finding my voice again, "the names she released. There was never any real danger, was there? There was no indication those people would become violent. Lives were ruined, and it's *your* fault."

"Everyone starts with the best of intentions," she says. "Even June. Now let's not pretend she's innocent." Her name, even now, shoots straight to my heart. "Put down the gun, please," she says to Cameron. "You're making me nervous."

This room is making me nervous. And I'm trying to find a place for everything she's telling me in my mind, to make sense of it all, make it fit with my understanding of events. It's too much all at once—my mother, Ivory, Edmond, June. The past life and this one are both different than I thought they were. So much bigger, so much more.

"The saddest thing is," Ivory says, "the US justice system refused to do anything with the results of the study. Because we're a system built on action, not thought. Even after the study, can you imagine?"

But the study was a lie, anyway. She used only the data that supported her theory, and she acted as if that were the *only* data. And, for the first time, I'm so grateful for our justice system.

"But the study enabled us to get further grants, to perform

further research, and then, well, then the lovely June Calahan came into the picture. She and Liam hacked their way in— unbelievable, really—and they honestly believed. They truly were something else."

"*You* were the blackmailer," I say, as I understand what must've happened back then. June, releasing information. Everyone knew she was in the database. And Ivory, seeing the opportunity. Getting away with blackmail while using June's name.

Ivory shrugs. "Me, the people who work with me . . . I'm not the only one, dear. I'm just the beginning. Blackmail is the short game. It's not just money. If a person doesn't want that information released, we can get them to do near anything."

Ava, I think.

She walks toward us, even though Cameron is still holding the gun.

The clues weren't leading me to any shadow-database, they were leading me here. We're all here, looking for the database, looking for the next step, but this is as far as I'm meant to get. This is the end. This is it.

What June left me is not access to a database, it's the truth. It's the person who was blackmailing, the beginning of the conspiracy, the longest of the long games. A falsified study, the conclusion—that criminal history is passed on—used to blackmail those in power, or those with money. It's Ivory Street at the center. The money was never with June. The money was here. It's in her fancy car and the bricks of her house and the metal points of the fence. June was the scapegoat.

"Did Liam know, too? Or was it just June?" I ask.

"I assume they both knew *someone* was committing black-mail under June's name, though they didn't know *who*. They tried to deny it of course." I remember her voice on the recorder: *I did not blackmail or bribe. The truth will not die with me. It will still be here, waiting for me.* "But it wasn't until after Liam's death, when June was hidden away with nothing but time, when she apparently mined the database herself before we figured out how she was getting in. I guess it was too late. She copied the data she needed, the souls with criminal activity, and all the relevant variables, and replicated the study on her own . . ."

"All this for money? People's lives for money?"

"Oh, no, Alina. Not money. Though, to be fair, the money is nice. But control is better. At first, the study was a source for more funding, but it became so much more. Once June began speaking out, we decided we could do the same, attaching her name to it. But more importantly, we could wait. We could use what we knew to sway people, influence policy, public opin-ion. We could support certain people, get them into positions of power, and then use that information *later* to force them to act in our favor. The only thing greater than money is power. Who controls the country? Not the president, or Congress, or the people, even. They're all figureheads. Puppets. Chess pieces. It's the people in the shadows who determine what we see and how we see it. Who determines where funding goes, what bills go forward, how the media spins events? What gets reported, what gets covered up? Who decides what is *wrong* and what is *right*? Perception is *everything*."

I remain silent. I imagine June hearing this same thing and what she must've realized: that she ruined lives, yes, and she ruined them for nothing. She was warning people for nothing. She was wrong. I imagine the guilt in her stomach, the regret in her heart. *What next, June?*

"Who's in charge?" I ask. "Is it you? Are there others?"

She waves her arm. "It doesn't matter. There will always be someone. The name doesn't matter, it's the idea behind it. Ideas do not die, Alina."

"How do you get into the database?" Casey asks.

Ivory turns to look at her. "That I cannot do for you. I'm the one who controls the information, not the one who gets it. There's a protocol to it. That's not my part. I only had direct access during the studies."

"*You* can't," I say. "But someone can. Who is it?" I ask. *Where next, June?*

Ivory remains silent, staring down the empty barrel of Cameron's gun.

"We know you can get information. One thing, just one thing," Casey pleads.

"I told you I can't," she says. And then she smiles. "But I can take you to the one who can. I'll bring you to him. I'll trade you for it."

But Ivory deals in lives and lifetimes, and I don't want her anywhere near us. Not any of us. Casey's about to barter away everything we have. "Casey, want a drink? The kitchen is just down the hall," I say. I try to use the random eye-movement code that she does with her brother, but I probably come off looking deranged. But this woman broke June, and she would break us in a heartbeat, and I will not give her that chance.

"Okay," she says slowly, and they walk, single file, from the office into the kitchen.

Just in case, I sit at her computer, which she's already logged into, and perform a search for Ava London, but there's nothing here.

I pick up the phone and hit Redial and see the number on the display. Then I sit at her computer and type in the number in the search bar, and her contact list pulls up. *Mason Alonzo.*

Alonzo. The Alonzo-Carter Cybersecurity Center. Holy crap. The person she called. The person she works with.

I was right—it is easier to break a person than to break a code, but June wasn't the one who did it. Ivory did.

His information is listed below, the number highlighted beside his name, with an e-mail and a physical address.

Mason Alonzo is currently a professor of computer science at Elson University back in the city. The address is on campus. Looks like I'm about to see my first college as well.

I stand up, my nerves on edge.

I should cover my tracks.

I should empty Ivory's gun, sitting beside me on the desk.

I pick it up, and I point it at the computer, and, remembering what Cameron said about being able to get one shot off with nobody noticing, I fire. The computer makes a noise as the bullet hits metal, but the gun is silent, and this, I think, is the most dangerous type of weapon. I fire round after round, the smell of mechanical burning from the computer, sparks flying, wires sizzling.

And then I walk out to join them.

"Time to go," I say, and I point to the dark stairwell beside the kitchen.

"What are you doing?" Ivory's knuckles are white as she grips the counter. Cameron gestures toward the staircase. I walk ahead of them, down the first few steps, just to make sure. But it's just as Ivory said. A cellar full of wine. Dark and musty. Windowless and comfortless. Cold, but not deadly.

"Don't worry," I say, leading her inside. "Someone's coming for you, right? In the meantime, this is just a containment." I close the door, and she pushes back against it. But I'm stronger. I lean close to the door. "It's for your own protection," I say. And then I turn the deadbolt.

She's still pounding on the door, screaming through it, as we prepare to leave the kitchen, leave the house, leave this all behind.

"I can give you something no one else can," she calls. "It's the same offer I made June. Your freedom. I'm in a unique position to get you out of here. I pull a lot of strings."

It's a tempting offer. I have my answers, but I still can't see how to get from here to freedom on my own. If it's even a possibility in this lifetime. And now Ivory is offering it to us.

But the price will be our silence.

Noise can be dangerous. But there's also a danger to silence. It's everything we discovered, still going, for seventeen years. It's a gun firing with no sound. It's me, on an island, with no voice.

"We'll take our chances," I say.

I picture June running for the woods, looking over her shoulder.

And then I realize.

June said no.

I can see her now, so clearly, running from this home, stopping at a bank, not even worried about the police picking up on it. She was terrified for her life. She left herself a message, just in case, like she promised she would. *The truth will not die with me.* But she never made it back to the hideaway.

I am not the danger, she had said. *I am not the threat. I am the bell, tolling out its warning.*

More than that, she was going to blow the whistle.

I hit my palms against the closed cellar door, and Casey sucks in a breath. "*You* got her killed," I say. "*You* did it."

"I didn't do anything," Ivory says. "I'm not a killer."

"No," I say, "you just pull the strings, right?"

But she doesn't respond. I want to feel anger, for how June and I have both been wronged, some drive for revenge, but instead, I am filled with a surge of adrenaline, of appreciation, of awe. What June was willing to do for us both.

"Alina?" Cameron asks. "What next?"

"Let's go," I say.

Cameron gives me a look, but he doesn't question me. Doesn't even hesitate as he swings his bag over his shoulder. He doesn't look back.

"Where are you going?" Ivory asks. "What do you think you're going to do? You won't get far, Alina. June didn't. You won't."

"Let's go," I say again. This was the end for June, but it will not be for me.

"What do you think you'll do?" she calls. "You have nothing."

"Don't you remember?" I say. "I am the bell, tolling out its warning."

And right now, I am the threat.

I am the threat and the warning and the whistle, all rolled into one. June made mistakes, and she tried to right them, and I think how hard that must be in your own life. To admit to it, and to try to change.

I wonder if I owe her this, or if maybe I owe myself this.

June died for this, and I may yet, too.

"I'm going to the source," I say to Cameron and Casey outside the house. "I'm going for the proof." For June, for me, for everyone. I will not ask them to risk anything more, to come with me any farther. If I have to go it alone, I will.

I run straight for the car, in broad daylight, in the middle of the street.

They follow me.

chapter 23

IT TAKES TWO HOURS to arrive on campus. It's just outside the city, but close enough to not be segregated from the community. People of all ages wander the sidewalks in front of the buildings that border the city streets, but as we drive through the entrance, the street narrows, and the people disappear. I'm not sure whether it's because it's summer or because it's almost dinnertime, but this place feels like a ghost town.

Cameron navigates the winding side roads, following signs for different sections of campus. Expanses of grass extend out to either side, and old stone and brick buildings break up the landscape. Once we pass the buildings, we find ourselves on an alley street with several homes that all look alike—as if they were built as part of the school but converted to homes later. The address for Mason Alonzo is for a brick home on this alley. "Should we check it out?" Casey asks. "He's not home, right?"

"Right," I whisper, imagining him on his way to Ivory. Cameron backs out and retraces our path a bit. We leave the van in

visitor parking and walk the rest of the way. Mason's home is
about halfway down the street. We don't stop as we walk past it,
but I take my time looking in the front window as we pass. The
house is old, narrow, covered with ivy, and has turrets like a
castle. Mason may not be home, but the house is not empty. I
can see through the window, through the open curtains, two
teenagers, or maybe a little older, and a woman I'm assuming is
their mother, sitting at the dining room table. They're mostly
ignoring each other—the boy looking down at his cell phone
under the table; the girl moving pieces of food around the plate;
the woman bringing dishes in and out and answering the ringing
telephone—but there's still a wave of jealousy stirring inside me.

Cameron pulls me close, puts an arm around my shoulder,
and I spend way too long wondering if this is part of our disguise or if he just wants to do it. Casey pauses and separates
herself from us, waiting for us to walk about fifty feet before
she starts moving again.

Disguise, then.

Okay, then.

We stop at the end of the alley, and Cameron puts his hands
on my waist, tips his head so it rests against mine, as if we're
sharing a moment, but it's a lie. "We can't go in there," I say.
"We have to find his office in the school."

"I know," he says. "We need to get back to the van. There
aren't enough people out here. We'll be noticed."

I nod against his forehead, though I want to stay this way,
to keep on pretending that this is our normal and something

like this moment could last forever, but I know it isn't safe. He pulls me close as we walk back to the van. Nobody seems to notice us in the visitor lot, so we crack the front windows and move to the back, hoping nobody knows we're here.

"One at a time," Cameron says. "We leave here only one at a time. It's too risky." He squeezes Casey's shoulder. "Me first," he says.

I grab his arm. "What are you going to do?"

"I'm going to see if these buildings are locked, and if they are, I'm going to find a way in. Casey, then you can see what you can find in his office, wherever that is. Once you find what you need, it's all yours, Alina. Sound good?"

I don't answer, and neither does Casey, but it does actually sound good. But every time he leaves I feel this overwhelming terror, that he is risking too much, that this is the last I will see of him. It has always been only myself on the line. I'm not used to worrying about others.

Casey doesn't speak the entire time he's gone. In the dark of the van, as the sun drops below the horizon, at first I think she's sleeping, with her head leaning back against the wall. But then I see her lips just faintly moving, and I wonder if she's praying. I'm scared to break her trance, so I close my eyes, and I try to imagine all the possible outcomes of this moment. But all I can see are the people who would stop us, who would punish us. All I can imagine are the words people will say, twisting the facts into their own version of events. The rooms that will hold us; the places that can contain us.

And then I am picturing that truck going over the bridge seven years ago, and my mother holding my wet and tattered body to her own as she pulls me from the ocean. I am imagining the lullaby she sings: *Duérmete, mi niña, duérmete, mi amor, duérmete, y nos vemos en la tierra de sueños* . . .

"What does it mean?"

I open my eyes to find Casey watching me. I must've been saying it aloud. "Literally, 'go to sleep, my girl, go to sleep, my love, go to sleep, and we will see each other in the land of dreams.'"

It's the only place she said I could find her.

"It's nice," she says. "Soothing."

I close my eyes again.

Because in this moment, it truly is.

Cameron doesn't knock before opening the back doors, and it makes us both jump. The streetlight is on behind him, and the sky is completely dark beyond.

He hops inside and says, "Doors are locked, but I have an access card." Then he looks at Casey. "You can yell at me later."

"I would never," she says.

He climbs over us and starts the car.

"Where are we going?"

"Hiding the car," he says. "After hours, security will run checks."

We drive behind a building, and he eases the van underneath a willow tree, out of sight, its hanging leaves covering us like a blanket. He gets out, removing the license plates—"Just in case," he says—before handing the access card to Casey.

"Do you know what you're doing?" he asks.

"Computer lab. Find his office. Get in. Get out." She nods to herself, leaving off everything important she intends to do in that office. *Find the way Mason accesses the database. Find Ava. Find proof she's still alive.*

Cameron grabs her arm as she leaves. "Stay safe, Case," he says.

"Be right back," she says.

We sit across from each other in the back of the van, not speaking, not touching. Everything between us, that got us to this point, hovering in the air. Every choice we've made, in this life and in June's, hanging in the balance. Tomorrow is only hours away. Tomorrow this will all be done. Tomorrow we'll no longer be bound to one another.

"What are you going to do after this?" I ask him.

"I guess that depends on what happens in the next few hours."

"What do you want, then, if you could do anything?"

He stares at me. "That's a dangerous question, Alina. Because I can't. I can only think about today. And the only thing I want right now is the girl sitting on the other side of the van."

Such a simple thing to want. Such a simple thing to give him. I crawl across the space between us, but he meets me before I get there, pulling me on top of him, one of my legs on either side of him, as he leans against the wall. I kiss him as if this is the last time, because it might be. I kiss him like it will have to last in my memory for the rest of my life. I kiss him like I've been imagining doing since the moment I let the pieces of glass drop from my fingers in surrender.

I feel his teeth softly against my lips, and I remember the blade that got us here. That got me out. I pull back, place my finger on the sharp point of his false canine, and say, "How'd you get this?"

He runs his tongue across it, but his eyes never leave mine. "Lost it in a fight. Had a friend take me to a place that would do this, for a trade. Before I went into the system. I don't like the idea of being stripped to nothing but my fists."

And here I thought it was just for me. But it was for him, before that. Because there are other prisons besides mine. More dangerous ones. I think, in truth, I could've had it worse. A prison where I am left and forgotten. A prison where I have no access to information or education. A prison where I have no hope. I think of June, hiding alone underground. I think of Cameron, locked in a cell. His soul was not meant to be caged, either.

"Never had to use it, thank God," he says.

"It saved me," I say.

He nods. "Casey told Dom about it. I guess they were brainstorming how to get a blade onto the island, and she mentioned this." He bites down, and I hear the sound of teeth on teeth. "She told him about this, and I guess he figured, why not just use *me*?"

And so, here he is. And here I am. "This is what got you involved?"

He shakes his head, and his nose touches mine. "I would've gotten involved either way."

"Regrets?" I ask.

"None," he says. "On the contrary. You?"

I smile and say, "None," the moment before I kiss him again. My hands are on his shoulders, and then they are lower, on his waist, and then under his shirt. He pulls me so we're chest to chest, stomach to stomach, hips to hips, and my hands trail up his back until I feel the ridge of the scar. "What about this?" I ask.

I lean back, and he lets me pull the shirt up over his head. I have never seen this look on him before. I like it. I love it. "Tell me," I say, overcome with the rush of power.

"Random attack," he says. "Outside a convenience store. Happened when Casey entered the National Guard training, and me and Dom were setting up the cabin. Dom was inside the shop, stocking up on supplies. I was out, loading the trunk with our first batch of stuff, and some guy jumped me from behind." His body tenses as he speaks. "There was a knife in my back before I could even process what was happening." I feel the shudder roll through him. "Took my wallet and left me there, bleeding in the parking lot."

I run my fingers along the scar—it covers the span of at least four ribs. I am imagining him bleeding on the blacktop, and I cannot stand the way the scene looks in my head, even though I know it isn't real.

"I know Dom's a dick, and probably a psychopath, but I

couldn't go to a hospital, and I couldn't reach Casey. He took me somewhere safe, gave me some drugs, stitched me up right. He's got some good in him somewhere, Alina." He laughs. "Or maybe he needed me too much."

While talking, his hands have made their way under the hem of my shirt, onto my bare waist, and I cannot speak. I want to get impossibly closer. I want to back up to the far wall. I am full of want. He trails his fingers up my stomach, until they reach the fresh wound that had once been a scar on my third rib. "Tell me this story," he says.

"It's a long story," I say. "And you already know it."

"I like hearing you talk," he says.

"I was a baby, just a baby in a nursery, and they stuck a needle in my back," I whisper. "They said I was June Calahan, and so they cut, right here," I place my fingers over his, over the scar, "and put a tracker there. Then my mother cut through the same line, and she took the tracker out. They came for her, threw her in jail, cut through the scar tissue, and put the tracker back. And it stayed that way for seventeen years."

"You still had the scar," he says.

"Mm-hmm. And then this boy showed up in my bathroom—"

"Boy?" he asks.

"Guy?"

"Good enough."

"So this guy shows up in my bathroom, and he takes a freaking blade from his jaw, and I think, who *is* this boy—sorry, *guy*—with a freaking blade in his jaw? And he cuts the tracker from me again. And then he stitches me back up, even though he doesn't know how, and then he touches the scar, and he asks how I got it . . ."

"You tell the best stories," he says, raising my shirt off my stomach. "Let me tell you about this girl I met . . ."

I feel real and solid. I feel his heart through the layers of his rib and muscle and skin, and my own. I feel his lips, brushing against mine, as he is talking. And when I cannot take it any longer—of being so close, and yet not close enough—I make him stop talking. I press my lips more firmly on his. And his arms become solid around my back.

The moment is filled with all the never-haves and never-wills and every possible outcome of the day. In short, the end is coming—the end of this, whatever this is—and right now it looks like a cliff. Like the end of the world. I kiss him—even though I understand, like Casey said, that this is not the time—because we're hurtling toward it. "We'll be okay," I say, waiting for him to say *of course we will*, but he doesn't.

He moves away from the wall, rolls onto his back, and drapes an arm across his eyes. So I sit beside him, and I run my fingers up his stomach, and he doesn't move—he stills. I trace the muscles, the skin, up to the bones of his rib cage, and I bring my face down to his chest, resting my cheek against him. His free hand goes to my hair, down to my shoulder, and he holds me to him like that. "Cameron," I say.

My heart is in my head and my stomach—everywhere all at once—when we hear footsteps racing toward us.

I back away, back against the front seats, my hands

groping for anything I can use to defend us. The back doors start shaking, and Casey's voice carries through in panicked nonsense.

Cameron opens the double doors, and Casey doesn't take a second to chastise us or even take in what was happening, or what was about to happen. "He's here," she says, and she can't calm down.

"Who?" Cameron asks, but she's staring over her shoulder, pulling us out the back. Cameron barely has time to pull his shirt back on.

"Dominic," she says. "Dominic is here."

We run along with her, to the side of an academic building. The doors are all locked, but Casey slides the ID through the card reader and pulls us inside. We race down the hall until we reach the next door, leading to a glass-walled atrium that spans the distance between buildings. There's another hall, off to the side, but we stay where we are, contained in the safety of this building—two exits, one hall, and we can see them all.

"I saw him get out of his car," Casey says, her voice shaking. "From the window of the computer lab. He was walking down the road in your direction. I ran—he didn't see me, too busy staring at his GPS screen. I sprinted ahead through the trees to get there first."

"Did he see the van? How did he know where we were?" I ask.

"I don't know," she says. "I don't know. Maybe—"

The sound of the door being pulled against the lock echoes through the hall, and Casey grabs my arm. "Is that him?" I whisper.

"How the hell would he know we were here?" she whispers back.

Cameron creeps into an open classroom and cranes his neck around the window before diving back down behind the desk. He motions for us to stay away, out in the hall, and keeps low as he exits the dark room. "It's him," he says.

We don't speak as we stay pressed against the wall, but we hear Dominic moving around the building. His footsteps pace the perimeter, he pushes at the windows—gently first, then with more force. It won't take forever. If he wants a way in, he will make one. Brick walls and glass windows and locked doors are not enough.

I grab them both by the hand and start running down the long, dark hall. There must be someplace else. Someplace to hide. "Tunnels," Cameron says. "In the winter, students use tunnels to get from building to building." We can use them, too.

"Mason Alonzo's office is on the fifth floor of the next building. We head that way. And then we get the hell out," Casey says.

Where the stairs go up, they also go down. There's a door at the bottom of the stairs, and it's also locked. Casey uses the student ID to gain access, and we race down the murky hall toward the next building. There are a few computer stations down here, and a few storage units for A/V equipment. There are no windows. We stay in the tunnel, hidden underground. Safe, for the moment. But I worry.

I worry because he found us once, in the van.

I worry because he found us again, moments later, in the building.

"He's tracking us," I say.

chapter 24

WE STAND, STARING AT each other, in the muted glow of the basement hallway. We look at the clothes that don't belong to us and the shoes that we've been wearing since the sewer. "Shit," Casey says as she strips them off.

Cameron removes the tooth from his mouth, flips the blade, and runs it through the rubber sole of his sneaker in sharp, harsh lines. He drops it to the ground, finding nothing, and picks up the next. He tosses each shoe, getting more frustrated each time, as he finds nothing. He checks Casey's shoes. My shoes. Strips of rubber litter the ground. Still nothing.

We search each other frantically for things that came from our time together with Dominic. I take the blade from Cameron as he examines his watch—it's sharper than I imagined. Cameron takes off his watch and uses the butt of the empty gun to smash it, his fingers sorting through the battery, the display, the metal pieces. He throws the fragmented pieces across the room with a grunt. He does the same with Casey's watch.

Casey dumps her bag, June's notebook and the papers in a heap on the floor, and runs her fingers through the fabric.

I take the blade to the buckles of the bag, tearing them off, but still, we find nothing. I fold the blade back in half, tucking it inside my closed fist.

I lift the bottom of my shirt, feel the patch of skin over my ribs, the fresh stitches done by Cameron's hand.

He grabs my hand, pulls it away, his fingers sliding between mine, and looks into my eyes. "We got it," he says. "I got that out of you. If there was something else, your guards would've noticed, or they would've found you. It's not you."

I should feel relief.

But I watch his mouth, the way his lips turn down in worry. I step closer to him as Casey takes apart the empty gun, which even she must know is a long shot.

"Cameron," I whisper, and he freezes at the way I'm looking at him.

I bring my fingers to the bottom of his shirt and then underneath to his back. I run my fingers up to the scar running the length of four ribs. He sucks in a breath and takes a step back, tearing off his shirt as if it has the power to burn him. He spins, his back facing us, his fingers stretching, reaching, for the scar.

Casey's staring as well. "Oh, God," she says. "Please tell me you were conscious when Dom stitched you up."

He stares at Casey. Then at me. The panic in his eyes, the answer. His silence, the answer.

"*No*," she says. Then she turns to me, her breath coming in a panic. "Where would he put it? Where's the tracker?"

I feel sick, and I have no answer. "Take it out. *Take it out*," she says.

It could be on the underside of any of those four ribs. Under muscle, under cartilage. His scar is at least five times the length of my own, and I am imagining five times the damage, five times the pain, five times the blood.

"I don't . . . I don't know."

I passed out when Cameron removed mine. I choked on a scream and passed out, and Cameron knew exactly where to look, what to do.

"Pack the bag back up," Cameron says, in a voice eerily low. Casey looks confused but places everything back inside—June's notebook, the studies, the hard drives—her hands shaking. "Now pick it up," he says to me, and I do, the fabric hanging limply over my shoulder, hoping this is part of some master plan that I don't understand that will save us all.

Now what? I think. I look at Cameron. *Now what?*

"Now go," he says.

Casey puts her hand to her mouth. "I'm not leaving you here while—"

"I'm sure he hasn't come here unarmed," Cameron says. "If he gets to us, he can use us to get into the database. And if he gets in the database—he can't. You can't let him."

He's right, of course. Even if I can prove the study wrong— that we are not bound to past criminal nature—still, this information in the wrong hands is terrifying. What of the people who seek revenge? Nothing good can come from this information being public. This information is dangerous. Ivory was right: it's power. In the wrong hands, it's destruction.

The door at the far end of the hall shakes as someone pulls against the lock. Dominic has made it into the building, and has followed us this far. Casey chokes on a sob, because she knows. We have to go.

He takes a deep breath. "Now give me the gun," he says.

And suddenly I have this image: *It's Christmas Day, and it's starting to snow . . .*

No. Not again. Not. Again.

I have a grip on the bag, but Casey pulls it off my shoulder, hands him the gun, mumbling a string of curses under her breath, and she places it in his hand. She raises her eyes and says, "I'll come back for you. I promise."

He looks at her, nods slightly. Then he looks away. "Take everything," he says to her. "Don't leave it with me. And Casey? Be fast. Get what we came for, and then you and Alina get the hell out of here. Promise me."

She doesn't say a thing, but her eyes say everything in the moment before she runs toward the door at the far end of the hall, where Dominic is not. She's waiting for me, but her hand is already on the metal bar, ready to make a run for it. She's crying without making a sound. She is so strong.

Cameron turns to me, but I'm shaking, the fake tooth with the blade in the palm of my hand. Something that saved me. His freedom for mine. The whole world in a balance. The only weapon he has left, other than his fists, other than the empty gun, is this tiny blade.

My freedom for his.

"I'm sorry, Alina," he says, as if this is somehow his fault.

"Don't," I say.

I kiss him for all I'm worth. "*I'm* sorry," I whisper as I back away, the warmth from him fading quickly.

He shakes his head. "It's okay. This was all for nothing if he finds you."

And I think, *It's all for nothing if I leave you*.

And so I kiss him one last time, and I push the button on the blade, so it is now twice the length. I shut my eyes, and I lean my forehead against his, and I ask for strength. I contort my face into calm and brave before I open my eyes again. I hold up the blade, watch as his eyes go wide.

"Try not to scream," I say.

chapter 25

"NO," HE SAYS, HIS hand around my wrist.

"Run," I say to Casey. "Run now. I'll get it out of him, I promise."

I hear the door open, but it doesn't close. She's watching us both, and then she looks straight at me, straight into me and says, "I know you will." The door closes, and then it's just us in this empty hall, and silence—Dominic has left the door, but he'll be back. He'll be back with a way in next time. We need to be fast.

"You have to go. There's no time," he says. "It's okay, Alina."

There's nothing okay about him and Dominic and an empty gun. There's nothing okay about leaving him behind.

June left Liam. She left him. I could never do that. I'm not her. This means more than the truth. *He* means more than the truth.

"Then lie down and stop wasting time," I say. "Because I'm not leaving you. You're coming with me."

"The database. The proof—"

"I don't care," I say. But that's not exactly true. It's more that there are degrees of caring, and degrees of truth, and what you want and what you need are very rarely the same thing.

"And when I pass out and you have to escape and I'm a sitting duck with no gun? And he can use me as leverage against Casey? Against *you*? What then?"

I don't know.

"You're going to have to trust me, Cameron."

His eyes are still wide, but he lies back. I press my lips to his one last time as I straddle his chest. "Well, I guess there are worse ways to go," he says, trying to laugh.

"Do me a favor?" I say. He cocks his head to the side, and something inside me splits in two. "Please don't pass out." He nods, a promise we both know he has no control over. "Now flip," I say, and he twists on the hard ground from his back to his stomach.

Then there is nothing between me and the long, white scar. I can feel his ribs, directly below. Dominic must've placed it along the scar somewhere. I try to channel Cameron when he did this for me. His calm, steady breath. His calm, steady hand. Impersonal. Efficient. But as I bring the sharp point of the blade to his flesh, this noise escapes his throat, and all I can think is *Cameron*.

I press down, and his body stiffens. I try not to think as I push down at the top of the scar, until I feel some resistance under the skin, as his whole body twitches, tenses—but my vision goes a little blurry. The blood starts coming then, and it comes fast, and I realize that *I* will need to be fast. Faster. Before there's too much blood, before there's too much pain.

One shaky breath.

One steady hand.

Go.

I move the blade in a quick stroke down the length of the scar, deep enough to find a hidden tracker. And at first Cameron must be trying not to hurt me, but he gives in, digging his fingers into my legs on either side of him, leaving bruises, I'm sure.

There are tears streaking down from the corner of his eye, along his nose, to the concrete floor beneath him. And there are tears clouding my own vision as well. "Almost, Cameron," I say. And then I dig my finger inside his back, and I press it down onto his rib, feeling along the edge, and he screams. "Oh, God, I'm sorry."

It's not on the first rib, not that I can tell—just bone and tendon and muscle, all soft along the smooth surface. But my hands are covered in blood, and Cameron's back looks like he's just been stabbed, because he has.

I bite down on my lip to keep from crying, and I picture a spot in the distance to stop the nausea, like Cameron taught me. And I keep my eyes closed as I run my finger along the second rib.

I feel something, something different—just over the muscle— and I take the blade and make one more cut, prying it out, and Cameron goes still. It's smooth and narrow, but it's covered in blood, and I have to wipe it off with the bottom of my shirt to be sure—the thin tracker, a curved piece of metal, out. It's out. I throw it to the floor and I crush it under the butt of the empty gun, over and over again.

But the cut that spans the length of his scar is bleeding more than I imagined it could. I ball up his shirt and press it against the wound, and I hold it there while he remains motionless. I strip the shoelaces from our ruined sneakers, and I use the blade to slice off a long piece from the bottom of my shirt, and I use both to bind his shirt to his back, looping the material around his shoulder, applying as much pressure as I can to his wound in the process. He recovered from this cut once before. He will recover again.

And then I flip him over—his eyes blink open and slowly reclose. I quickly pull him to sitting, because I'm not sure if he can do it himself. "Cameron, wake up. Cameron, I got it," I say.

"'Kay," he says, and he reaches for my face, as if he is talking in his sleep.

I close my eyes and ask for strength, but the only feeling that floods through me is a sharp wave of panic.

I guess that will have to be enough.

I take my hand and bring it down hard and fast across his face, my palm stinging, the blood from my hands staining his face.

His eyes pop open, and I say, "Get up."

He tries, and my God, I love him for it. He holds on to my shoulder as he pulls himself to standing, and I am so thankful for the muscles I have earned over the past year, pushing myself upright, and bringing him with me in the process. For once, they are useful. "We have to move," I say.

We're both covered in blood, and it's trailing behind us as he bumps into the wall while we walk. I have butchered him. I was not careful, or calm, or efficient. I was fast, and I was brutal. I wish I were better.

"Thank you for waking up," I say as we make it to the door.

He leans into me, and for a second I'm scared he'll pass out again. But he stays on his feet. He's trying to say something, but his back connects with the door, and he winces.

"Don't," I say. "I'm sorry. I know I made a mess of you. Please, if you're going to be mad, be mad later. We have to move." We have to move before Dom comes. We have to move before he passes out. *Please*, I think, *let him not have lost too much blood. Please.*

We have to move to the fifth floor, and that thought alone seems insurmountable.

We push through the doorway, and I see the stairs. "Don't look up," I say. I'm saying it for myself, but it will probably help him as well. I start moving, step by step, and his bare feet stumble alongside mine. He's got half his weight on me, and half on the railing, or against the wall, but at least we keep moving.

I try not to notice the walls, smeared with his blood, that we're leaving behind. Who needs a tracker when you have a blood trail?

Please let Casey be okay, I think. *Please let her get what she came for,* I think. *Please let all of this be worth it for them.*

"Get off the wall," I say when we reach the landing for the third floor. I take my bloody hands and smear them across the entryway to the hall. I run down and try to leave a trail of blood, transferring what's on my hands, my body, to these concrete walls.

Cameron wavers in the middle of the landing. He looks pale but his expression is alert. He's here. He's back. "No more blood on the stairs," I whisper as I race back toward him, but even that echoes. He leans on me but manages to support himself—by sheer willpower, I'm sure—as we make it to the fifth floor, where Casey should be.

The hallway is dark and silent, but we are barefoot and alert.

There's an open doorway.

The sound of her voice.

And the sound of another.

Cameron rushes by me, and I put my arm out, trying to stop him—but he keeps moving, almost running, until I catch him by the arm and hold him back.

Patience, I want to tell him. But I don't dare speak. I keep my back pressed against the wall and pull him beside me as I walk closer to the room.

"It's just one name," I hear Casey say.

I hear a gravelly voice speaking, aged and smoke laden. "It always starts with just one name. It never is, though. It never ends."

Casey's voice is shaky, and I want to tell her to be calm, be brave. Though I have no bravery and no calmness to spare her.

"Ivory said she would trade me for it. She said you could do it. Didn't she tell you?"

"Ivory Street would throw me under the bus in a heartbeat. I didn't go to her when she called, though I'm sure she expected me. No, I waited here. I waited for you to come to me." Ivory must still be in the basement, waiting, waiting, for someone to come. "But you are not the one I'm waiting for. Where is she?"

I hear the sound of knuckles cracking, and I smile. Casey, buying time. Casey, gathering herself. "Alina? Oh, she got bored with this whole thing," she says. "Took her freedom and ran with it." God, I love her. I do.

He laughs. "You're a terrible liar. All youthful arrogance, like June was."

I ease my head around the entrance, and I can see only the back of him. Slacks with deep wrinkles, as if he's been folded up inside them for days. A plaid collared shirt, and a sprinkling of gray hair along the base of his skull. From the back, he looks perfectly nondescript. Perfectly like anyone else. He takes a step forward, and I expect his knees to creak. A generation passed since the picture I saw of him was taken—when he first set up the Cybersecurity Data Center.

Casey sits behind his dark-brown desk, facing me—the room is full of computers and machines with periodically flashing lights, and there's a door to the side that must lead to his work lab—because there's a window in the door, and I can see the blue blinking lights behind it. Her face looks unnaturally white in the glow of the monitor. She doesn't see me. There's a wall of windows behind her where I can see the reflection of the monitors and the man before her, but I worry he will catch a glimpse of me in the reflection as well. I pull myself out of the doorway. "How badly do you want this, single, solitary name, child?" he asks.

"Badly enough to break Alina Chase out of her containment," she says.

"Good," he says. "Then that's the price. Alina Chase for the name."

She pauses. "I can't. I don't know—"

"That's the price, and your time is running out."

I peek again. He doesn't seem to have a gun, so I'm not sure why he's saying that. I don't see any immediate danger—he's just an old man in a computer lab. He has his cell phone out, and he holds it up to her. "I called the authorities as soon as I was sure you all were here. Your price went up, child. Two million dollars for information leading to the capture of Alina Chase. How long do you think they will take? If I were you, I'd want a pretty good head start."

Casey stands, the sound of the chair scraping along the floor out from underneath her as she moves away from the desk. She takes one last, longing glance at the screen. "Am I free to go then?" she asks.

"I'm sure I cannot stop you," he says, stepping aside.

All this for nothing.

Her name for nothing.

I've got my answers, even if I can't prove them.

I stand in front of the open door, even though I feel Cameron's hands reaching, and then losing, a grip on my arm.

"Hello," I say, and the old man spins around.

He smiles, his eyes crinkling at the corners, his lips cracking as they pull farther apart. "You're even smaller than I imagined," he says. "Such a little thing. Such a big mess . . ."

From the front, he looks like anyone's grandfather. Sparkling eyes, thick glasses, crooked and slightly discolored teeth, and a stomach that hangs over his waistband. Years and years since that picture was taken. A lifetime, for me. "We have a lot in common, Alina Chase," he says. "We should talk, truly. Ivory Street got me, too, with the past life. Ensnared me for a lifetime of doing her bidding." He licks his lips, and I wonder who he was in the past life, and who he was in this life, before Ivory Street.

Ivory Street must have discovered something about Mason Alonzo. About his past life. Must've learned something he didn't want revealed and coerced him with it.

"Her study was a lie," I say. "She falsified the data. Only included the data that supported her theory. You don't have to do her bidding. She has nothing on you."

His face twists—first down, then up—before he speaks. "Yes, she does. Everything I've done since then, child. Everything I've let her do since then. I *gave* people to her. I let her see data that should've been protected at the highest level. I let her use it. *That's* my crime now." There's a sound of bones popping, but I don't think he's moved. Maybe it was his jaw. Or maybe it was Casey, standing behind him. "I suppose," he says, "when all is said and done, my crimes in this life will far exceed the last. So be it."

I see it in his eyes: he is that selfish. He doesn't want to go back, to drag it out into the light. He is fine with the situation. With the power of it all. "You don't have to do this," I say. When all I'm thinking is *please, don't do this.*

And then he laughs. "Now I get it. Now I get why Ivory was so set on making sure you were found and then contained. It didn't make sense to me back then: why June and not Liam? It wasn't the fear of the information June left about accessing the database—we closed that door anyway. It was this. What you just told me. That June knew the truth, and that she left that for you."

"Ivory had me contained?" I ask.

"She had you sought out—it all happened so fast. And there was no precedent for it. She left no time for debate. Act now, act fast. She pushed, and someone listened. I don't even know who it was. She has a lot of people in law enforcement wrapped around her finger. Of course, now I'm wondering if she wasn't just a bit spiteful that June figured her out. If it wasn't meant to be a punishment, after all."

I am filled with pure rage, that Ivory was the force behind my containment. I hate her. I hate her and I hope she stays locked in that basement for eternity. But I try not to let it show on my face. I take a deep breath, and I focus on the faces of the people I love instead.

I see my mother, free somewhere, and my father, still in prison.

I see Cameron.

I see Casey.

I see June.

And again I think of her—I see her walking away from me, a small smile as she looks over her shoulder, her blond curls swaying with each step, blue eyes looking straight into mine. I close my eyes, and I thank her for all she has done, and what she was trying to do. That she believed in redemption, in her own life. She discovered she had made a horrible mistake. She was wrong, and she was going to reveal it anyway. She was going to take herself down with them. She was the bell and the whistle. If only she had lived . . .

I feel her in me—the parts of her I like, the parts I struggle against, all of them—and I gather her close. I think I must love her, anyway. She was beautiful, and she was wrong, and she was brave. I want to see my own life stretched out before me, like she must have, and think not of myself but of truth, and who it belongs to. There is nothing selfish in her soul. Maybe she wasn't born good or bad. Maybe her choices were both. Mostly, though, they were her own.

As are mine.

"Is that it? The shadow-database is in there?" I ask, gesturing behind him. Casey said it would have to be big to store everything, but it seems impossible that it would just be sitting here, in his office.

"No, no, there's no complete copy. This is just a piece of it. Just a storage unit—the information we've accessed over the years," he says. He points to the computer on his desk. "It's all linked. Whatever we access gets copied and stored for when we might need it. The data Ivory pulled for the study. The souls we pulled after, with the new names attached, it all gets copied and stored right here. Funny, huh? How it's just sitting here, in my lab, mixed in with my other projects? Ivory convinced me, very persuasively, to leave a portal open for myself—to set this up—when I went back in to upgrade security. The irony, right? She's no different from anyone else, not June or Liam or you, even. Once you get in, you can't let it be. Too much power in that knowledge. Too much you can do with it. Like moths to a candle, flitting around it while your wings are on fire."

Casey's expression is pained, and she's about to say something. "Don't," I say, even though I'm looking at Mason.

"In you go," he says, gesturing to the room behind us.

"Give her the name first," I say.

"You are in no position to be bargaining. Can you beat two million dollars?"

I surely cannot.

Except then Cameron stands in the entrance, leaning against the doorjamb, the empty gun in his hand. "They're both coming with me."

Mason looks at the gun and laughs. "You think I'm afraid of death? What's to fear, really? Another chance with another life . . ."

I catch Cameron's eye and then Casey's. "It's okay," I say, going willingly into the room. I turn the handle and back inside, the door falling shut in front of me. It's colder in here, and dark. There are machines, but nothing like the simple computers I'm familiar with. Just equipment, small lights flashing blue and red and green. June. Me. The history of our souls, humming across this sterile room.

I watch through the square window as the sound of the key enters the lock, and the lock turns in the door, sealing me inside. And I listen to their voices on the other side.

Mason Alonzo sits at the computer, but first looks at the gun in Cameron's hand, spins around to the windows, and slides one open. He pushes at the screen until it pops, then tosses the single key five floors down into the bushes below. "The gun," he says.

"That wasn't the agreement," Cameron says, raising it at Mason—who looks like he is, actually, a bit scared of death after all. "Alina for the name."

Mason nods and tilts his head toward Casey.

She keeps her eyes closed, not looking at him or Cameron—or me, behind the door window.

"Ava London," Casey says.

chapter 26

MASON PAUSES FOR SEVERAL seconds before his fingers tap against the keyboard.

My time is now. This is my chance. I'm alone in this room, and a copy of the data I need is before me. The data that was in the study, and the data left out. The proof is stored inside. I can clear June's name of blackmail. I can free us both. I just need to figure out how to transfer the data. How to copy what I need . . .

"I know this name," Mason says, and I go back to the window in the door. Mason pushes back from the desk, turning his body away, averting his eyes, as the information pulls up onto the screen.

He keeps his back to Casey, to Cameron with the gun, and I know this cannot be good.

Casey moves behind the computer, her face too close to the screen, her eyes too wide, and Cameron, looking way too pale, on the other side of the room.

"I want you to know," Mason says, "that I am not responsible." He turns from the window, talking to Cameron since Casey still has not moved. "I get the names, that's all. I cannot predict who will go along and who will run."

I close my eyes, and I picture June running. I picture Ava running. I know what happens to both.

Casey cannot move from the screen. She cannot speak. Cameron pushes off the door frame, the gun held with more intent, more authority.

"She had just accessed her inheritance," Mason says. "Crooked money left behind by a very crooked soul. They had plans for her, and how she should use that money . . ."

I know, from Mason's words, from Casey's expression, that Ava has a soul before and a soul after.

I know from the tears running silently down Casey's face.

I know from the tension in Mason's body.

And Cameron knows, too. His body, leaning limply against the door frame. The gun hanging loosely from his slack fingers.

I press my hands against the glass—I want to go to them.

Mason keeps talking to fill the silence. "Do you know who that is? That name before Ava?"

Casey looks at Cameron and says, "She received a huge inheritance when her entire family was killed. Then a year later, she went on a two-day killing spree before being gunned down by the cops. She snapped."

"That she did," says Mason. "Afterward the police discovered that she was the one who killed her family. I think, more than anything, Ava was afraid she might do the same. Couldn't concentrate on what we were saying. Couldn't think of what we were offering. We gave her time, but she couldn't get past it. The fear of who she might be, that was worse than the fear of us revealing that information. And so she ran. As if you can run from yourself . . ."

I back away from the door, my limbs trembling, my breath shaking. This cannot be what we've traded everything for. This cannot be what we're left with. There's no meaning in this. There's nothing for us here.

I look at what's surrounding me. The servers that tower over me, the machines humming through the room, the power lights flashing with life. The information Ivory used for her research is in here somewhere; Mason said as much. In here is the proof. But in here is also the thing that binds us in this life to the last. In here is the thing that June died from, that Ava died from. This room is a prison. It's a prison full of information that some would twist to contain us.

But the information is stored on machines. Wires and cables and electrical circuits. I know what to do with them. I know what to do with all this information.

I studied this. How to make things. A phone. A stun gun. A fire.

It does not take me long. I strip wires with my teeth, and I pry circuit boards from their computer units with my fingernails. I know exactly what to do.

There's yelling in the other room—it's high and nonsensical, and I try to shut out the pain in Casey's voice, but I can't. It seeps into me, the contagiousness of grief, as my fingers fumble with the exposed wires.

I smell the smoke before I can see it.

Like something changing. Something happening.

Something dying.

Something coming to life.

It sparks and singes the tips of my fingers, and I drop the wires. The smoke curls in dark clouds, crawling upward—the promise of destruction.

But then the smoke becomes something more, something I cannot escape, multiplying and giving life to itself, sucking the oxygen from the room—how insidious smoke is when set free. How dangerous it becomes in a closed room.

I did not imagine how suffocating smoke could be, but here, in this room, it burns my lungs before it destroys the machines. I suck in air, but it's poison. I try to breathe, but the room is full of a grayness that burns my eyes, and so I close them. I lean against the nearest server, sinking to the ground, the sound of sparks igniting behind me.

He can get me out. I know he can. I know he will.

I close my eyes, and I imagine instead.

I imagine Cameron, uninjured, smiling before me in the open doorway. And Casey, finding her sister. My father, being released from prison. And my mother, pulling me from the water.

I listen for the sound of his voice through the door. But the noises have changed. The sound of grief has turned to panic, to rage. There's another voice out there now.

I feel a sudden burst of clearer air in my lungs. The door is open in front of me, and Cameron pushes through the thick smoke. I see his pale face, and his arms pulling me up, as the sparks and smoke become something more. Becoming flames, becoming fire.

I barely make it out of the room before Dominic has me by the arm. Casey is frozen in the hallway. Mason is frozen beside her, his face unreadable. And Dominic stands among us all. Cameron was right—Dom didn't come unarmed—he moves the gun quickly from one to the next as smoke fills up the space around us, the fire alarm blaring, the sprinklers overhead, the lights flashing at the exits.

"What did you do?" he shouts over the alarm. "What did you *do*?"

"It's gone!" I shout back, but my voice comes out raspy. I cough, but my lungs feel too tight. And the heat on my back, the smoke growing thicker. "We have to *go*."

"No," he says. "Fix this!" He grabs the fire extinguisher with his free hand and thrusts it at Casey. "Fix it now!"

Mason is screaming for help, but I don't know what he's looking for: help for his lab, help from the man with the gun, or help from us. Which is the most dangerous. Cameron is beside me with an empty gun, but he's in no position to be fighting. It's a miracle he's still standing.

"The police are coming! The firefighters will be here! Campus security. We can't be here!" I say, shaking free of Dominic.

I grab Casey's arm and head down the hall. Dominic fires a

shot at the ceiling to stop us. "You don't get to do this," he says. "You don't get to *decide* this."

Except I already did. "There's nothing here anymore. I destroyed it. It's gone."

Dominic stares into the smoke and then strides back to me, taking me by the arm again. "For them, and not for me, Alina?" he asks, like I have betrayed him. And maybe I have. I don't like the look on Cameron's face. The empty gun in his hand. What he might use it for.

Go, I mouth to him. I turn to Casey. *Please. Go.* But they do not.

Mason grabs the fire extinguisher, trying to salvage what's left of his lab. Dominic watches, stunned, angry, all the things I'd be in his place. But there's a gun in his hand and a price on our heads, and he is a man with nothing left to lose.

"Liam and June were wrong," I say. "And June was trying to set it right after Liam's death. The study was a lie. We're not bound to be the people we once were. We can take a different path."

He fixes his eyes on me, the gun tight in his fist.

"Did you hear me?" I ask, because I have to yell over the alarm and my voice is barely working. "We're not the people we were!" But his face twists, his fingers tighten.

"I don't believe that," he says. "And neither do you." He doesn't want to believe it, because if he does, he's staked his life on something that no longer exists.

"I can't help you," I say. "There's nothing left here. Let me go. Please. We're running out of time."

He doesn't move, but he doesn't raise the gun, and I guess that's as good a sign as any. I yank my arm from Dominic, and he lets me go. I wonder if there's still a chance for him. If he believes in redemption. In this life, for *this* life. I believe it. I believe it's not too late, for any of us.

The fire trucks are coming. The authorities are coming. Everyone is coming. "Dominic," I say, because I do owe him something—or maybe June does, but I am the only one here. "Run."

"They were willing to die for it, once before," he says.

"Not for *this*," I say. "Not for *data* or money or power. Dominic. *Run.*"

He runs, but he runs in the wrong direction. Into the room with Mason, trying to save the information.

I feel a twinge of regret for this man—who believed we had a love and a purpose that transcended one lifetime. Maybe it's possible. Maybe it happens. But we're more than just the history of our soul. More than DNA. More than our past lives. We're the choices we've made in *this* life. Every one of them, giving us purpose.

We run down the hall, Casey leading the way, and I hear Mason and Dominic shouting behind us, for water, for blankets, for anything as the lab goes up in flames. But I hope it's too late. I hope it's destroyed. I hope there's nothing left.

Because as we race down the hall, down the stairs—all of us in stunned silence—I know there's nothing left for us, either.

Nowhere left to go. Mason told Casey he called the authorities. We don't have much time.

But time for what? *What next, June?* She doesn't answer.
She never has. The only one who's been here, this whole time,
is me.

We race down the stairwell out into the night, and we stumble
across the grass, across the road, to our hidden car.

Casey wordlessly yanks the keys from Cameron's hand, as
he's leaning against the side of the van, bleeding and coughing
underneath the willow tree. I pull him into the back with me,
and Casey begins to drive, despite the sirens. But they're coming from everywhere. I don't know whether it's the police for
me, or the fire trucks for the building. Cameron rests against
the inside of the van, his head in his hands.

Casey idles at the end of the street, then randomly turns
down an alley. We're still on campus, and there are only so many
ways out. She stops for a moment, pulls something out of her
bag, and extends her arm to the back without looking at me.
It's Mason's phone, the one he had in the office. I don't know what
she intends for me to do with it, until I see that she's already set
it to video recording.

Cameron raises his head, looks at me, and takes the phone.
He points it in my direction, and the red light flashes, recording. "Talk," he says. "Make them believe."

I'm covered in blood and soot in the back of a stolen van, in
clothes that don't fit, with a bag of hard drives and a notebook
that belongs to June—and this is all we have. Nothing else.
There's nothing left to do. Action, nothing. Words, everything.

I look straight into the screen, but I have no idea how to make them believe.

I guess this is the part where I trust in myself and humanity. That the words, the truth, will be enough. Please, let them be enough.

I begin to talk.

"My name is Alina Chase," I say, and my voice is still raspy from the smoke. I clear my throat and begin again. "My name is Alina Chase, and seventeen years ago I was placed in containment because of a lie. June *did* leave me something, but not the way into the database. She left me the truth, the reason she was killed." I hold up June's notebook, now tattered and crumpled, and I say, "She discovered that the study on violent souls was a lie. Fabricated by a woman named Ivory Street, and potentially others, to control people in power and affect public policy and laws. And when that didn't work, she used it for money and power, blackmailing others with this information and framing June. June wasn't innocent, but she wasn't guilty of that. We're here on the campus of Elson University because this is where the information is. Mason Alonzo is a professor here now, and he left himself access to the database at Ivory's request. There's a portal he can access through his office, and he stored the data they accessed in his computer lab." I hear the sirens, getting nearer. "His lab is on fire now."

This story I'm telling is not just mine and June's, but everyone's. It's Casey's and Cameron's and Ava's, and it's the story of the others who have been kept silent.

"Ivory Street is locked in the cellar of her home. Dominic Ellis is the third person involved in breaking me off the island. He was once a guard. He wanted access to the database, and he thought I could give it to him." I think of telling about his soul, about Liam White, but that is not mine to tell. "But it's bigger than blackmail. They've been using people. Moving people into positions of power to give them whatever they want. I was contained because Ivory Street saw me as a danger to her scheme. Not for any other reason. But I am not the danger. I am not the threat."

Casey stops the van, backs up, turns it around. My heart picks up speed. Faster, I will need to go faster. And do better.

"The other people who rescued me . . ." I reach for the phone, and Cameron hands it to me. I point it at him for a moment, and then to Casey as she drives. I hold the phone myself, and turn it around, facing me. "Cameron and Casey London. They've been looking for their sister, Ava. She was approached by these people—blackmailed because of who they said she was in her past life and the inheritance she had just accessed—and when she wouldn't do what they said, she ran." I take a deep breath. "June ran, too. But you're not allowed to run."

Casey slams on the brakes and turns around. "We can't get out of here in the van," she whispers, but I'm sure the camera is picking up her voice. I nod, and I speak into the camera once more.

"They've done nothing wrong, other than seek the truth to help the sister they love. They are the most selfless people I know. My name is Alina Chase, and this is the truth. I'm tired of running. I'm going to get out of this van now, but before I go, this is what we have." I show June's old hard drives, and I methodically flip through page after page of the notebook for the camera, committing them to the memory of this machine. "June replicated the study, with *all* the data. The results are not the same." I take the gun from Cameron, open the back doors, and toss it outside. "We are unarmed," I say, and then I hit End.

Casey takes the phone, and though she's still sucking in air—from crying, I think, and not the smoke—her fingers move effortlessly across the screen. "Posted," she says.

"Where?" I ask.

"Everywhere," she says. "It's been e-mailed to news stations and uploaded directly to video-sharing sites in its entirety."

We get out of the van where the alley dead-ends, and Casey says, "Are we running?"

I'm not sure if Cameron *could* run, even if we wanted to. Even if we had somewhere else to go. I picture June and Liam's hole in the ground. I picture June, alone, for over a year. I understand why she came out of the woods. Why she risked it all.

"I'm done running," I say. I gesture toward the phone in her hand. "That will have to be enough."

Casey drops it to the ground as the first red-and-blue lights pull up the street and stop in front of us. Two more cars soon follow. And the helicopters circle above. I look up, and I see several have the symbols for different news stations. For once, I hope this will keep us safe. We have no weapons. The police are here, shouting instructions through a loudspeaker. I hold my hands up, straight over my head, and I turn around like they tell me to. And I place my hand on my collar when they tell me to, lifting my shirt so they can see I have no weapon, slowly spinning around. I do everything they tell me to, and I hope that Casey and Cameron do as well, but I'm scared to look, to turn—I'm scared if I make even one misstep, they will see some element of danger. I walk backward, like they instruct, and the shouting grows. I drop to my knees, like they insist, and the footsteps race toward me.

I feel hands on my arms and metal on my wrists and a knee in my back. I cannot see Casey or Cameron as I'm yanked to my feet and led to the back of a police car. Someone guides my head so I don't hit it on the roof, and then I'm tossed across the seat, no free hands to brace my fall. The door shuts behind me.

I can't see what's going on outside, through the chaos of the people. I can't hear what's happening, through the static of the radio. I can't do anything more.

I close my eyes, and I picture my mother out there some-where. I wonder if she sees the news. What she thinks of this. Of me.

chapter 27

I AM KEPT IN a hotel room, somewhere near my island—
where the original event took place. They are careful not to call
my escape a crime, because that implies I had been held captive. But still, I am kept. It is not a prison, or a containment.
Not exactly. But it *is* a room with a guard just outside—it's for
my own protection, I am assured.

I spent one day inside a cell while they sorted everything
out, but they could not hold me any longer without charges.
Not even for my own protection. Not with the public watching
so closely. Not with the endless debating on television, which
I have now come to love. It may save me this time, public opin-
ion. Which is all law really is, anyway.

We make our laws, and then we must suffer for them.

I've been in this place for six days now, and I'm growing
anxious.

Casey, Cameron, and I were kept in different rooms, paid

for by public donations to our cause. Yet again, I have become a cause.

Cameron spent the first two days in the hospital, and he was here for only one night before he and Casey left for their sister's memorial. I felt better when Casey was in the same building, but she and Cameron have been gone for four days now.

Even when they were here, we had very little contact.

We were watched at all times. We were never left alone together. I know we were all walking a line, each afraid to cross it.

Casey hadn't spoken about her sister other than that one morning over breakfast, before Cameron returned. "I just don't feel like she's gone," she said.

But the thing is, she's not. Just like June isn't. Not entirely. I hope that thought gives her comfort.

Ivory and Mason are under investigation—kept under house arrest—but Dominic is gone. Disappeared through the tunnels during the chaos.

I am the only one here, once again.

The news reported that Casey has struck some kind of deal in the days after the memorial. And, they say, if she is free, then the logic goes that Cameron should also be free. And then maybe *I* will be free. But in the meantime, I am not eighteen yet, and there are legal loopholes to examine and stories to dissect and truths to create.

My lawyer said that part of Casey's deal will be her cooperation with the federal division of cyber crimes—I guess technically they have recruited her. Part of me thinks this will make her happy, that she will love it, but I haven't had a chance to ask her. I don't know if I will. I don't know whether she will come back.

Cameron and Casey will not need the public's funds any longer. They don't have to come back here, once they are set free. He and Casey will inherit the money that Ava had left to herself in her previous life. Once they are free, they will truly be *free*.

I tried to catch Cameron in the hotel lobby as he left for the memorial. But I barely got a chance to say anything other than sorry as he and Casey were ushered past me, through the open glass doors and into the back of a black SUV, disappearing down the road.

And so I am in a room, alone, with a television and a laptop and a window blocked by trees—no view in, but no view out, either. With a guard outside and the media out front and a lawyer who sits in the lounge all day and doesn't let anyone question me anymore.

The news is on again—this time, it's a talk-show-style debate about Ivory Street and the falsified study. They cannot disprove the study for certain without going back into the database; but they also cannot prove it. They show June's math on the screens, pictures captured from the video I took in the van and enlarged for all to see. Our fates will be decided by the public. Not science. Not law. I know that.

We cannot be reduced to numbers. A human being isn't quantifiable.

Even if we could find out for sure—whether one life affects the next, whether our nature is predetermined—people keep saying it's better not to know. There's too much at stake. Too many consequences. We want to believe in free will here. We want to believe in the power of redemption here. That we are always capable, for this life or the last, of making each life worth something.

What I would give for that chance—what I *have* given for that.

Nobody's sure what to do about Dominic. Where he fits in the balance of good and evil, right and wrong. If Cameron, Casey, and I are to be free, then shouldn't he be as well? I think about telling the investigators about the gun, and the way he pointed it at Casey, the way the bullet grazed my skin. That's a crime with a standard punishment. An accepted consequence.

But part of me does believe in some sort of karmic justice, and my soul cost him his life once before. I do not want to be responsible for the containment of his soul anymore.

I have given them the location of the hideaway, so sure he would be there. And the cabin, too, but it had been destroyed. It doesn't seem fair to me that he should be out there when I am still being held. But then I think of June, driven underground, unable to show her face. Out, but not free. And then I think that maybe it's fitting.

There are different types of prison, after all.

Besides, Dominic has too many cards to play. He's too smart. He'll strike a deal if he gets a taste of containment—maybe end up like Casey. I don't want to be anywhere nearby when he crawls out of the woodwork. I need to shake myself free of his obsession as well. I have this fear that he is in a basement somewhere, watching us. Hacking into the security feed of the hotel, watching my keystrokes on the computer. Sometimes I write him notes, typing and deleting them in a blank document, just in case he is watching.

Go live, I tell him. *Live* this *life*.

Sometimes I type *I'm sorry*.

I don't know for sure whether he's alive or dead, but he's a ghost to me either way.

I'm lying on my stomach with the laptop propped up between myself and the television. I scroll through a new article I find and stop at the bottom, at the comments section. It's become an obsession, reading the comments on the articles and the blog posts. I probably shouldn't, but I cannot stop. The opinions vary, but the majority are in support of my freedom. Many offer their homes, their names, their help. I've read thousands. And still I cannot stop.

Because the first article I read, three pages down in the comments, I found this, sent from an anonymous account:

I wonder what you dream of, niña. I hope you find it.

And I remembered that commenter from the article we read in the school computer lab.

Where she might go, one can only dream.

So I began an endless search, every place our video feed appeared. Every news site, every blog, every online journal. I read every comment, searching and searching for more.

I've found 107 comments. Every one from an anonymous source. Every one the same:

I wonder what you dream of, niña. I hope you find it.

There aren't any comments left on this one yet. So I close the article and bring up that video feed of my mother, the only time she spoke to the press. I watch it again, even though I know it by heart. But I like to see the shape of my eyes mirrored back at me as she speaks. In truth, there's a lot I get from her. Not everything comes from June, from my soul. We are more than that—a combination of genetics and the soul and the experience of our lives. And something more, I am sure.

"I used to sing her a lullaby," she says on the video. "Same as my mother used to sing to me. She can find me there, in her dreams." I see myself reflected in her. Her eyes. Her resistance. Her refusal to barter with lives. And her ability to bide her time, to trust that I might find her.

Go to sleep, and we will see each other in the land of dreams. Tierra de Sueños.

She can find me there, she told the media—she was telling me. *Find me there.*

I am not supposed to leave. It's for my own protection, I am told. But there's a gaping void the size of a lifetime that can fit between "not allowed to" and "not supposed to." I have read the comments. I have listened to the news. I believe they will let me go. I believe that if I walk out that front door and turn down the street and wave good-bye, nobody will stop me.

I am not okay with waiting for someone else to decide my fate.

But I sit here, still, on the seventh day, growing anxious and antsy and claustrophobic.

I sit here still, because after I said sorry to Cameron as the lobby doors slid open, he leaned in close, placed his cheek against mine, even though the cameras were on us. And he whispered, "Wait."

Because he knows. I will not stay here long.

My lawyer has requested a meeting over lunch, which I am all too happy to take, because it's in the dining hall and not this room, and she will not allow anyone to follow us.

She's eating a salad with slices of fruit and nuts sprinkled on top, and I order the same because my mind is ten thousand miles away.

"I'm working on declaring you an emancipated minor," she says. "Are you okay with that?"

I shift in my seat. Emancipated means free, so at least this is in the right direction. "How long will this take?"

She chews on her lettuce for an eternity before speaking. "First, we file a petition with the court. Then we go from there."

"Sure," I say. "Let's file the petition." But I am used to laws that are bent to contain me, not a court that grants me freedom. It makes me nervous. It's a nice thought, though. It might just work. Too bad I won't be sticking around long enough to find out. Maybe they can emancipate me in absentia.

· · ·

The guard to my room is returning with his sandwich delivery at the same time I'm walking down the hall. I slide my key into the door and nod at him. He nods back, his mouth full of bread and chicken as he slides into the chair.

I step into the room and I smile—there's a bag in the corner that does not belong to me, and there's a guy standing beside it, leaning against the wall. I turn on the television, turn the volume up high, before going to him.

"You waited," he says before I get to him. He's quiet, and I'm not sure if it's because of the guard outside or because of where he just was and what he went through.

"Of course I waited," I say.

He smiles, but he doesn't come closer.

I do not know what to do with this new Cameron, this version of him who has lost a sister. "How's Casey?" I ask, which seems like the safest way to find out how he is.

He shrugs. "Okay. Devastated and angry, but she'll be okay. Better today than yesterday. Better yesterday than the day before." He pushes off the wall then, meets me halfway. "Ava's been gone for a year, Alina. It's . . . there's some comfort in knowing the truth, even if it's not what you were hoping for."

"You're okay," I say.

"I'm okay," he says. "Better now that I'm here."

"You came back," I say.

His eyes shine. "Of course I came back."

He leans closer, but there's a commotion in the hall. I turn the volume down on the television and hear the guards speaking to each other. "Cameron checked in, but he's not in his room. Have you seen him?"

Cameron laughs. "I wanted to come see you before heading to my room. I didn't know if there were rules about room visits, so I figured it was a better plan to just not find out . . ."

I knock on the door and tell the guard, "Cameron is fine." And the commotion stops. I don't think anyone knows if there's a protocol for this.

But then the talking picks up again.

He rolls his eyes. "I'll be out in a few minutes." His face goes serious. "What's the plan, Alina Chase? They're not going to let me stay much longer."

But just in case, I move the lock at the top of the hotel door, to slow them down.

"You better sit down," I say.

I sit beside him on the edge of the queen bed and show him my laptop, the comments I've found, the video of my mother. I sing him the lyrics. He's watching me with his head tilted to the side.

"She's telling me to come," I say.

"Are you sure it's her? It could be anyone—it's anonymous."

"Yes. No. I'm not *sure*," I say. "But I believe it is." How insidious a belief can be, coloring all of my decisions. I shrug, playing it off, closing the laptop. "But if not, I hear there's an ocean. Maybe I'll finally learn to swim."

He smiles and pulls me close, his hands around my back, his face close to mine. "I think it's her. I hope it's her."

So do I. Hope must be contagious, too. And, I think, if I am so full of the hope that maybe she has waited these seven years for me after the failed escape, then maybe so is she. Maybe she has hope still that I will make my way to her.

I pull back from him, and I tell myself to look brave, look calm, don't cry. "I have to go," I whisper.

For a second, I think he'll try to talk me out of it. To be honest, I hope he tries. "I'll come back and find you," I say. "I promise."

But he stands and goes to the window, where he picks up his bag, pulling it open. "There's still some room," he says. "I packed light."

And when he sees the look on my face, he smiles and says, "One more crime, for old time's sake? Honestly, I've kind of missed it."

He pushes the screen from the window, but there's a two-story drop. I reach out, my hands testing the nearest branch. "You sure?" Cameron asks.

"Ha," I say. "How's your back?" I ask. "Can you do it?"

He holds my waist and helps me hoist myself onto the branch. I wrap my legs around it and scoot closer to the trunk, and I laugh as he mumbles, "Of course I can do it."

We make our way down the tree, branch to branch. Cameron stays close, in case I need an extra hand—or in case he does. We drop the remaining distance together, and I laugh as he stumbles on the landing. He puts a hand over his shoulder, reaching down his back. "I have an injury, don't mock me—some girl saved my life by taking a knife to my back. Such is love, so I hear."

And then he's the one smiling and I'm the one stumbling, but he's definitely not wrong. "So I hear," I say.

There's no pattern to falling in love. At least, nothing I can understand. Not something I could see beforehand. Not something I can decipher after, either. Trust can be earned, piece by piece, like links of a chain. But love is more like faith, or belief: it's a leap. It's hurtling over the edge of the cliff and trusting you will not drown.

"What are you thinking about?" Cameron asks. He's looking at me as if he can read something on my face, but it's also a challenge.

"You," I say, and I feel my smile mirroring his.

He closes the distance between us. "Just so we're clear," he says, "I'm here because this is the only place I want to be."

"Outside a hotel?"

"*Alina*," he says. "I'm trying to tell you something."

I already know. But I love how he wants me to be sure of him.

"Clear," I say, the second before he kisses me.

There's a commotion nearby, near the corner of the hotel, as we pull apart. And I see a single reporter, his camera on his shoulder, his press badge swinging across his button-down, his eyes fixed on me and Cameron. I pick up Cameron's bag, swing it over my shoulder, and hold up my hand in greeting. He holds up his free hand as well. I smile—at him, at the camera—and I wave good-bye.

"Wait," he says, as I turn away. Cameron takes my hand, and I can feel the tension in his grip—he's ready to run. But the man rests his camera on its side in the thick grass, fishes inside his pocket, and tosses a set of keys in our direction. "It's the black truck near the playground," he says, gesturing through the trees. "If you're looking for a ride."

"Thank you," I say.

We race through the trees until we hit a park. I see children running across the grass, a girl with her head tipped back on the swing, a baby in a carriage while a woman rocks it gently back and forth. Some of them look at us, some of them smile. Some look away. But nobody stops us.

The children go back to their game. The girl stretches her feet to the sky. The mother goes back to her baby.

I want to believe it's Genevieve, with her head tipped back, staring at the sky, and Ava, being rocked to sleep, beginning her life again right now. I hope, whoever they are, that they have a good life. I hope they live and love and know that there are people who love them back—in this life, and the last.

"I really can't wait to teach you to swim," Cameron says, hanging an arm over my shoulder. "I mean, seriously, you're horrible. It's like you have no natural instinct for survival."

He opens the door of the mud-covered truck, and I climb in before him. "I bet you don't even know how to *drive*," he says.

"Add it to the list," I say.

"I've got a long list," he says.

I sit beside him on the bench seat in the front of the truck. Nobody follows us as we pull out of the lot, then onto the highway. Every few minutes, he catches my eye and smiles, and I can't help doing the same. I spend a lot of the drive daydreaming—no nausea at all. Imagining what waits for us.

In my mind, I can see it already: feet in the sand, Cameron in the water, and my mother's voice, calling me inside.

But for now, Cameron is sitting beside me and we're in the cab of a truck, heading south. Next, we'll get out and cross the river on foot. We'll make it there, to Tierra de Sueños and whatever awaits us.

We will make it.

I know we will.

acknowledgments

THANK YOU TO EVERYONE who helped usher this book from idea to draft to finished product. I am so fortunate to have all your guidance and support.

My agent, Sarah Davies, whose thoughtful advice I rely on from the first pitch to the final book—and beyond. I'm so lucky to have you in my corner.

My editor, Emily Easton, who championed this idea when it was just a handful of pages and a chat over dinner, and who knew exactly what I was hoping this book would become—and showed me how to get it there.

The entire team at Bloomsbury, including Jenna Pocius, Patricia McHugh, Nicole Gastonguay, Lizzy Mason, Erica Barmash, Beth Eller, Linette Kim, and Courtney Griffin; and the teams at Bloomsbury UK and Australia, including Rebecca McNally, Natalie Hamilton, and Emma Bradshaw. It's such a pleasure working with you all!

My talented and thoughtful critique partners: Elle Cosimano, Megan Shepherd, Ashley Elston, Jill Hathaway, and everyone at Bat Cave 2013. I'm so thankful for your feedback, and your friendship.

My mother, who will read every draft of everything I ever write; and my father, who tells everyone who will listen about my books.

And my husband, Luis, who declared this one his favorite idea.

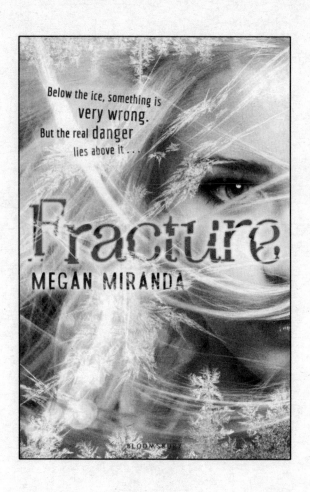

WHAT WOULD YOU SACFRICE FOR LOVE?

The truth is
hard to share . . .
Impossible to forgive.

Vengeance

MEGAN MIRANDA

BLOOMSBURY

OUT NOW

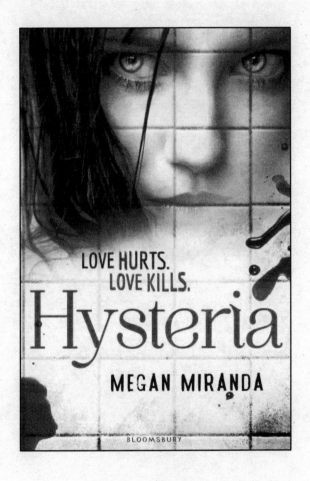